With big dreams of being a publishe
11-year-old girl writing *Beverly Hills 90210* fan fiction before fan
fiction was even a thing, **SHANN McPHERSON** has been writing
angsty, contemporary romances for most of her thirty-something
years.

Living in sunny Queensland, Australia, when she's not writing
Shann enjoys making memories with her husband and cheeky
toddler son, drinking wine, and singing completely off-key to
One Direction's entire discography.

Where We Belong

SHANN MCPHERSON

ONE PLACE. MANY STORIES

HQ
An imprint of HarperCollins*Publishers* Ltd
1 London Bridge Street
London SE1 9GF

First published in Great Britain by
HQ, an imprint of HarperCollins*Publishers* Ltd 2020

ISBN: 9780008381974

Printed and bound in Great Britain by
CPI Group (UK) Ltd, Croydon, CR0 4YY

For Niall

Chapter 1

I push my glasses up my nose for the millionth time, and while holding my breath and with one eye narrowed, I wipe a tiny smudge of frosting from the silver turntable holding Mr. and Mrs. Robertson's fiftieth wedding anniversary cake. It may have taken me two full days and most of last night, but I've finally finished. Exhaling the breath I've been holding for a beat too long, I take a step back to really appreciate my craftsmanship. Four layers of lemon and blueberry perfection, covered in a fluffy whipped buttercream frosting, decorated with beautiful red roses, delicate peonies, and a smattering of baby's breath, all of which have been hand-piped by yours truly.

I place a hand on my hip, smiling proudly. "Alice Murphy, once again you've outdone yourself," I whisper under my breath, mentally high-fiving myself.

The bell above the door to the shop jingles, pulling me from my musings, and I walk through from the kitchen to the front of the store, still smiling at the thought of my latest masterpiece.

"Welcome to Piece O' Cake," I sing in a cheerful customer service voice. "How can I help yo—" Stopping dead in my tracks, my eyes go wide as I gawp at the unexpected figure standing in the middle of the shop. He's shadowed by the afternoon sun shining in through the windows, backlighting him to nothing more than a darkened silhouette, and I blink hard, unsure whether or not I'm imagining things. But then he speaks. And I would know that voice anywhere. This is definitely not my imagination playing tricks on me.

"Hey, Murph." The shadow takes a step forward, coming in to the glow of the overhead lights, and I'm immediately enamored by that all-too-familiar grin.

"N-Nash?" I gasp.

His smile is bright and those eyes. I'd remember those eyes anywhere after spending such a big part of my life dreaming about them.

"Oh my God!" I scream, covering my mouth with trembling hands until I finally come to, ripping off my apron before practically throwing myself over the counter. Jumping up, I wrap my arms around his neck, and emotion gets the better of me as I stand there in the familiarity of his warm embrace with tears of happiness streaming down my cheeks.

He's here.

The love of my life.

He's home.

The May sun simmers gently upon my shoulders. Birds chirp in sync, their chorus singing through the air. Butterflies flutter aimlessly, whisked away by the gentle breeze. And, in the distance, a child is giggling full of an infectious happiness that I can feel through to my soul. I can't possibly wipe the smile from my face. I couldn't, even if I wanted to. Nash Harris is actually here, by my side, as we walk beneath the canopy of the lush magnolia trees. The moment couldn't be any more perfect.

"What are you doing here?" I ask incredulously, my cheeks stinging from smiling so hard.

"I wanted to see you." Nash stops, turning to me and pulling my hands into his. "Actually, Murph, I *needed* to see you."

I look up at him, our eyes meeting as his thumbs gently stroke the backs of my fingers. But when I catch sight of something unfamiliar in his gaze, something unsettling, my heart sinks a little in my chest. I know Nash. Something is wrong. He continues smiling that same beautiful smile, but I can see it in his eyes.

"Nash, what's wrong?" I ask, suddenly worried. Is he in trouble? Oh, God. Is he sick? I wouldn't be able to handle it if something happened to him. Not to my Nash.

"I'm fine, Murph." He shakes his head once with a light chuckle, dismissing my concerns, and then, letting go of one of my hands, he reaches into the back pocket of his jeans, causing my eyes to widen of their own accord. For a moment my mind begins to get carried away with itself. Between the chirping birds and the fluttering butterflies, the beautiful warm sun, and the backdrop of the inky river reflecting the fluffy white clouds in the sky, it's all too perfect. And, as he reaches into his pocket, I begin to wonder if Nash Harris is about to drop to one knee and make all my dreams come true.

The realization that Nash doesn't have a ring box in his hand snaps me from my reverie. Instead, he presents me with an envelope. And not just any old plain white Staples envelope, but a sparkly gold one, made of real fancy paper. My brows pull together in confusion as I look back up at him, meeting his eyes once again.

"What is this?" I ask, tentatively taking it from him. But he doesn't answer. He just takes a step back, letting go of my other hand and scratching at his lightly stubbled jaw as he watches me, waiting. He's nervous. So am I. And, right now, I almost wish something *was* wrong with him, because I have a terrible sinking feeling in my belly that whatever this is, I am not going to like it one bit.

I lift the tab with my index finger and pull out a single piece of card. Looking closer, I push my glasses up my nose, and it takes my eyes a while to adjust to the dim light of the shadows

3

cast by the overhead trees. But then I manage to read the words embossed into the card in my hand, and in that moment, it feels as if my whole world comes crashing down around me.

Mr. and Mrs. Howard E. Hutchins request the pleasure of your company ...

I stare at it—the invitation—reading the words over and over again as a painful ball of emotion wedges itself into the back of my throat. Suddenly I find it difficult to breathe. "W-what is this?" I finally ask, trying so hard to keep my voice from quavering. I glance up with a tight smile I know doesn't even come close to reaching my eyes. "You ... You're getting m-married?"

Nash nods slowly, the ghost of an uncertain smile playing on his lips.

A flush heats my cheeks, and I know tears are imminent, but I try to keep what little composure I have, looking down at the invitation in my trembling hands in an attempt to avoid his eyes.

"I wanted to tell you in person," Nash says. His words are soft and gentle, as if he knows what they're capable of doing to me.

"Wow." I try so hard to sound excited and happy, but I know I'm not even close to pulling it off. My heart is breaking. Actually, no. It's already broken. And then I do a double take, looking closer at the invitation, and I actually can't even believe my own eyes. "Next *week*?" I shriek, finally forced to meet his gaze.

"Yeah." Nash tucks his hands into the front pockets of his jeans, shrugging a little sheepishly. "I know it's sudden. But with my final year of med school coming up, and Anna studying for the bar, if we don't do it now, we'll probably be waiting another whole year, and we really don't want to wait any longer."

"Anna?" I ask, looking down at her name embossed in shiny black lettering on the invitation. *Annabelle Victoria Hutchins.* I can only imagine what she looks like. Her name is elegant enough. I bet she's tall and beautiful. Thin and probably blonde. Nothing like me, Alice Murphy. I once thought Alice was a beautiful name.

Beautiful like Alice in Wonderland. But Murphy? Bleh. When all the guys started calling me Murph, I just went with it. Because, let's face it, I'm certainly no Annabelle Victoria Hutchins.

"Yeah." Nash's wistful smile is enviable as he ruffles a hand through his sandy blond hair. "Murph, you're gonna love her. She's great. She's a lawyer. Well, she will be once she passes the bar. She's so smart. And funny, and kind, and … Well, she's just perfect." His blue eyes actually glaze over for a moment while he gets carried away with himself, and I wince as the bitter taste of bile begins to rise up the back of my throat.

Thankfully, before he can gauge my reaction, Nash turns, continuing to tread the stone path that trails down to the boardwalk at the river's edge, and I follow, still speechless as he proceeds to talk. "I was coming out of my favorite juice shop. You know, the one on the same block as my dorm? And Anna was walking with her head down, looking at her phone." He chuckles, scrubbing a hand over his smiling lips. "She collided headfirst with me, and my smoothie spilled all over the both of us."

I smile, but really, all I want to do is cry. But I swallow the emotion, clearing my throat. "B-but, isn't it a little soon?" I ask, adding a casual shrug to try to lighten my question. "I mean, when I came up to visit you for New Year's you were … *happily* single." I meet his eyes with a knowing look. He and I slept together after a drunken night of celebrations on New Year's Eve. It had been a night of promises, the night I thought everything was going to change. I thought this was going to be our year. And now he's marrying some woman named Anna?

"What's it been? Like, a few months?" I guffaw, shaking my head in exasperation.

Nash looks at me, and I can see he wants to say something, but he's hesitating, considering my question. "I guess … when you know, you just know." He shrugs, looking down to the ground a moment before tentatively meeting my eyes.

Never before have I imagined someone's words could feel like such a brutal kick to the stomach, but he's just about crippled me with that.

"Yeah." I look down at my hands as they twist together. "I guess I wouldn't know."

We continue along the boardwalk and, despite the obvious shift in the air between us, Nash keeps talking about his wonderful, perfect Anna, and their impending nuptials. All the while I'm considering whether or not to just jump into the murky water of the Chelmer River and save myself any further torture. He's killing me, and he doesn't even know it. Or, worse. Maybe he knows exactly what he's doing, and he just doesn't care.

The thing about Nash and me is that we have a past. It's more than just the occasional New Year's hookup. He's not only my best friend, he was my first crush, my first kiss, my first love, my first everything. He and I were childhood sweethearts who actually thought our love would last forever. But life managed to get in the way and, after we left for college to live our happily ever after together in New York City, my mother's illness brought me back to Graceville, and our love suffered. I literally went from seeing him every single day, to every third weekend of the month, then every other month until we finally ended things and visited one another when we could.

Now, he's marrying someone who isn't me, and I'm still stuck in Nowhereville, Georgia, running my dead mother's bakery. Suddenly I begin to wonder how different things could have been if she'd never fallen sick. It's not like I haven't thought about it over the years, but now the what could've beens are as real as my broken heart.

"So? Will you do it?"

Realizing I haven't been listening, I glance up from the wooden planks at my feet, meeting his hopeful blue eyes, and he offers me a knowing smirk. "Our wedding cake! Will you *please* make it?" He nudges me playfully with his elbow. "I know it's late notice, but I always did love your cooking."

So, not only has he flitted into town on a whim to tell me he's marrying another woman, he also wants me to make his damn wedding cake? I … I … I can't even. I swear, it takes everything I have not to give him a piece of my mind. But the longer I gape at him, finding nothing but innocence and sincerity within his eyes, the more I know I have no way of saying anything but yes to this boy. I've never been able to say no to him, and I can't start now.

"Of course." I smile with a nod. And then, because I need to get the hell away from him, I glance down at my watch, not even really paying attention to the time. "Actually, I have to get back to the store," I say all flustered and pathetic. "A customer is coming by to pick up their order."

"Okay." Nash grins. "I have to head into Chelmer to pick Anna up from the airport."

At the mention of *her* my stomach twists at just how real this whole situation is.

"We're having a small get-together tomorrow night at the club."

"The club?" I ask, quirking a brow.

"Harrington Country Club." He nods. "That's where we're staying for the week to prepare for the wedding."

My face scrunches up at the thought. Nash Harris at a country club. It doesn't make sense. We used to make fun of the rich kids who came into town every summer to stay at Harrington's. We'd sneak onto the golf course through the pine forest, steal their golf balls before they could get to them, and laugh at how long they would spend looking for them. Now, Nash is one of them, and I feel sick at the thought.

I'm suddenly brought back to the now by a pair of strong arms wrapping around me in an all-too-familiar embrace, and that unsettling feeling in my belly is immediately gone. I find myself smiling as I rest my cheek against his shoulder, closing my eyes and breathing him in. He smells like him, like he always has, like home.

"You're my best friend, Murph."

My eyes fly open as I remain in his hold. Best friend? Those two words are suddenly like a slap to my face. I slowly pull back, finding him looking at me with that same innocence he's had his whole life and I sigh, forcing another smile onto my face as the realization comes crashing down upon me like a ton of bricks. I've lost the love of my life.

Chapter 2

For two hours I've been torturing myself. While designing a rough draft of the cake I'm now making for the love of my life's wedding to a woman who isn't me, I've been going over mine and Nash's last night together, wondering how I'd managed to get it all so wrong. I thought we were going to get back together. The only reason we broke up in the first place was because of the distance. I couldn't leave Graceville, not when Momma was sick, and especially not after she passed away. I had so much to do here; everything had fallen into my hands. So I was stuck here, and Nash was in New York City at college.

We both agreed that the distance between us was too difficult and we broke up, but it was never really final. We continued to see one another. We continued to talk almost every day. We even continued to share 'I love you' texts before bed. Of course I'd thought we were going to get back together, eventually. Nash and I were meant to be together. So, I surprised him by flying up to New York at the last minute on New Year's Eve. The flights cost me more than I could afford, but I just had to be there with him. He couldn't get home for the holidays because he was scheduled at the hospital. And when I'd spoken to him over the phone he sounded so sad, so forlorn. I made it my mission to be there with him.

9

And he'd been so surprised to see me, but there was something else, as if he was actually relieved that I was there. We spent the night in Times Square with a million other revelers, drinking cheap wine, freezing our butts off in the snow while waiting for the ball to drop. And, when it did, when the clock struck midnight, when the fireworks started to explode from the sky, Nash turned to me. He grabbed my face with his gloved hands, steadying me with a look that took every ounce of my breath away, and despite the deafening sound of a million people singing along to 'Auld Lang Syne', I heard every ounce of yearning in his words when he told me he missed me, kissing me in a way he'd never kissed me before.

I look down at the design I've sketched, and I shake my head, scrunching the paper into a ball and tossing it in the direction of the trash can. With a heavy sigh, I look around me, at the place I've called home my entire life. Momma's bakery was always my safe space, the one place I could come and feel as if everything in life was good, no matter how far from good things truly were. But now, it suddenly feels like my prison, the one place that's kept me trapped here, the reason I'm not the woman marrying Nash.

I need to get the hell out of here before I completely lose it and drown my sorrows in what's left of today's cream cakes in the display cabinet. My already rounded hips are relying on what little self-control I have. I need to go home, have a long, hot bath, and lose myself in a cringeworthy Netflix series and the box of Girl Scout cookies I keep stashed away for times of crisis, like this. But, just as I finish locking up the store and turn to my car parked out front, my eyes zero in on the flashing neon 'End Zone' sign across the road, and I'm like a moth to a flame; I don't even remember so much as crossing the street and, yet, here I am pushing my way through the saloon doors like I own the damn place.

The End Zone is the only bar that exists in the tiny town of

Graceville. It's the kind of place with sports memorabilia hanging on the walls, a couple of pool tables taking up most of the space in the back, flat-screen televisions displaying every kind of sport you can imagine, and an old restored jukebox playing classic hits. Everyone knows everyone, at The End Zone, and everyone knows everyone else's business. It's comforting, though. It's like the family home I unfortunately no longer have, the same family home most people wish they had.

As I walk in, my eyes narrow. The place is dimly lit and eerily quiet, which is no real surprise since it's only four o'clock in the afternoon. Aside from a couple of die-hard regulars, Bob and Leroy, sitting in the booth by the front windows, sharing a pitcher of beer, I'm the only other person. I wave to the two men as I make a beeline directly for the bar, taking a seat on one of the stools. I search for service but, after a few minutes of waiting, I give up waiting and reach over the counter, grabbing a bottle of whiskey before plucking a glass from the overhead rack.

"What the hell are you doing, Murph?"

I roll my eyes, ignoring the familiar voice coming from somewhere behind me while I continue to pour myself the shot that I need so bad. The warmth of a body sidles up beside me, taking a seat on the very next stool, and I can feel his eyes watching me, but I ignore that overwhelmingly imploring gaze as I throw back the whiskey without even wincing at the afterburn as it trails down the back of my throat, because that's how pent up I am.

"Huh," he muses from beside me and I cast a sideways glance to see him nod once. "So, I guess this means you saw Nash then, huh?"

I turn with a quirked brow, meeting his dark emerald eyes and I sigh. Harley Shaw is and always has been the proverbial pain in my butt. It's nothing sinister. I don't hate the guy. He just he knows me too damn well. I've known Harley for as long as I've known Nash. The two of them were the very best of friends before I came along and stole Nash for myself. Of course, Harley

11

was always hanging around like a bad smell. He was the third wheel we just couldn't seem to escape. We grew up together and, for the last few years, with everyone off at college and grad school, or working in the city and starting their adult lives, Harley's really the only person I've had. He's like the older brother I never had. The confidant I never knew I needed. He knows me better than anyone, maybe even better than I know me. And because of that, right now, I know he knows the pain I'm going through, and that only frustrates me more.

Even though I don't answer him, I catch him nodding in understanding from my peripheral vision. But, instead of further chastising me for reaching over the counter of his bar and pouring my own drink, he grabs the bottle from me and pours another, pouring one for himself, too, and that's exactly what I need right now. Someone.

"He's 25 years old." I balk, downing my second shot. "I mean, who even gets married at 25?"

Harley says nothing, choosing instead to listen. And I thank God that he does. I don't need someone trying to correct me, or argue. I want to vent—I need to let it all out—and the only person I have right now who will listen is Harley, and he does, so I continue. "Does he even *know* this woman?" I laugh once under my breath, shaking my head as I stare straight ahead at the shelves of liquor bottles lined up behind the bar. "Who the hell marries someone after knowing them for just a few months?"

I throw a hand in the air in exasperation, curious as to why Harley isn't nearly as incredulous as I am. This whole thing is ridiculous. Why am I the only one who thinks so? And, at that thought, I swivel on my stool, gawping at him, watching as he casually sips his whiskey with little to no emotion, his eyes trained on the television overhead playing some English soccer game.

"Did you know about this?"

Slowly, his eyes flit to the side, and he carefully places his glass onto the counter as he turns to face me, albeit reluctantly. "Well, yeah." He sighs, adding a casual shrug. "But, I mean, I *am* his best friend."

"So am *I!*" I yell, slightly offended. "At least, I *thought* I was."

"Yeah, but—" Harley stops to gauge me, hesitating momentarily. "I've never slept with the guy, Murph ..."

I sigh heavily, my shoulders falling as I stare down into my empty glass. He's right.

"I don't know," Harley continues. "He seems happy. Granted, I haven't met the woman but from what he's told me, she's good for him. Maybe ..." He trails off, pulling his bottom lip between his teeth and glancing away. I can tell he's battling with his words, his clenched jaw working overtime.

"Maybe *what?*"

He finally meets my eyes again, and there's a sadness within his gaze, a resignation of sorts as he sighs. "Maybe it's time you let him go." Before any more can be said, he stands from his stool and moves behind the counter to serve a customer who's just walked in from the street. He offers me a sad smile as he pours beer into a frosted glass, but it's a smile I can't return. Because, once again, he's right.

You know how they say if you love something you should let it go, and if it comes back to you then it's yours, and if not, well then it was never meant to be? Well, I call bullshit on that. If you love something then hold on to it for dear life, because once it's gone, it's gone for good. And suddenly you're left sad and alone in a bar on Main Street, wondering where it all went wrong, crying into your second glass of whiskey at four o'clock in the afternoon.

While Harley busies himself with restocking the cold room behind the bar, I find myself thinking back to the day I met Nash Harris, back to when a 9-year-old girl first met the love of her life.

I'd never had a lot of friends growing up. For most of my life it had just been me and Momma. My father left before I was

13

even old enough to remember him, but that was fine with me. I didn't need anyone else. I'd always preferred my own company. I had a wild imagination and a love of books, so whenever Momma was busy with the bakery, I'd sit on the curb outside the store with my head buried in a book, makings friends in the characters I read about.

When I was 9, I started getting bullied by a kid at school named Billy Connor. He always tried to steal my lunch. It became second nature. I'd know I wasn't going to be able to eat whatever Momma packed for me, so I'd stock up with an extra breakfast muffin in the morning, and hide it in my book bag for the afternoon when I was usually starving.

One day, I'd been clutching my NSYNC lunch bag as if it were my lifeline, walking through the school halls with my head down, desperate to make it outside safely without being intercepted by Billy and his band of bullies. But, of course, with no such luck, I was accosted in the corridor, slammed up against a locker with such force I dropped my lunch to the floor as I clutched the back of my throbbing head. But I'd expected it. I'd been waiting for it. I knew it was going to happen. What I hadn't been prepared for, however, was Harley Shaw coming to my defense.

Harley had always been popular. Even in the bottom ranks of elementary school, he was the most popular guy in all our class. I think it had something to do with being so good at sports. Apparently, when you're 9 years old, being athletic is the equivalent of being a rock star, and Harley Shaw was like the Justin Timberlake of Graceville Elementary. And he saved me that day, in more ways than one. He made Billy Connor pay for stealing my lunch by dragging him into the girls' bathroom and flushing his head down the toilet until he begged for both mercy and my forgiveness, and he made sure he and his mean friends never even looked twice in my direction ever again. And they never did. Never again was my lunch stolen.

Still to this day I don't know why Harley went out of his way

14

for the dorkiest girl in class he'd never once spoken more than five words to, but he did, and I will be eternally grateful. Not just for saving me from Billy and his friends, but if he hadn't stepped in that day I might never have felt that tug in my heart, that dip in my belly at the sheer sight of the piercing blue eyes of his very best friend when he'd swept in to ask if I was okay while Harley was busy making Billy pay. When he'd taken hold of my hand and led me to the school nurse's office to get the bump on my head checked out, I knew, even at 9 years old, that I had fallen head over heels in love with a boy named Nash Harris.

"What the hell are you smiling at?"

I startle from my thoughts, looking up from my glass of whiskey to see Harley sitting beside me again, this time lifting a bottle of beer to his lips. I can feel my cheeks blush of their own accord, giving me away completely, and I try to hide my smile behind my glass as I look straight ahead at nothing in particular. "I was just thinking of that first day," I admit. "Back in fourth grade when you flushed Billy Connor's head down the toilet."

Harley chuckles to himself at the memory.

"That was the day we all became friends." I look at him, seeing him nod as he stares down at his beer with a faraway smile of his own, and I know he knows it too. It wasn't just the day we became friends; Nash, Harley and me, we became family that day. It was the day my whole life changed.

Chapter 3

I stand in front of the mirror that hangs on the back of my closet door, staring at my reflection with serious contempt. You know when you're hoping for a particular look, and you really think you're going to pull it off, but then you see yourself and wish you'd thought things through better? Well, that's me right now. I'd driven forty miles, all the way to Chelmer, to the Westfield because it has a Macy's, and I spent a couple hundred bucks on my outfit for tonight. I wanted something sleek and sexy, sophisticated and elegant. Something not at all like my usual self. But contact lenses always make my eyes burn like hell, and I simply cannot get away with wearing a bodycon dress with hips like mine.

The first thing to go is the contacts. Straight in the trash. I've worn glasses since I was five years old and, unfortunately, they aren't going anywhere anytime soon. I tug off the constricting dress that feels like it's suffocating me, and I toss it to the floor before rifling through my closet.

Finally, I'm dressed in a navy dress that sits mid-thigh and flares out from the waist, concealing my hips, thighs and butt. I team it with my shiny red Mary Janes to add a splash of color, and I wear my tortoiseshell glasses. Painting my lips a cherry red to match my heels, I leave my auburn hair natural, falling around my shoulders.

I look at myself in the mirror for a long time, taking in every little detail of my outfit. Unlike the look I'd been hoping for, it definitely isn't sleek, sexy, sophisticated or elegant, but then, neither am I. And I can't pretend to be someone I'm truly not. I'd never pull it off and it would only end in embarrassment. And tonight's the night I'm meeting the woman who is marrying the love of my life. The beautiful, wonderful, perfect Annabelle Victoria Hutchins, at least that's the impression I get from the social media profiles I've spent the best part of the last twenty-four hours stalking. She's literally perfect, and beautiful, and everything in between. I can't possibly risk embarrassing myself. Not tonight. Not in front of her.

I've had almost an entire day to come to terms with the fact that Nash is no longer mine, nor will he ever be mine again. And it hurts more than I could have ever been prepared for it to hurt. Last night was spent crying into a half-empty bottle of wine while listening to my Spotify playlist of saddest songs. I cried so many tears. And even now, with no more tears to cry, it still sits like a painful lump at the back of my throat.

I'm not sure how I'm going to be able do it: go there tonight to celebrate with them, spend the rest of the week making their wedding cake, and watching on Saturday as they become husband and wife while acting as if everything is fine when deep down it's anything but okay, like a rusted blade slicing through my gut. But, when the doubt begins to get the better of me, I remind myself that first and foremost, Nash is my friend, and I owe it to him to be the happy and supportive Murph that I've always been. But it still kills me like crazy.

As I sit at my dressing table fastening a small gold hoop into each of my earlobes, I think back to the night I first realized I'd fallen in love with Nash Harris. I was only 14, but even at an age when marriage should have been the last thing on my mind, that was the night I thought maybe I would one day be the woman lucky enough to become his wife.

I woke with a start. My eyes flew open as I searched the darkness surrounding me. My heart raced without me knowing why. But when something hit my window, I breathed a sigh of relief realizing it was the tapping of the glass that had woken me from my dreams. Throwing my covers off, I crawled down to the foot of my bed, and pulled the curtains aside. I looked down to the front yard, gasping at the silhouette standing by the elm tree. His hood was pulled low over his head, covering most of his face, but I could tell it was him, and I knew immediately something was wrong. He hadn't come here in the middle of the night since the last time.

Suddenly my heart felt as if it had climbed to the back of my throat. Jumping out of bed, I shoved my feet into my slippers, tiptoeing past my momma's bedroom, hurrying as fast as I could downstairs. I stopped at the front door, holding my breath a moment before lifting the latch and pulling it open. The cool night breeze blew in from outside, shocking me, and I shivered.

"Nash?" I whispered through the silence, searching the front yard for him.

A shadowy figure appeared from behind the thick trunk of the elm tree, and I watched with a furrowed brow as he limped unsteadily through the darkness. When he came into the light of the moon, I couldn't help but gasp at the sight of him. With a split lip and a black eye, he was hunched forward, clutching his side, his face distorted in pain with every step he took. He stopped on the porch in front of me, and I could feel my eyes prick with the threat of tears. But I knew it was my job to remain strong. He needed me. So, without saying a word, I ushered him inside, quietly closing the front door behind us before taking his hand in mine and carefully helping him upstairs.

Nash sat on the edge of the tub, his head bowed and his

shoulders small and cowering. He'd taken off his sweatshirt, and when I'd first caught sight of the painful red welts lashed across his back and the purple bruises covering his ribs, I wasn't sure if I should have woken my momma. I was terrified. I couldn't be sure he didn't need to go the hospital. But Nash pleaded with me not to say anything to anyone, so I didn't say a word. I tended to him as best I could, as quietly as I could so as not to wake Momma. As I padded the open welts across his back with anti-septic ointment, I could feel a wayward tear trail over the curve of my cheek. I quickly wiped it away with the sleeve of my pajama shirt. I couldn't let him see me cry.

"What did he do to you?" I whispered under my breath, unsure he'd even heard me.

"Belt." Nash's hushed voice was full of an uncharacteristic fragility that just about broke my heart. I closed my eyes a moment, an involuntary shudder coursing through me.

"I hate him," he hissed between gritted teeth, flinching away from every one of my tender touches.

So do I, I thought silently to myself. "I'm so sorry, Nash."

Nothing more was said between the two of us. I did all I could to ease his suffering, and he sat silently. He was so strong through the worst pain imaginable, and all the while my heart continued breaking for him. He didn't deserve this. Nobody did. I wished I could help save him from his horrible daddy.

Nash and I lay together in my bed, side by side, staring up at the shadows cast from outside as they danced across the ceiling to an imaginary tune. I reached under the covers, finding Nash's hand by his side, and without a word, I took it in mine, lacing my fingers through his, holding him tight.

"I'll always be here for you, Nash." My voice was a whisper, but the silence seemed to make my promise echo through the air around us.

Holding my hand so tight as if he couldn't possibly bear to let me go, Nash rolled onto his side. He looked at me for a long moment, his mischievous eyes sparkling through the muted light of the moon seeping in through open curtains.

"One day some lucky guy is gonna come into your life and steal you away from me," he whispered back, pulling my hand closer and enveloping it in both of his, holding it tight.

Never once breaking our hold, I rolled onto my side, facing him, our noses a mere hair's breadth from one another. For a long moment we simply lay there, staring into each other's eyes, our silence speaking volumes.

"Nobody is ever going to take me away from you," I said in a hushed tone.

My eyes moved down to his lips. His perfectly pouted lips, glistening in the darkness. I was only 14 years old. I'd never been kissed.

Suddenly something unexpected came over me, something I knew he felt too. I'd never experienced it before, but out of nowhere my belly twisted low in my gut, and my heart stammered, thumping heavily in my chest. It was an unfamiliar feeling I didn't necessarily dislike. Every day I had dreamed of my very first kiss, of Nash's lips on mine. But it was just a dream. It was all a dream that would never come true, because this was real life, and happily ever afters were just in books.

"You're my best friend, Murph." Nash leaned in even closer, resting his forehead against mine. "I don't know what I'd do without you."

I smiled, closing my eyes a moment, breathing him and his words in. Looking at him again, I blinked once, watching him so closely it was as if I could see straight through to his soul, and it was beautiful. "We'll always have each other," I whispered.

Nash leaned forward, pressing his lips to my forehead, and I gasped, not having expected such an intimate closeness from him. "Just the two of us," he said so softly. "Forever and always."

I looked up, meeting his eyes, and when I caught the ghost of a smile pulling at his lips, in that instant I knew everything in the world was perfect. Deep down butterflies swarmed in my tummy *as I realized maybe—just maybe—one day, I would get my happy ending, after all.*

The sound of a car horn pulls me from my past and I startle, shaking my head free of the reverie clouding my mind. My phone vibrates and I glance down to see a notification from Uber on the screen. Peering through the curtain I see a silver Toyota idling at the curb. With one last glance at my reflection, I exhale a heavy breath and collect my purse. And, with my heart a little heavier than it had been only moments ago, I know it's time to face my past, now or never.

Chapter 4

Harrington Country Club is certainly not the type of place I frequent in my spare time. It's the kind of place a girl like me just doesn't belong. Women with handbags worth more than my car, dripping in diamonds and pearls, accompany men who exude wealth and stature. And, here I am in my old dress, wearing shoes I dug out from the very bottom of a bargain bin during the Black Friday sales at Nordstrom's two years ago, smiling nervously at the club host as I walk through the grand entrance, scared I'm going to be asked to leave.

"Can I help you, miss?" the host asks, crossing the foyer to reach me in such a hurry it's as if I'm trying to sneak in.

I straighten a little, squaring my shoulders. "I'm here for the Harris-Hutchins dinner party." I lift my chin a little higher as if I'm the kind of woman who frequents the most exclusive country clubs every Saturday night.

"Certainly, ma'am." The man nods and smiles down at me. "Just through the main hall, past the gentlemen's lounge, and into the formal dining room."

"Thank you." I nod on my way past him, trying not to outwardly roll my eyes at the fact that this is the kind of establishment that actually entertains the idea of a gentlemen's lounge.

The formal dining room is even more exquisite than the foyer, and I'm rendered speechless when I walk through the double doors. A perfectly planned maze of beautifully decorated tables fills the space, complete with candles, fresh flowers, and fancy silverware. Soft music resonates throughout, accompanying the sound of gentle voices murmuring amiable dinner chitchat. As much as I try to pretend as if I do, I certainly do not belong in a place like this.

"Murph!"

I stop mid-step, looking to my right and breathing a sigh of relief to see Nash through the sea of pompous country club members. And, for a moment, I'm left breathless by the sheer sight of him. He looks incredible. His sandy hair is a little messy, like he's been running his fingers through it all day. His azure eyes seem to illuminate the otherwise dim light of the room, sparkling beneath the low-hanging crystal chandeliers. He's dressed in a navy suit that looks as if it was made to fit only his body. I've never seen him look so put-together, so grown-up, so handsome.

"Murph, over here!" Nash yells out again, chuckling this time as if I'd not seen him.

I come to, snapping myself out of my daze. His hand is in the air, beckoning me over and that same boyish grin I fell in love with years ago beams as he waves me over.

"Hi." I smile awkwardly, approaching the long table set up in front of the floor-to-ceiling windows that overlook the eighteenth hole lit up like Christmas, providing a spectacular backdrop.

Nash makes his way to me and, before I know it, he has me wrapped in his arms. He holds me so close I can feel his breath fanning over the sensitive skin at the base of my neck and, again, I'm breathless, speechless, and everything in between. The things this guy is capable of doing to me without really doing anything, I swear he might just be the death of me.

"I'm so glad you're here," he whispers, pulling back and holding me at arm's length. "You look beautiful, Murph. Real beautiful."

I roll my eyes at his compliment, feeling my traitorous cheeks blush.

"Come." Nash takes my hand in his, holding it tight. "I want to introduce you to Anna."

My heart falls at the mention of her, as if somehow in the last three minutes spent rapt in everything Nash, I'd forgotten the reason I was here. I try desperately not to let my smile fall but, when I'm led to the striking blonde woman I remember from my social media stalking session, tentatively standing from her chair, looking from Nash to me and back again, the overwhelming happiness I felt just moments ago has all but disappeared.

Is this some kind of sick joke?

She's the epitome of beautiful. Even more beautiful than the photos on her Instagram. In fact, beautiful doesn't even cut it. She's tall—at least five foot ten – plus however many inches the stiletto heels she's wearing are. She's thin, with an enviable amount of cleavage on display. Her skin is luminous, soft and flawless; it's as if she's actually glowing from the inside. Long blonde hair that shimmers like glitter and she's dressed in a slinky red dress that hugs her strategically placed curves. I can't help but stare at her while realizing every one of my fears have been confirmed; Anna isn't just everything I'm not, she's everything a girl like me could never be.

Immediately I feel as if I pale in comparison to a girl like Anna Hutchins, and I really want the floor to open up and swallow me whole. Being in the same room as someone so sickeningly perfect, so naturally charming, is definitely not good for my already dwindling self-confidence.

"Anna," Nash begins, looking down at me with an endearing smile I suddenly want to slap right off his face for reasons unbeknownst to me. "This is Murph."

"Oh my goodness." Anna beams, covering her smiling mouth

24

with each of her perfectly manicured hands. "I can't believe I'm *finally* meeting the infamous Murph."

I stiffen a little. Infamous? What does that even mean? What am I, some kind of funny story he likes to tell all his new rich college friends about? I eye Nash dubiously but he just grins down at me, wrapping an arm around my shoulders. "All I do is talk about you, *and* Harley of course, and everything we did growing up together," he explains, but that doesn't make me feel any better.

"I'm so happy to meet you." Anna smiles, apparently over her sudden shock of coming face-to-face with my apparent infamy. Ducking down to my level—which is humiliating in itself—she wraps her arms around me in an embrace I can't say I'm all too comfortable with. I hesitate a moment before reluctantly lifting a hand and patting her back a few times, feeling as awkward as possible. I'm not usually one to hug a stranger and, let's face it, she's a stranger; I don't care how tightly she has my best friend wrapped around her dainty little finger.

"Harley!" Nash yells from beside us, and that's my cue to pull away from the slightly overbearing Anna, straightening my dress as I glance at Nash who is, once again, holding his hand in the air.

"Hey, man!" he calls out.

I turn to see Harley approaching and, for a moment, I find myself actually stunned. What the hell? He looks good tonight. Surprisingly so. I've never seen him so dressed up. Wearing a pair of neatly pressed khakis and a white button-down, which helps to accentuate his athletic build and tan skin. Even his chestnut hair is perfectly styled away from his face, instead of in its usual disarray.

I'm shocked. His look tonight is in stark contrast to his usual ripped jeans and End Zone T-shirt he wears every day at the bar. Hell, he even wore his damn football jersey to prom, complete with a sequin bowtie. The guy has never looked like this before, and I find myself unable to tear my eyes away from his as he smiles, flashing his dimples and all. He oozes charisma as he weaves his way through the table maze.

Reaching us, Harley throws his arms around Nash, and I force myself to look away from him, my eyes flitting to Anna who is watching the boys' exchange with an adoring smile, her perfectly straight white teeth glistening. Everything about her annoys me. I can barely contain an eye-roll. I force myself to turn away from her to stop the annoyance from consuming me from the inside out, and my gaze shifts to Harley once again. On closer inspection, I realize perhaps he isn't as put-together as I had initially thought, the Men's Warehouse tag poking out from the back of the starched collar of his shirt proves that, beneath the façade, the usual Harley is still there in all his glory, and I bite back a grin.

"Hey, Murph." Harley offers me a smile.

"Hey," I murmur in return, again forcing myself to look away from him. I don't know what's wrong with me. Maybe I just need a drink. I begin searching for a waiter, craning my neck over the sea of country club diners as Nash and Harley continue talking with one another, but then I overhear Nash introducing him to Anna, and everything stops.

"Harley, this is Anna, the love of my life—"

At that, I snap my head back to look at them, my jaw gaping at his words. *The love of my life?* As if his words aren't bad enough, I'm forced to watch on as he offers her the most adoring look, and it's heartbreakingly obvious just how enamored he is of her. My hands ball into fists by my sides and something unexpected comes over me, something I hadn't been prepared to deal with tonight. As I watch Nash slap Harley's shoulder, introducing him, the words are like hot lava as they burn their way up the back of my throat. I couldn't even stop them if I tried.

"Anna, babe, this is Harley Shaw, he's—"

"My *boyfriend*." I find myself stepping forward without missing a beat, surprising not only myself with my completely fabricated and obviously blatant lie, but Harley and Nash as well, each of them gaping at me as an awkward silence settles between us. But, I don't stop there. I reach up and touch Harley's arm, trailing my hand down to his, intertwining our fingers together as I smile at Anna.

"Wait … What?" Nash gapes incredulously, looking from me to Harley and back again.

I swallow hard, trying desperately to keep my cool, but I can feel Harley tense up beside me. I look up and meet his eyes. His jaw clenches beneath his lightly stubbled skin and he flashes me a warning look, his green eyes glaring.

"Wait," Anna speaks up, laughing to herself. "You two are together?" she shrieks in absolute joy. I look at her, my smile faltering at her reaction, and it takes all I have not to tell her to shut the hell up as she cuddles up to Nash, clutching a hand to her heaving chest. "That is *so* adorable!"

My teeth grit together and I try so hard to return her smile, but she really is impossible not to outwardly cringe at.

"So, Wait. I-Is this— is this actually a *thing*?" Nash asks, looking between Harley and me, his smile a little forced if the look in his eyes is anything to go by.

I grasp Harley's hand so hard, squeezing it a little too tight as if he's my only lifeline, and I pray he'll just go along with whatever it is I'm doing. I don't even know what that is, but I hope like hell he'll just play along. I look up at him with an imploring gaze full of desperation and he meets my eyes momentarily, swallowing so hard his Adam's apple bobs up and down in his throat. "Uh—" A sound similar to that of a strangled laugh comes out of him, and he shakes his head before looking at Nash. "Y-yeah." He presses his lips together in the semblance of a smile, this time offering me an unexpectedly doting glance so unlike him it almost makes me laugh out loud.

Good job, Harley.

27

"We're … t-together," he says, clearing his throat a little at the end as if his own words leave a bad taste in his mouth. "We're together," he says again with a little more conviction.

"So *cute*." Anna smiles, flashing me a wink I'm assuming is her way of telling me she thinks she and I are kindred spirits of some sort. We're not. At all.

"Huh," Nash muses out loud, looking at the two of us with the hint of a confused smile lingering on his lips, one that reflects the bewilderment in his eyes. He seems to be considering something, studying us, and I try so hard to look happier than I've ever been while holding Harley's arm tight to stop my buckling knees from bringing me crashing to the floor. Thankfully, before any more can be said—before I can think of some other elaborate lie to announce out of the blue—a waiter arrives at our table with a tray of canapés, and everyone finds their designated seats.

As I take my seat beside Harley, I can feel a thousand questions radiating from him as he offers me a sideways glance full of trepidation. And the whole time I can feel Nash's eyes watching me too, assessing me from across the table. But I ignore them both. Instead, I pretend to be oblivious, busying myself with pouring a glass of wine from the carafe in the middle of the table. I've never been more desperate for a drink before in all my life. I need to get drunk. Because at least if I can get drunk enough, I can blame the alcohol for my night of unfathomable decisions.

Chapter 5

I swear, I've never sat through a more awkward dinner in my whole life. The entire time Nash was watching Harley and me like a hawk. He was pretending not to, quickly turning his attention to Anna or the dinner plate in front of him if I caught his penetrating gaze, but it was so obvious. And I couldn't help but take that as a good sign. He was clearly curious and confused, but could he actually be jealous?

"We need to talk," Harley whispers from the corner of his mouth.

"I know," I mutter back with a tight-lipped smile, avoiding his eyes and focusing intently on my pasta Alfredo.

"What the hell is this all about, Murph?" he hisses so low I'm sure I'm the only one who can hear him.

I look at him, noticing his jaw clenched even tighter despite his smile that looks so obviously forced, the way he's watching me, waiting for some kind of explanation that I just don't have. And, at that moment, I can see from the corner of my eye Nash is still watching us with piqued interest he's so clearly trying to conceal.

I find myself softening as I turn to Harley, cocking my head to the side with a small smile. "We can talk." I stare directly into his green eyes, which are so dark they're almost olive, and, for Nash's benefit only, I reach my hand up, tenderly cupping his cheek as I whisper, "Later. I promise."

Harley's eyes widen, and I can see him inhale a sharp breath at my unexpected touch. I have no doubt he wants to kill me for putting him in such a predicament. I can almost feel his skin crawl beneath my fingertips, and I don't know whether to laugh or cry at just how messed-up this entire situation is.

"Good evening, everyone."

I turn away from Harley to see Anna standing from her chair, her beautiful, effervescent smile lighting up her face as she looks around at everyone seated at the table.

"Thank you all so much for coming to our makeshift engagement dinner." She glances down at Nash, smiling that same adoring smile before continuing. "Everything happened so fast. One minute we were dating, the next Nash was on one knee in front of me, asking me to be his wife. So, since everything has been so rushed, we thought we'd get everyone together to start the beginning of our wedding week and celebrate our engagement," she squeals, excitedly clapping her hands together as the rest of the party surrounding the table cheers.

I hide my scowl as best as I can, taking a few unladylike gulps of wine from my glass.

"I've asked my maid of honor, Beth—" Anna pauses, smiling at a just as blonde, just as beautiful woman sitting at the opposite end of the table "—and Nash's best man, Harley—" she stops once more to acknowledge Harley, before continuing "—to say a few words tonight. To introduce themselves and get the party started. So, Harley?" She nods across the table to him. "If you'd like to say something, that would be wonderful."

Harley clears his throat, wiping his mouth with his napkin before casting me a sideways glance as he hesitantly stands from his chair. I take another drink of my wine, looking across to where Anna is giggling quietly with Nash as he presses a tender kiss to her cheek. My teeth grit together at their display of affection, so hard my jaw begins to ache.

"Hey, everyone." Harley waves a nervous hand in the air. "I-I'm Harley Shaw. Nash's oldest and therefore *best* friend." He flashes me a smug smirk while everyone who knows us chuckles, and I roll my eyes, continuing to drown my secret sorrows with wine.

"Nash and I first met in the sandpit in Kindergarten. He was crying because he'd peed his pants and he didn't want to tell the teacher in case the other kids made fun of him."

Everyone at the table roars with laughter, and I look across to see Nash's cheeks flush with embarrassment. He holds his glass of scotch in the air, nodding at Harley in mock appreciation.

Harley chuckles. "No, but seriously, I could stand up here and embarrass the hell out of my best friend with all the stories I have." He casts Nash a knowing smirk. "But then what would I talk about at the wedding reception?" Again, the party guests laugh. "I can tell you one story, though. This one isn't embarrassing, or particularly funny, but it sure is proof that Nash Harris might just be the greatest guy around."

Everyone settles in, watching Harley as he continues.

"We were 16. And those who know me and Nash know that when it comes to fathers we were both dealt a pretty ... lousy hand." He pauses, this time raising his glass at Nash, and Nash nods in understanding, something passing between the two of them and only the two of them. Harley takes a deep breath, continuing, "My father has always been a drunk. Hell, he still is. He used to come to my football games and stand on the sidelines drunk as sin, cursing at the top of his lungs, making a damn fool of himself and embarrassing me."

The mood around the table dwindles, and I shift a little uncomfortably in my chair because I know this story all too well, and it definitely isn't pretty.

"Well, this was the biggest game of my whole life. Division

One college scouts were coming to see me play. We were up against our fiercest rivals. I had to do a good job because my entire future rested on that one game." He takes another sip from his beer, managing a smile. "So, I wrangled the help of my very best friend who knew all too well about alcoholic fathers." He glances at Nash. "Nash went to my house before my dad got home from work, and he cleaned out all the alcohol. The beer. The liquor." He stops to laugh. "Hell, he even swiped a bottle of mouthwash from the upstairs bathroom."

Nash nods with a proud grin, shrugging to himself. "I'm thorough, if nothing else."

Harley looks down at the glass in his hand, taking a moment, and I glance from him to Nash, and back again, my eyes pricking with tears. "My father never made it to that game," he continues. "When he realized all his liquor was gone he smashed up most of the house and went to the bar instead of coming to the high school stadium. And I played one of the greatest games of my entire football career that night. And I can confidently say that it's because of this man right here." He indicates Nash with a wave of his hand. "Without him, I might never have got my scholarship to State. All my dreams came true that night, because of him."

Nash smiles tightly, but then his eyes find mine, a look within them so full of meaning, despite his failing smile. You see, I know the truth about what *really* happened that night. What happened is a secret Nash and I will take to our graves. To everyone else, Nash's bruises were a result of him falling off his bike in the woods, through the shortcut from his house to Harley's. Nash never told Harley the truth about that night, because he didn't want him to feel responsible for his best friend receiving the beating of his life just for helping him. But I know firsthand what happened, and to this day it still breaks my heart.

* * *

In a town like Graceville, Georgia, Friday nights were for football games, noisemakers, giant foam fingers, and not a lot else. But for me, Friday nights were for pajamas, Eighties teen movies and way too much ice cream. I didn't care for football. Even if Harley Shaw was QB1. I'd rather stick gum in my hair and spend all night trying to get it out, than sit in the high school football stadium surrounded by overzealous fans waving clappers in the air every time some footballer did something not even remotely exciting.

I was halfway through my all-time favorite movie when my cell phone chimed from my night stand, alerting me to a new text message. Curious as to who the hell was messaging me on a Friday night when everyone I knew was at the game, I blindly reached out and picked up my phone.

Nash: Can you please come here?

My brow furrowed in confusion.

To the game? *I replied, my face already scrunching up at the sheer thought.*

Nash: No, to my house.

I looked up, craning my neck to see out through my window. The street was cast in darkness, and the big elm tree in our front yard was in need of a trim, so I couldn't see all the way to Nash's house. But, immediately, my heart began racing in panic because I knew something must be wrong for him not to be at the game watching his best friend play such an important game. I jumped up, shoving my feet into my Converse and, without even stopping to second-guess myself, I hurried as fast as I could.

Outside, the night air was icy as I ran across the road to Nash's house. I came to a stop in his front yard, considering a moment. The lights were on, and his front door was hanging wide open but, thankfully, his daddy's truck wasn't in the drive. My heart was beating so hard in my chest, I was afraid it might crack a rib, but I continued up the front path, taking the steps two at a time before coming to a stop on the porch.

"N-Nash?" *I called, my voice wavering despite how desperately*

I tried to remain strong. "Nash?" I yelled again, slightly louder. But when he didn't answer, I took a hesitant step over the threshold, coming to stop dead in my tracks, gasping when I saw the state of the living room.

Picture frames had been torn from their hooks in the walls. Fist-sized holes gaped in the drywall. The base of a ceramic lamp was smashed on the hardwood floor. And there, in the middle of it all, was Nash cowered in the far corner, hunched into a ball, sobbing quietly.

Instinctively, I ran to him, falling to my knees on the floor before him. I wanted to wrap him in my arms but I didn't know how badly he was hurt and I didn't want to make his pain worse. So, I stopped myself, gently reaching a hand out and placing it on his shoulder.

"Nash?" I whispered, tears pricking my eyes.

He lifted his head so slow, and I was taken aback by the sight of him. He was bleeding from a wound just above his left eye. The right one was almost completely closed over it was so swollen. But most shocking of all were the red welts in the shape of obvious hands, imprinted around his neck.

"W-what happened?" I asked through a sob of my own.

"My dad. He— He f-found the liquor ..." Nash cried, coughing a little as he rubbed at the red marks at his throat.

"What liquor?" I asked, shaking my head in confusion as I gently rubbed his arm.

"The liquor I took from Harley's house so his daddy wouldn't get drunk and embarrass him at the game tonight," he sobbed, swiping almost violently at the tears on his cheeks as if he hated the fact that'd he'd been reduced to such emotion.

I had no idea what he was talking about, but it didn't matter. All that mattered was that he was hurt. Nash was in pain. And I had to help him. He needed me. "Where is he? Your father?" I asked, looking around at the state of the house, frightened his daddy might come back.

Nash shrugged. "He left."

"Stay here," I ordered. "I'm going to go pack you a bag. You're coming to my house."

"What about your momma?"

It wasn't that Momma didn't like Nash. In fact, she loved him like her own. But she knew a long time ago that there was a lot more to mine and Nash's friendship. Maybe she even knew before the two of us had even figured it out. So, Nash Harris sleeping over was not allowed. I had a feeling if she knew the truth of what happened between him and his daddy on a daily basis, she would have cleared out the room above our garage and moved him right in. But she didn't know, because I promised Nash I wouldn't ever tell a soul about his daddy beating on him. Looking at him now though, I wish I'd broken that promise a long time ago.

"It's okay. She's at Macon visiting my aunt for the weekend," I said quickly before turning and hurrying upstairs as if my life depended on it.

Later I sat on my bed, raking my teeth over my bottom lip as I stared at my cell phone. I should've called Momma to tell her. She deserved to know, and if she knew the truth, I know she wouldn't be mad at me for having Nash in the house when she wasn't here. But I just couldn't bring myself to do it. I promised him, and my promise was all I had. Chewing nervously on my thumbnail, I glanced up from my phone as my bedroom door slowly creaked open. Nash walked in, his hair damp from the shower I'd forced him to take. He stood in the middle of the room, his duffel bag falling from his hand to the hardwood floor with an almighty thud. He looked at me a little sheepishly, and the uncertainty in his eyes almost killed me.

"I'm going to get you some Advil." I jumped up and headed for the door.

Nash stopped me, grabbing hold of my wrist as I passed him, and I turned slowly, looking up at him. "Don't go," he whispered.

"I'm just going to the bathroom to get you some—" He silenced me with his index finger pressed against my lips, pulling me closer so there was no space left between us.

"I don't want no Advil, Murph," he said, his voice full of an unimaginable pain. "I just want you. I need you."

At those words, all the air in my lungs escaped me, rendering me breathless. I looked up into his eyes, my eyebrows knitting together in confusion. I knew what he was saying, but I couldn't possibly believe he was saying it. "Y-you want m-me?" I stammered.

He nodded. "I need you just to be here for me."

A flutter in my belly made my knees weak, and something I'd never felt before surged through me like a lightning bolt, bringing with it an ache in a place I hadn't expected, nor been prepared for.

"Please kiss me," Nash pleaded, closing his eyes, his head dropping forward as if he was in the most immense amount of pain.

I took a stuttering breath, considering for a moment, before reaching up on my tiptoes. With our mouths so close together I could feel the warmth of every one of his soft breaths. I brushed my lips against his. In an instant, his hands moved into my hair, urging me closer until we were nothing more than a flurry of lips, teeth and tongues in a frenzied kiss so full of need, want, and desperation that we became one.

I blink hard, pulling myself from the memories consuming me, forcing myself back to the present and looking up at Harley as he continues talking.

"My best friend risked everything to help me that night. Hell, he almost broke his damn neck falling off his bike on his way from my house back to his before my father returned home ..." Harley pauses, his face full of seriousness before his mischievous grin returns. "But that's the thing about Nash. He'll gladly go through hell and back to help the ones he loves the most. Anna, you're a lucky woman. Make sure you treat him right, because he deserves the world." He stops to meet Anna's eyes before raising his bottle in the air and looking around at everyone at the table. "To Nash and Anna."

"To Nash and Anna!" the entire table toasts in chorus.

I swallow the lump at the back of my throat, forcing a smile as I lift my wine glass in the air. My eyes flit, momentarily meeting Nash's once again, an unspoken truth passing between us from across the table before he turns to Anna, whispering something into her ear and leaning in close to place a kiss on her cheek.

I tip back my head, finishing what's left of my wine, placing the glass back down on to the table and lifting my napkin to wipe my lips. My cheeks flame as my heart sinks in my chest at the sheer thought that I've lost him. But it was me who saved him that night. It was me who was always saving him. And damn it, I am not going to give him up without a fight. I won't let Anna take him away from me. He needs me just as much as I need him.

Chapter 6

I can feel Nash's eyes on me as we stand together on the patio looking out over the immaculately landscaped golf course and all the way to the shadows of the pine forest lining the boundary in the distance, looming in the darkness. The moonlight reflects over the still lake, sprinkled upon the water like diamond dust. The stars twinkle high above, glowing like a million fireflies against an inky night sky. In the distance, a choir of crickets chirp through the woods, accompanying the soft tune of the music playing from inside the club as it seeps out into the calm night air, filling the silent void between us. It's almost romantic. Almost.

Yes, Nash's eyes are on me, but I pretend not to notice the intensity within his gaze as he continues watching me. I can't trust myself to look at him. I'm not sure what I might be capable of if I so much as chance it.

"So …" He finally breaks the awkwardness of the silence, nudging me playfully with his elbow as we continue down the steps. "You and Harley, huh?"

I swallow the guilt at the back of my throat, offering him a fleeting glance with a smile so tight. "Yeah." I shrug nonchalantly, focusing intently on my Mary Janes as we follow the flagstone path.

"I never thought I'd see the day Alice Murphy and Harley Shaw got together!" He laughs a somewhat derisive laugh, and it annoys me.

I look to see him glancing up toward the clear night sky, a slightly smug grin lingering on his lips, and I turn to face him, placing a hand on my hip. "What's so funny?" I ask a little abruptly.

He looks at me, his eyes widening a moment before he relaxes again, his smile returning. "Nothing." He shakes his head. "I just never expected the two of y'all to get together, that's all."

"Why?" I press. "Is it *so* hard to imagine another guy wanting to be with *me*?"

Nash's brow furrows, his mouth falling open. "What?" He gasps. "No, Murph. Of course not. Why would you even say that?"

Quite frankly, I don't know why I asked that. But, stubbornly, I fold my arms over my chest, shaking my head as I turn, continuing along the path. Nash falls into step beside me as we walk in an overwrought silence, thick and heavy with tension until we come to a stop overlooking the lake. He's still watching me. I can feel his eyes on me. But I choose to focus intently on the clubhouse as it glows in the darkness like a beacon in the distance.

"Why didn't you tell me?" he finally asks.

This time, it's me gaping at him, wondering if he can even be serious. "Well, that's fresh coming from you." I laugh. "Mr. 'Oh, by the way, here's an invitation to my wedding in a week'…" I quirk one of my eyebrows.

"Okay." Nash chuckles, obviously not missing the irony within his question. "I see your point."

I'm still annoyed, but I manage to let it go, huffing out a sigh with a nonchalant shrug. "It's no big deal, anyway."

"Are you kidding me, Murph?" He laughs again, his eyes blazing beneath the glow of the moon, bluer than I've ever seen them. "My two best friends are together," he continues with his hands in the air as if to further emphasize his point. "After everything we've been through, the three of us—" He stops himself, biting down on his bottom lip as he looks away a moment before recovering and offering me a smile that doesn't quite meet his eyes. "It's a *huge* deal!"

I suddenly feel sick to my stomach. I've never lied to Nash, before. I know I need to come clean. I owe it to him, and to Harley as well. Harley doesn't need to be dragged into my momentary lapse in judgment. It just isn't right. But none of this is right. Only a few months ago, I was with Nash in New York City, and we shared the most loving, most romantic night together. Now, suddenly, he's moved on, while I've been sitting around for five months waiting for him to come back to me, to profess his love for me, to give me the happily ever after I've been dreaming about since I was a 9-year-old girl. He's supposed to be mine. He and I are meant for one another; we always have been. I'm hurt and I'm angry, and if Nash has moved on, then I want him to know that I have too. And, with his best friend of twenty years, nonetheless.

But it's all a lie. And what am I supposed to say now? Oh yeah, about that whole Harley and me thing? I was just lying because I don't want you thinking I've been sitting around waiting for you for the last five months. Well, the last five years, actually.

Thankfully, before I can even begin to explain or confess my lie, we're interrupted by the sound of footsteps crunching over the loose pebbles on the path behind us. I breathe a sigh of relief, my shoulders sagging. But then I turn to see Harley walking toward us with his head bowed, his hands shoved deep into the front pockets of his pants, and my stomach twists. When he looks up, his eyes are full of an obvious trepidation as he tentatively approaches us. "Everything okay?" he asks, looking between the two of us as he rocks back and forth on his feet.

"Yeah, everything's fine ..." Nash chuckles, a crease of confusion pulling between his brow. "Why wouldn't it be?"

Harley glances at me with a questioning look, but all I can

offer him is a slight shake of my head, quickly averting my eyes. I stare down at my hands, cracking my knuckles.

"I'm happy for you guys," Nash says, moving forward and wrapping an arm around both Harley and me. "It's about time."

About time? I swing around, one of my eyebrows quirked slightly higher in confusion. "What's about time?" I study Nash, waiting for an explanation and his eyes flit from me to Harley, and back again. But before he can say anything, Harley interrupts the moment.

"I've gotta go. I have to stop in and check on the bar to make sure it's all okay." He rolls his eyes, continuing, "There's this new girl. She can't even pour a damn beer. I don't think she knows how to close off the register."

Nash nods, removing his arm from my shoulders so he can pull Harley into a manly embrace. The two share a hug, complete with a couple of friendly back slaps and a few murmured words I'm not privy to. Pulling away, Harley looks at me, awkwardly scratching the back of his neck. "Um, d-did you want a ride home … *babe*?" he asks through gritted teeth, adding the pet name as an obviously forced afterthought.

Nash watches closely, his eyes slightly narrowed.

"Yeah." I shrug, smiling at Harley as sincerely as I possibly can through the guilt and shame eating at me from the inside.

"Y'all didn't come together?"

I gulp, at a loss for words as Harley looks from me to Nash and back again before fixing his eyes to the ground while rubbing his stubbled jaw, clearly waiting for me to speak first.

"Oh, I-I—" I speak up with the first thing that comes to my mind. "I had a late customer consultation," I lie. "I've been commissioned to make a sweet sixteenth birthday cake for the mayor's daughter," I add, as if to further validate my excuse, and for a moment I don't even know who I am anymore. Does the mayor even have a daughter? I have no idea.

"But—" Nash pauses, his brow furrowed as he looks away a

moment before meeting my eyes once again. "But you were here before Harley."

Shit. I think for a moment. He's right. I laugh with a casual shrug. "Yeah, but you know Harley." I glance over my shoulder at Harley, careful to avoid his eyes. "He probably got sucked into some replay of a football game from five years ago on ESPN."

Nash laughs, nodding and smiling between the two of us, and I can feel Harley glaring at me as I exhale a breath of relief, ignoring him. "Well," I say with a weak smile. "Goodnight." I step forward, placing a quick peck on Nash's cheek. But as I go to move away, he holds me a little tighter, so close, and when I look into his eyes I find something I wasn't expecting deep within his intense gaze.

"Let's do something tomorrow," he whispers into my ear before pulling back and meeting my eyes with a knowing look. "Just the two of us."

Just the two of us? I can't say that my heart doesn't jump at the thought of being alone with him again after all this time. But why does he want to do something, just the two of us? Is he jealous? I nod, trying to keep the smug grin from claiming my entire face.

Harley flashes me a confusing look, one I can't read, before forcing a smile onto his face. Turning, he hesitates a moment, but then he grabs my hand, a little more roughly than necessary, and pulls me with him. Together, we walk in a silence so thick with tension, so overwrought with frustration, that I just know I'm in for it the moment we're alone.

Chapter 7

The drive back from the club doesn't take long. I only live on the other side of the pines behind the golf course but, with the tension reverberating throughout the silent cab of Harley's truck, three minutes actually feels like an excruciating lifetime. When we pull up to the curb outside my house, I exhale a breath of relief. I thought he was going to blast me the moment we were alone, but he remained silent the whole way. The only thing that gave away the fact that he's even remotely pissed off was the way his death-like grip on the steering wheel turned his strained knuckles a stark shade of white.

"Well," I say, reaching for the door handle. "Goodnight."

He doesn't say anything, so I climb down from the truck and close the door behind me. Tucking my hair behind my ear, I continue up the steps to my porch and fumble through my purse for my house keys, which is when I hear the porch steps creak behind me.

"Are you gonna tell me what the hell this is all about?"

I startle, turning quickly to see Harley right there. I didn't even hear him get out of his truck, let alone his footsteps approach on the path behind me. Yet, there he is, glaring at me, waiting impatiently for me to explain myself. Rolling my eyes, I push my glasses up my nose as I retrieve my keys from my purse. I unlock the door and continue inside, waiting for him to follow. I know he deserves at least some semblance of an apology, especially seeing as I can't give him the explanation he needs.

Harley walks inside like a man on a mission, pacing back and forth in the small foyer, his footsteps heavy on the cherrywood floorboards. I turn, watching him as I relax against the front door before pushing off and continuing past him and into the kitchen.

"Do you want a drink?" I call over my shoulder.

He follows me. "No, I don't want no damn drink. I *want* an explanation, Murph!"

I stop at the kitchen island, gripping the counter and taking a moment to collect myself. I've consumed far too much wine for such an intense conversation, and my head is already all over the place. To be honest, I really don't even know where to begin.

"Murph!" Harley presses, his gruff voice booming throughout the silence of my tiny house.

I reluctantly meet his eyes, folding my arms over my chest, considering him for a moment. "Do you wanna know what I've been thinking about all night?"

He stares at me, blinking once, offering an uncertain shrug.

"I've been thinking if Momma never got sick, I never would've had to drop out of college. And if I never dropped out of college, then maybe I'd be the woman marrying Nash …" I shake my head at my own words, ashamed to have said them out loud.

The hard look in Harley's eyes softens a little, and he takes a tentative step forward, glancing away as if in serious thought, as if my confession really affects him, and I know it does, because it's been his shoulders I've spent the last five years crying on.

"Me and him were so happy together after we left for college. Our lives were perfect. Everything was working out just how we'd always planned," I continue. "And then I get a phone call to tell me she has stage-four breast cancer?" I scoff, shaking my head once again at that memory. "I had to drop out, come home, look

44

after her and the bakery, every damn thing. All for what? For nothing. Because she *died* anyway. Just like that."

I look down at the floor as sadness overwhelms me, but I don't cry. I cried all my tears for Momma when she left me. And, I'm not even sad anymore. I'm angry. Angry that I was left all alone. Angry that I got stuck with the mortgage and the doctor bills I couldn't afford. Angry that I lost everything I worked so hard for. College is all I ever wanted, but it was taken away from me, and now it's nothing more than a distant memory. Something I *almost* had. Of course, I miss my mother. I always will. I'm just angry. I have been for five long years.

A heavy silence ensues, settling thick in the air between us.

"You know," Harley starts, his voice a little softer. "I lost everything, too. I was All-American. A five-star recruit. Hell, I was the nation's number-one high school quarterback, for God's sake. I had it *all*. I was a sure shot for the NFL draft ..." He exhales a heavy breath, his shoulders sagging in defeat as he looks down at his hands. "Then I had to go and blow not one, but both my damn knees during the season opener of sophomore year." He shakes his head, his brow furrowed. "I couldn't afford tuition on my own, so I had to drop out of college, too. I know all about losing everything, Murph, and it sure does hurt like a kick to the teeth."

I chew on the inside of my cheek, watching him as he continues.

"Life is nothing more than eighty, maybe ninety years of shitty circumstances all tied in together." He stares into my eyes. "But I still don't understand why the hell I'm suddenly your boyfriend!" He throws his hands in the air with an exasperated sigh.

"You really think I want Nash knowing I spent the last five years of my life stuck in this godforsaken town, just waiting for him to come back to me?" I'm laughing now, but my laugh is void of any humor. If I don't laugh I might cry, and I can't risk letting him see me break down. Not tonight. "You really think I

45

want him knowing I've been waiting around for him to realize he's supposed to be with *me*?"

"Huh ..." Harley seems to realize something at that point, looking at me a moment as he slowly nods. "So, that's what this is all about?"

I stare at him, snapping my mouth shut, realizing I've said too much.

"You're using me to—what? To try to make him jealous?" His eyes are wide with disbelief.

"It's not ... it isn't like that. I—" I begin to try and explain myself, but he interrupts my useless stammering.

"God, I can't *believe* you!" He rakes his fingers through his hair, tearing at the ends as he glances up to the ceiling.

"What?" I snap, offended by his reaction.

"We're supposed to be *best* friends." He laughs under his breath. "I never even knew you were—"

This time, it's me who interrupts him. "We are *not* best friends, Harley." It's totally the wine talking.

He gapes at me, hurt evident in his green eyes. "We're *not* best friends?"

"No." I scoff. "You and me, we're friends by default. Nothing more."

Shut up, Murph, I think to myself. *Just shut up.*

For a moment he looks a little flummoxed, like he can't possibly believe what I'm saying.

"Harley, you were quarterback of our high school football team," I say, as if it's brand-new information. "I ... I volunteered at the school library on weekends, for Christ's sake!"

His brows pull together as he gauges me.

"If it weren't for Nash, I doubt you and me would've even crossed paths, let alone be friends." Another silence is left in the wake of my words, only this time it's different. It's thick with something I've never experienced before, and suddenly I feel terrible. I don't even know why I'm saying what I'm saying. I

46

know it's a defense mechanism. But who the hell am I defending myself from? Harley? Why, when he's the only friend I have?

Harley finally nods, pressing his lips into a thin line as he continues looking into my eyes, his gaze imploring. I'm not sure what more he expects me to say—if anything—so I turn, ending our conversation and busying myself with filling the kettle with water.

"Well, I mean, if that's how you feel ..." he finally says, pulling my attention back to him.

I turn, watching him linger in the doorway, wishing I could tell him it isn't how I feel.

"But, Murph, you better tell Nash the truth, or I will," he warns. "I won't lie to him. He's my best friend." He pauses on his way out, adding, "I thought he was yours, too." He offers me a look that speaks volumes, one that makes me feel about three inches tall, before turning and walking out. And as I remain standing there all alone in the kitchen, listening to the front door slam shut, my thoughts drift a mile away, back to the day my entire world as I knew it came crashing down around me.

Walking out of my Literature class, I smiled as the sun's rays finally managed to break through the heavily looming snow clouds. New York City had been shrouded in a gloomy gray blanket and, in turn, doused with snow for what felt like the entire month of February. So, the warmth of the sun was almost magical as I walked through Washington Square to meet Nash for a bite to eat before our afternoon classes. The moment I saw him sitting there by the fountain, my heart skipped a beat. He looked incredible and warm, dressed in his NYU sweater with his pea coat over the top, as he stared down at the textbook on his lap, rapt with whatever it was he was reading.

God, I love that boy, *I thought to myself as I stopped a moment just to stare at him, appreciate him. I was still completely enamored even after all these years.*

"Nash?" I waved, continuing toward him through the throng of students, tourists, and office workers from the nearby buildings taking advantage of the sun during their lunch breaks.

He looked up from his book, his blue eyes lighting up with his grin as he found me through the crowd. As I approached him, he stood, but I was interrupted by my cell phone vibrating in the pocket of my jeans. Pulling it out, I looked down to see my mother's beautiful face flashing on the illuminated screen. My eyebrows pulled together instinctively. She never called me during the day. She only ever called at night to see how my day went.

"How was your morning?" Nash asked, leaning in to place a kiss to my cheek.

"Hold on just a sec." I turned away from him, answering the call. "Momma? Is everything okay?" I asked before she could speak.

"Hi, darlin'." Her voice sounded different, strange, like it wasn't really her.

I shoved my index finger into my ear in an attempt to hear her a little better over the city noise, walking away from the three girls sitting by the fountain laughing loudly together.

"Hi, Momma," I said with a tight smile, my heart climbing higher and higher toward the back of my throat. Deep down, I knew something was wrong. "Is everything okay?"

"Sweetheart," Momma began, her voice soft and a little broken. "I'm afraid I have some bad news ..."

As I strained to hear her soft voice over the noise I'd become so accustomed to, I glanced back over my shoulder to see Nash watching on with interest, his eyebrows knitted together as he watched me intently while I listened to my mother. But then, when everything around me began to go dark, when the beat of my heart became so deafening it was all I could hear, I watched as Nash dropped his textbook to the ground, running toward me with a look of fear in his eyes. I didn't even realize I'd fallen into a heap on the cold concrete until Nash dropped to his knees, pulling me into his arms.

It looked as if his mouth was trying to say something, screaming

something, a vein in his neck protruding against his smooth skin.
I couldn't hear him. All I could hear was those same words repeating
over and over and over in my head. "Stage-four cancer ... Too late
... I'm dying ..."

The whistling of the kettle brings me back from those heart-breaking memories haunting my mind, and I shake my head, collecting myself as best I can. That was the day it all ended. Everything. That was the day I lost my mom. Although she didn't pass away until about six months later, I lost her that day. In fact, with that one phone call, I lost everything. College. Momma. That was even the day I started losing Nash. Everything I loved was just snatched out from underneath me without warning, with one simple call.

It's funny how your life can go from exceptional to devastating within the flash of an unexpected minute, and there's nothing you can do about it when it happens.

Chapter 8

With the smell of cinnamon and sugar hanging in the air throughout the bakery, I have a little kick in my step, some gusto in my belly and a smile on my face as I open up the store for the after-church rush. I've been up since four o'clock, baking test batches for Nash and Anna's wedding cake for them to try tomorrow and, if I wasn't so excited, I'd probably be exhausted. But Nash wants to hang out today. Just the two of us. He said so himself, last night. There has to be a reason behind it. I know I wasn't imagining it when I saw the flash of jealousy in his blue eyes as he watched Harley take my hand when we were leaving the country club. I saw it with my own damn eyes.

I'd sent him a text earlier to see what we were doing, where he wanted me to meet him, but that was forty-five minutes ago. Now, I keep finding myself checking the time in between customers, wondering what the hell is even going on. It's almost eleven when I finally get to catch a break from the morning rush. With a heavy sigh, I take a sip from my glass of iced tea, drumming my fingers against the countertop, watching the clock on the far wall tick so excruciatingly slowly, it's as if each second is mocking me. When I'm just about to give up and resign myself to the tray of freshly baked éclairs out back in the kitchen, my cell begins to ring, and I almost dislocate my shoulder trying to reach into my back pocket in time to answer it.

Nash.

"Hey!" I smile through the phone, trying not to give away my relief.

"Hey, Murph." He chuckles from the other end as if he knows I'm more than excited to speak to him. "I got your text," he continues. "Sorry, Anna and I got stuck talking to my grandma at brunch."

My smile falls at the mention of *her*. Not his grandma. I've always loved Nash's grandma. My smile falls at the mention of *Anna*. But I force myself to cheer up, remembering that look of jealousy in his eyes last night. "Okay … So, did you still wanna hang out today?"

"Well, that's why I'm calling you," Nash says, and I can tell by the tone in his voice that our plans have been canceled. My shoulders sag involuntarily. "I'm surprised you didn't know, actually—"

"Know what?" My brows pull together in confusion.

"Harley called me this morning," he begins and, at the mention of Harley, my heart stops dead in the center of my chest. Oh God. Did he tell Nash the truth about my lie like he threatened he would last night? I'm on the verge of a panic attack. I almost miss it when he says, "He said he's having a barbecue at his house. You didn't know about it?"

My thoughts come to a crashing halt in the back of my mind. A barbecue? My eyes narrow into slits as I glare straight ahead at the glass cake display, as if it alone has done me some sort of an injustice. My jaw clenches at the thought of Harley. He knew Nash and I were supposed to hang out today, and he's gone and fabricated a stupid barbecue as some kind of a diversion. What a jerk.

"Murph?" Nash's voice interjects my thoughts. "You there?"

51

"Yeah." I manage a smile despite my anger, exhaling the breath I've been holding. "I forgot all about the ... *barbecue*," I lie.

"So, I guess I'll just see you there, then?"

"Yeah." I nod to myself, pressing my lips together to contain the profanities threatening my composure. "I'll see you there, Nash."

Our call ends, and it takes everything I have not to throw my phone across the store in frustration, but my moment of anger is interrupted by Mrs. Wilcox, the sweet 82-year-old wife of Reverend Wilcox, walking into the bakery with a beaming smile mostly hidden beneath the wide brim of her church hat, and I can just tell she's bursting at the seams to collect her weekly apple and custard turnover to have after her Sunday lunch.

"Mrs. Wilcox." I smile through gritted teeth, tucking my hair behind my ear. "Just the usual for you on this fine Sunday?"

"Oh yes, please, Alice, darling." She nods, looking through the glass at all the sweets, her eyes lighting up.

I haven't been to church in a long time. Ever since Momma passed. When she was taken from me, I wondered what the point was, going to church and sitting through an hour-and-a-half sermon while Reverend Wilcox blathered on and on about our Lord and savior. Momma went to church every single Sunday, rain or shine, and a fat lot of good it did her. After Momma's death, I began to wonder what the point was of anything, really. So, I haven't been back. The reverend visits me here at the bakery every Thursday morning. He pretends he's just here for one of my famous peach muffins, but his efforts to try to convince me to come back aren't as stealthy as he believes them to be. Maybe one day I will go back to church. Harley's always trying to tag me along with him. But I just can't. For now, I just don't see the point.

"Oh Alice, sweetheart, I heard Nash Harris is back in town." Mrs. Wilcox flashes me a knowing look. "Marrying a woman from *New York City*."

I can't help but bite back my laughter. The way she refers to Anna as the woman from New York suggests she's some scandalous harlot. I press my lips together, nodding as I carefully wrap up the turnover.

"Such a shame," she muses, offering a sad smile. "I always thought it would be the two of you walking down the aisle of the church."

I shake my head, placing the pastry into a paper bag and handing it over the counter. "Nope. Not me," I say with a nonchalant shrug, and, although I know I shouldn't, I just can't help myself. "And, in fact, they're not getting married in the church, Mrs. Wilcox. They're getting married in the chapel at Harrington Country Club."

Poor Mrs. Wilcox. Her jaw drops and she actually turns sheet-white as she clutches a hand to her robust chest. "Harrington Country Club?" She gasps. I nod, trying so hard not to smile. "Well, I *never*." She mutters something else under her breath, shaking her head to herself. "You just wait until I see that boy's grandmother at our weekly book club, tomorrow morning." And, with that, she turns and waddles out of the store with her apple turnover nursed carefully in her arms, murmuring something under her breath I can't hear.

"Have a good day, Mrs. Wilcox," I sing cheerfully as she exits, chuckling to myself.

I glance at the clock just as Sarah, my weekend helper, comes bounding in through the door, her cheeks flushed from the warmth of the midday sun. I breathe a sigh of relief, untying my apron, and she follows me through to the kitchen, jabbering on about her excuse for being late. Something about a fight with her boyfriend, Tyler, this morning. I don't allow her to see my eye-roll, but I really don't care.

"I have to go," I say, handing Sarah the keys to the bakery, which she proudly tucks into the pocket of her pinafore. "I have a barbecue."

"Oh yeah, I heard the news," Sarah says, leaning on the island counter and watching as I pack my things into my purse.

"What *news*?" I flash her a look.

"You and Harley Shaw. Official." She waggles her eyebrows up and down. "I saw it on Facebook last night."

"Facebook!" I shriek, gawping at her, but she just nods, as if news of my relationship status circulating social media isn't a big deal. "Wow. News sure does travel fast in this town ..." I sigh, rolling my eyes once more.

"It does when you nab the town's hottest, most eligible bachelor." She smiles a lustful smile, and I can only imagine she's momentarily daydreaming about Harley, and I can't help but wonder if her older brother, Seth, knows the way she idolizes one of his best friends.

"Don't forget to lock up." I place my apron onto the stainless steel counter, pulling Sarah from her reverie. "And turn off the gas this time." I offer a warning look, which she meets with a sheepish smile as I hurry out to make it to Harley's stupid barbecue.

With a Tupperware container of cupcakes I took from the bakery, I pull up outside Harley's house. Huffing out a sigh, I sit in the car for a moment, glaring at his isolated home in the boondocks, almost completely hidden by the tall pine trees overcrowding the sprawling front yard. I'm not in the mood for this today. Closing my eyes a moment, I take a few fortifying breaths in through my nose, cleansing myself before hopping out of the car. I smooth down the front of my shirt, tuck the container of cakes under my arm, and proceed up the driveway, hearing the sound of people having far too good a time coming from around the back of the house.

The moment I step through the side gate, I really wish I'd just stayed at home. My eyes roam the expansive yard, zeroing in on Anna's bevy of beautiful bridesmaids huddled together on lawn chairs, cackling in sync to something that cannot possibly be that funny. They remind me of those mean girls at every single high school in America. All beautiful. All blonde. All bitches. Of course, I have no grounds on which to base my assumption. I don't know if they're mean or not. I just dislike them because they're with Anna, and I don't like her because she's with Nash. Petty? Absolutely.

Turning, I cross the yard, walking up the steps of the deck to where Seth and Kevin, Nash and Harley's friends from high school, are sitting, drinking beers with a few guys I've never seen before.

"What'd you bring, Murph?" Kevin asks, eyeing my Tupperware container.

"Salted caramel cupcakes," I say, placing the container on the patio table while I scan the backyard for a glimpse of Nash.

"You made 'em?" Seth asks, overly excited.

"No." I shake my head. "Your sister made them yesterday. Something about a new recipe she found on Pinterest, or whatever. I just let her go for it so she wouldn't annoy me while I was doing the books."

Seth laughs at the mention of his little sister, Sarah, the apple of his eye.

"Where's Nash?"

"Inside."

Taking a deep breath, I continue inside, stepping into the kitchen, but I stop suddenly, finding Nash and Anna together—really together—kissing as if they've not seen each other in forever, and it takes everything I have not to outwardly gag. I clear my throat, looking down to the floor.

"Oh, hey, Murph." Nash chuckles. "You finally made it!"

I look up to see him sheepishly wiping his mouth with the back of his hand, and I feel my cheeks blush. "Yeah."

"You look cute, Murph," Anna coos, looking me up and down, and inwardly I cringe. Cute? I'm literally wearing jean shorts, a Falcons' T-shirt, an old flannel shirt over the top, no makeup whatsoever, and a pair of scuffed Converse. Far from cute. I don't know what she's playing at. The moment I look at her, finding her just as beautiful as the night before—maybe even more so—I hate her. But then, my eyes trail downward, taking in the plain white T-shirt she's wearing, the one emblazoned with *Future Mrs. Harris* across the front in big bold letters. I suddenly have this overwhelming feeling that she secretly has it in for me. It's as if she's taunting me. I don't just hate her, I actually despise her.

"Murph, are you coming to Myrtle Beach?" Nash suddenly asks.

"Myrtle Beach?" I quirk a brow in confusion.

He nods. "Yeah. The bachelor party. We've got this really cool rental house right on the beach. Just me, Kev, Seth, a couple of guys from New York. And, Harley, of course."

Of course. I try to act unbothered. "No. I have some things to do around here."

He shrugs, and Anna starts, looking at me with bulging blue eyes. "Oh my God!"

"What?" I stare at her, waiting for whatever it is she's suddenly so excited about as Nash picks at chips from a bowl on the countertop. She clutches at her chest dramatically, and I just blink at her until she gets to whatever it is she feels so inclined to tell me. "You can come to the bachelorette party," she says as if it's the greatest idea since sliced, gluten-free bread. "We're having it at a retreat in the mountains. Facials. Massages. Manicures and pedicures. The works! Please say you'll come?"

I almost choke on thin air from her unexpected invitation. She can't possibly expect me to come. I couldn't honestly be expected to go. Not with her, the woman marrying the man I was supposed to end up with. And a retreat in the mountains? It's hardly my kind of thing. To be honest, I'd rather jump headfirst into an open shark tank than spend a night with Anna and her girlfriends. "Actually, on second thought, I'll go to Myrtle Beach," I say, trying not to make myself too obvious. And both Anna and Nash look at me, so I add with a smile, "It'll be nice to spend the time with Harley." I'm almost certain I can taste throw-up in my mouth.

Nash makes a cooing sound, Anna openly gushes, and I try so hard not to roll my eyes.

"Is he around?" I ask, forcing myself to look away from where Nash's hand rests casually on Anna's slender hip, his thumb tenderly stroking the smooth skin showing where the hem of that damn T-shirt has ridden up slightly higher, exposing her perfect skin. Not a single stretch mark in sight.

"Garage." Nash nods in the direction of the door, picking a chip from the big bowl on the countertop. "He's getting some ice from the back of his truck."

"Babe, stop!" Anna slaps his hand playfully. "No more chips. Think of the wedding photos. You're going to break out and bloat up!"

Nash rolls his eyes, doing as he's told and pushing the chip bowl as far away as he can, and for some reason that makes me real sad. He's like her little dog, doing as he's ordered. Turning quickly, I hurry through the internal door that leads to the garage, desperate to get the hell away from the two of them.

The garage smells of gasoline and freshly mowed lawn, and immediately I can feel my allergies threatening what little composure I have. I sniffle, wiping my nose with the sleeve of my shirt as I step down into the cluttered darkness, illuminated only by the tiny window at the top of the garage door. When I spot Harley, I pause, resting against the side of his truck. I take a moment to watch as he effortlessly lifts two bags of ice and a case of beer from the back. He's wearing a flannel with the sleeves ripped off, exposing his strong arms, most of which are covered in tattoos. The top few buttons are undone, showing off his inked chest.

For a few seconds, it's as if I'm in some kind of a trance I can't snap myself of out of, and I hate every second of it, but I still can't tear my eyes away from the way his muscles move beneath his skin. It's almost hypnotizing.

Harley looks up in time to see me standing there, gaping at him like a creeper, and a knowing smirk pulls at his lips as I shake my head free of the crazy thoughts running through it. "Oh, hey, *babe*," he says, smoothing his hair back from his face, his eyes raking up and down my form. "Like what you see?"

I roll my eyes and shake my head at him. "What the *hell* are you playing at, Harley?"

"What?" He shrugs, offering a look of innocence, despite that same smug smirk playing on his lips.

"What's this all about?" I wave a hand in the air to indicate the party currently going on outside.

He shrugs again. "Nothing. I just thought I'd throw my best friend a barbecue to celebrate his impending nuptials," he says with a knowing grin. A real shit-eating grin—dimples and all—one I desperately want to slap straight off his stupid face.

"You knew Nash and I were planning to hang out together today." I point an accusatory finger at him. "And then suddenly you throw an impromptu barbecue?" I scoff, folding my arms across my chest while glowering at him.

Harley just stares at me, that same infuriating smile ghosting over his lips as he looks me up and down.

"And, besides, I thought you were gonna tell him everything? You sure did threaten me last night," I add, tapping my foot impatiently. "Well?"

"I thought about it." He stops, and glances up at the exposed beams overhead as if considering the idea. "But then I realized this might be more fun."

I shake my head, confused by his words.

"You know," he begins, going back to stacking the cases of

58

beer from the bed of his truck. "Anna has some pretty hot bridesmaids." I blink at him, a crease pulling between my eyebrows. "A single guy like me, a couple cute bridesmaids ..." He trails off, quirking one of his eyebrows. "You don't think maybe I would have liked to take advantage of my single status this week?"

"Ugh!" I cringe, scrunching up my nose at him. "You're a pig and a half, Harley Shaw!"

"No," he interjects. "I'm a single guy who would've liked to have a little fun. But now, I'm stuck pretending to be with a woman I, quite frankly, can't even stand right now."

If I cared about a thing he said, his words would have hurt. But I don't, so they didn't.

"Oh my *God*, Harley!" I clutch my hands at my chest in mock shock. "I'm *so* sorry I got in the way of you man-whoring your ass through a group of conceited Park Avenue princesses all week long! How *inconsiderate* of me." I offer a smug smile of my own. "You can thank me now for not contracting some disgusting STD."

He rolls his eyes.

"Why must you sabotage everything?" I murmur with a huff.

"You're the one planning on breaking up a damn wedding!" He balks, a look of exasperation in his wide eyes. I narrow my eyes at him, considering my own words. But when I open my mouth to speak, he beats me to it. "He's my best friend, and he's *finally* happy!"

I snap my mouth shut, looking at him in stark shock. I hadn't been expecting that and, while it's true, I just can't bring myself to agree. "But he was *happy* with *me*," I say, my voice obviously less confident than it had been only moments ago.

"Yeah, he *was* happy with you." Harley nods, stepping past me with a big bag of ice in each of his hands. "But that's the past, Murph." He looks down at me a moment, something earnest within his green eyes. "Don't you think maybe it's time you move on? Nash sure as hell has."

He walks back inside the house and I'm left alone in the musty garage with nothing but the floating dust particles to keep me company, and my shoulders slump in resignation as I allow his sobering words to sink in.

Chapter 9

I sit on my own for most of the afternoon, my mind busily running away with itself.

Harley is occupied at the grill, drinking a beer, trying to ignore Anna and Nash who are shamelessly sucking one another's faces right beside him. The bridesmaids are clearly gossiping among themselves. Most of Nash and Harley's friends are glued to the television inside, watching some baseball game. And I'm on my own, nursing a big bowl of pretzels, watching YouTube videos on my phone on the latest fondant craze, secretly wondering whether anyone would even notice if I get up and leave.

"Hey, you okay?"

I jump, looking up to see Nash sliding into the patio chair beside me. He offers a cheeky grin, his eyes flitting sideways before he reaches his hand into the bowl of pretzels on my lap.

"Yeah." I smile, placing the bowl onto the glass tabletop after he carefully selects a handful of pretzels. "Anna won't be happy if she catches you eating pretzels," I tease. "Think of the *wedding photos!*"

"She'll get over it." He chuckles, shoving a few into his mouth. "Is everything okay between you two?" he asks, his brow slightly furrowed as he casts Harley a sideways glance.

I look to where Harley is at the grill, drinking a beer while talking and laughing with one of his friends, and I nod. "Yeah," I say with a nonchalant shrug. "Why wouldn't it be?"

What? Just because I'm not giving him an over-the-pants hand job like Anna is practically doing to Nash every time she's near him, something has to be wrong?

"I'm real glad you and Harley are together," Nash continues, his eyes still focused on Harley. "He deserves a woman like you."

I'm not sure if that's a compliment or not, and I almost scoff out loud.

Harley looks over at that moment as if he knows we're talking about him. And, with a small smile, he lifts his chin at me, adding a wink before busying himself with flipping the burgers. He's actually kind of good at this whole pretending thing.

"He's a lucky guy," Nash adds, flashing me a knowing smile before getting up and walking away.

What?

I shake my head in an attempt to clear the confusion suddenly clouding my mind. Harley deserves the best … He's a lucky guy … Nash Harris is seriously beginning to confuse the hell out of me. If he thinks so highly of me, then why the hell did things end between us all those years ago?

I hadn't seen Nash since the funeral. He'd stayed to help as much as he could, but he had to get back to school for midterms. Plus, I'd kind of wanted to be alone while I tried to pick up the pieces after my mother's death. But six weeks was a long time to go without seeing the love of your life, particularly when the rest of your world was lying at your feet in tiny, jagged pieces.

Piece O' Cake suffered while Momma was sick. I'd tried as hard as I could to manage the orders that continued flooding in, but between looking after her, taking her back and forth to the hospital, and tying up loose ends just before she passed away, it was almost impossible to keep the store afloat.

With everything we owned of value sold off, I'd been living off beans and working around the clock so I could try get the store back up and running. But, doing everything on my own was more difficult than I had ever imagined. Thankfully, I had one thing going for me. My mother had taught me how to bake when I was just 7 years old. I was her shadow in the kitchen when I was little. Watching her like a hawk while licking every spatula, I learned all I needed to know. I knew I'd never be as good as she was, but it was the gift she'd passed on to me, and I'd hoped and prayed it would help me save what was left of her legacy.

I'd been busily working for weeks on the grand reopening, and I had spent a good chunk of Momma's insurance money on radio advertising, signage, balloons, children's face painters, you name it. It was what would hopefully bring Piece O' Cake back from the proverbial dead. Nash was supposed to come home to help me. But then, something came up.

"What do you mean you can't come?" I cried, my cell phone clamped between my cheek and my shoulder as I busily frosted a batch of cupcakes.

"You know how I was telling you about that accelerated program they're running at Sacred Heart?"

"Yeah," I lied. He probably did tell me, but likely my mind had been elsewhere, as it had been ever since I'd found out Momma was ill.

"Well," he began, his voice tentative, "I got in. Can you believe it? I actually made it. But … it begins this week."

I placed my piping bag down, my hands gripping the stainless metal countertop as I tried desperately to take a few steadying breaths.

"Are you there, babe?"

"Yes," I sighed, shaking my head. "So, when do you think you'll be able to come home?"

He hesitated, and I could almost hear the trepidation in his silence.

63

"Nash?" I asked a little more urgently than I would have liked.

"Probably not until Thanksgiving ..."

My jaw dropped.

"Two months?" I cried.

"I know, I'm sorry, babe."

I could feel tears burning at the backs of my eyes, but I refused to cry. I'd cried enough over the last few weeks, I couldn't spare any more tears.

"Maybe you could—" Nash went to speak, stopping himself halfway.

"Maybe I could what?"

He paused a moment, and all I could hear was the sound of the New York City traffic bustling in the background of his call. It was a sound I hated when I'd first moved up there. A sound I never thought I would get used to. A sound I now miss, terribly, because all it does is remind me of what I'm missing out on being down here in Graceville, Georgia, a town with literally two sets of traffic lights and three roundabouts, and no such thing as a morning rush hour.

"Maybe you could come back to New York?" he suggested. "Back to school. You could take catch-up classes, and we could—"

"Nash," I interjected. "I can't go back to school. I can't afford the tuition, and I have this place to run. I'm-I'm not coming back to New York."

"What? Ever?" His voice was high-pitched and incredulous, and I imagined his blue eyes bulging.

I took a deep breath, preparing myself. I hadn't been expecting to have this conversation with him over the phone. I'd planned on telling him when he came home this weekend to help with the reopening. "I have to stay here," I began to explain, considering my words. "I can't lose this place, Nash. My mother worked her whole life for the bakery. It's been in the family for three generations."

Silence ensued.

"S-so you're not coming back to New York?" Nash finally asked, and there was something behind his question—a harsh tone within his voice—that immediately pricked the skin at the back of my neck.

"No," I stated vehemently. "I'm not coming back, Nash."

"Well then," he said with a derisive laugh that held no hint of humor. "I guess there's nothing more to say."

I pressed my lips together, picking at a loose thread on my apron. "I guess not."

"I've gotta go," he murmured. "I'll call you later."

And with that, our call ended. No I love you. No I miss you. Not even a goodbye.

I stared down at the half-frosted cupcakes, so many conflicting emotions running through my mind. And those tears I'd been trying so hard to keep at bay began falling relentlessly. Looking around at the kitchen, I realized something. This was my life now, whether I liked it or not. And, without warning, an anger I'd never felt before got the better of me. Or, maybe it wasn't anger. Maybe it was the feeling of resignation or resentment. I don't know what it was but, without even considering the consequences of my actions, I released a scream that had been pent up inside me for far too long.

Lunging forward with as much strength as I could muster, I swiped at the cupcakes, the mixing bowls, the ingredients, everything, watching as it all went crashing to the floor in an almighty clatter before I went down with it straight after. As I buried my tear-streaked face into my hands, I cried for everything I'd lost. Momma, college, Nash, my life as I'd known it. It felt as if everything was falling apart and there was nothing I could do about it.

But then, something I hadn't expected. I startled from my sobs by the sound of scuffing footsteps coming from the doorway through to the kitchen. Wiping my eyes, I sniffled, looking up, and my jaw dropped as fresh tears fell.

No, I thought to myself. It couldn't possibly be him.

With sad eyes, he offered a lopsided smile I could tell was for my benefit only. I could see the pain his own smile caused him deep within his sad eyes. But still, he smiled. And, with a slightly staggered limp, he took another step forward.

"Hey, Murph."

"Harley?" My voice croaked through my emotion as I looked him up and down. He was skinnier than I'd ever seen him look. His cheeks were hollow, and he had dark circles beneath his eyes. Dressed in a faded T-shirt and basketball shorts that hung low on his narrow waist, I zeroed in on the knee braces securing each of his knees, and the crutch he kept himself upright with, secured under his left arm.

"W-what are you d-doing here?" I gasped, scrambling back up to my feet. "I thought you were still in hospital!"

"I discharged myself." He nodded, looking me up and down before his glassy eyes met mine. "I needed to come home ..."

I stared at him as tears pricked my eyes and emotion overwhelmed every fiber of my being. There, before me, stood a boy so broken, inside and out. After losing everything he'd worked so hard for all his life, at a time when he should've been recovering, here he was.

A sob escaped me, but I didn't care anymore. The tears flowed freely, streaming down my cheeks as I ran across the kitchen as fast as I could, crashing into his chest. And, with our arms wrapped around one another so tight, I'm sure neither of us could breathe properly. I cried against his chest, feeling some semblance of comfort in the familiarity and warmth he provided, and for the first time since losing Momma, I didn't feel alone.

Pulling myself from my overwhelming thoughts, I look to where Nash and Anna are laughing and giggling together, and I sigh, looking down at my hands as I think of the past five years. That phone call hadn't been the end of mine and Nash's relationship. We managed to drag it out for longer than we should have, and I don't even know why. It was hell for the both of us. Visiting one another when we had the time and the money. Talking as much as we could over the phone. But then, our conversations became labored, forced. And our visits became few and far between. Although it was obvious where we were heading, we'd each been too stubborn to end it. Unfortunately, our ending came long after both our hearts had been broken.

"Burger?"

I look up to see Harley standing over me, a paper plate in his hand with a cheeseburger on it, and something comes over me—an emotion I hadn't been expecting—and I feel tears prick at the backs of my eyes when I suddenly realize something as if for the first time. The day I'd lost Nash, I gained Harley. He was there for me when Nash wasn't. It was Harley who had helped me pick up all the pieces when I needed someone the most.

I swallow the emotion balling at the back of my throat, managing a smile as I take the plate from him. "Thanks."

Expecting him to walk away and go back to his friends, much to my surprise he takes the seat right next to me, and I feel his gaze watching me intently while I pick at the burger bun.

"Are you okay?" He cocks his head to the side, studying me.

I nod, eating a slice of pickle, avoiding his eyes.

"Murph?" Harley leans in closer, lowering his voice a little and I force myself to look at him. "I've known you for fifteen years. We may not be *best friends*, according to you, but I know you well enough to know when something's wrong." A small smile plays on his lips, hinting at his dimples, and his green eyes are dubious as he continues watching me.

I shrug. "I didn't mean what I said last night."

His eyebrows pull together as he studies me for a long moment.

"About you and me. About our friendship being forced." The words are like poison on my tongue, and I shake my head at myself, unable to believe I even said such a thing last night. I take a deep breath, blinking away those infuriating tears. "You're my best friend, Harley. I don't know what I'd do without you."

I half-expect him to offer me some smartass comment like he normally would, but he doesn't. In fact, he doesn't say anything. Instead, he reaches out, his hand squeezing my knee once, a small smile of understanding curving his lips upward as he stands back up and returns to the grill to continue plating the burgers.

Chapter 10

The afternoon sun finally retreats behind the tall pines, offering a reprieve to the blistering warmth and, with the cool shade it provides over the backyard, the guys decide to play a game of flag football, with Nash and Harley as the team captains.

Normally I'm not one for sports. There's just something barbaric about it all. Plus, I'm terrible at any and every physical activity, and far too competitive for someone as unfit as I am. But, when Nash chooses Anna first up, I stand from my seat so fast the thing falls back against the decking. I meet Harley's eyes with a pleading look. He just has to let me play.

"Okay." Harley chuckles under his breath, a look of confusion in his eyes as he meets my stare. "I pick Murph."

"Aww, cute ..." Nash laughs, teasingly, nudging his friend with his shoulder.

Harley shakes his head at him, watching me with a curious look in his eye as I approach him. "What are you playing at?" he asks from the corner of his mouth while Nash busies himself with choosing his next player. "You *hate* flag football."

"What are you talking about?" I look up at him, fluttering my eyelashes innocently as I push my glasses up my nose. "I *love* football ..."

"*Flag* football, Murph," he reminds me with a warning look. "Flag!"

I roll my eyes, dismissing his halfhearted caution with a brush of my hand. Smiling to myself all the while, I began imagining Anna's flawless face being pushed into the mud by yours truly.

Ten minutes into the game and Nash has the ball, laughing and dodging Harley's defensive line, while I'm stuck on the sidelines because I'd been sent off for two minutes for tackling Taylor, one of Anna's bridesmaids.

Taylor had the ball, and she was running toward the makeshift end zone. I saw her flag flailing in her wake, and I should have grabbed it. But I didn't. I'm not sure what I was thinking. Maybe that's just it. Maybe I wasn't thinking. All I knew was that I couldn't let her score, and my natural instinct was to stop her, any way I could. So, snapping into action, I picked up speed, sprinting as fast as my short legs would allow. I was just lucky she wasn't really putting in any effort; I'm pretty sure she was only playing in an attempt to be cute in front of the guys, because I somehow managed to catch up with her and, in an instant, without even thinking, I launched at her. And I mean *launched*. I wrapped my arms around her shoulders from behind so tight, my feet actually lifted off the ground.

Our collision seemed to happen in slow motion as our bodies tumbled together, until Taylor fell to the ground in a pile of mud with me landing on top of her, my glasses flying right off my face. She pushed me off, screaming and crying. Apparently, she bit her tongue, but I doubt it was as bad as she was carrying on about since there was no sign of blood.

So, while I wait on the sideline for my penalty time to count down, Taylor sits on the patio with a bag of frozen peas pressed against her chin, glaring daggers at me as if she's hoping looks might actually kill.

After an interception, we have the ball again, and Harley leads a huddle when he waves me back onto the field. I run toward the small group, sidling up next to him as he explains the play to the team. "Murph, this is your ball." He looks at me. "You're the shortest."

I stand as tall as I can, gaping at him with my hands on my hips. "Hey!"

He offers an unapologetic smile. "Sorry, but you'll get through Nash and Kevin without them being able to touch you."

I roll my eyes, submitting to my five-foot-three fate.

Beth, Anna's maid of honor, shoots me a warning glare as she steps back from the huddle. Folding her arms over her chest defiantly, she looks me up and down in disgust. "I am *not* playing with *her*." She shakes her head. "She almost *killed* my best friend!"

Killed? Bit dramatic. I try not to laugh out loud, looking to the ground as I bite back my smile.

"It was an accident," Harley says, trying to placate her. "Isn't that right, Murph?" He nudges me with his elbow, and I glance up, trying so hard to remain poker-faced, but the absolute look of horror in Beth's eyes makes it difficult. I mean, you'd think I actually did kill someone the way she's looking at me.

"Yeah." I nod, pressing my lips together to stifle my threatening laughter. "Total accident."

Harley claps his hands together. "Win big, on three," he shouts, holding a hand in the middle of the huddle. We each put our hands over his, and I watch Beth flash me a narrow-eyed glare as she reluctantly reaches in, her long, skinny fingers hovering over the top of mine.

"One! Two! Three! *Win big!*" we yell in unison before breaking apart and taking our positions on the improvised field.

Harley's play consists of him faking a handoff to his friend, Seth. He then crosses to me, handing me the ball, and I tuck it under my arm, turning and checking my path before running with everything I have toward our end zone. I dodge Kevin, and then Nash, laughing when Nash slips on the grass and falls on

71

his butt. I slip past Whitney, another of Anna's blonde brides-maids, but then, not looking where I'm going, I slide on a patch of mud, and I almost fall to the ground, stumbling unsteadily and fumbling the ball.

"Go, baby!" I hear Nash yell from the other end of the yard.

I turn to see Anna running for me, her blonde hair flapping in the breeze as she giggles and laughs, successfully dodging the mud before reaching for me, and I panic. I'm taken by complete surprise as she comes at me from my blindside, so of course my natural instinct is to throw an elbow out in defense. I was just trying to scare her off. I didn't actually expect to connect with her. But I do connect with her. Hard. And poor, unsuspecting Anna crumbles to the ground in a heap, clutching her right eye and screaming bloody murder at the top of her lungs.

"Anna!" Nash runs toward us.

Like a deer caught in the headlights of a rusted old Ford, I freeze, looking around to see everyone hurrying over, their eyes wide and their faces stark. Nash drops to his knees, carefully helping his fiancée from the mud as she continues bellowing while her bridesmaids crowd around her, pushing me out of the way a little aggressively.

"I'm sorry, I didn't—" I try to apologize, but it's pointless. No one is listening to me.

"Let me have a look," Nash says, gently cupping Anna's face and taking a closer look to assess the damage.

I crane my neck to see, finding the skin around her eye already red and swollen, and I take a step back, clamping my bottom lip between my teeth.

"Can someone get some ice?" Nash yells.

Anna continues crying.

Under any other circumstance, I probably would laugh because, let's face it, I didn't even hit her *that* hard. But she has a wedding in six days. I can't laugh. I'm not that callous. I feel bad—terrible, in fact—I didn't mean to hurt the girl, I just got carried away. And this is why I never play sports.

"Jesus, Murph!" Harley hisses coming up beside me. I look up to see him shaking his head at me while trying to conceal his smile.

"I didn't mean to," I gasp. "It was an accident."

"If I have a black eye on my wedding day, I swear to God, I'm canceling the whole damn thing!" Anna sobs, absolutely beside herself with distress.

"It's okay, baby," Nash conciliates her. "Let's just sit down and put some ice on it. You'll be fine."

I stand back, watching Nash help Anna as she staggers unsteadily, gripping his arm tight. He flashes me a look, one I can't really read. I'm not sure if he's angry with me, disappointed, or perhaps even sorry. Either way, it's a look I've never seen in his eyes before, one that makes my stomach twist painfully in my gut.

"Wow, that looks really bad!" Kevin laughs, coming in closer to get a look. Anna glares at him, and instinctively I whack him in his tactless belly in an attempt to silence him.

I move quickly, running toward Anna and Nash as they head toward the patio steps. "Anna, I'm so sorry." I reach out, touching her shoulder, but she flinches away from me.

"Murph, just leave it!" Nash snaps, offering me a warning glance over his shoulder while shaking his head.

I pull my hand back looking between the both of them. "I swear I didn't mean to. I was—"

"You gave her a black eye!!" Beth is on me like a rabid dog, violently pushing me away before hurrying to help her best friend, following them as they disappear inside the house.

As I stand there, covered in mud, feeling all eyes watching me as if I'm some kind of homicidal lunatic, I sigh, looking down to see that I've still got the damn football tucked under my arm.

"Are you okay?" Harley asks, suddenly beside me again, his hand on my shoulder, squeezing gently.

I look up at him, nodding once. But I'm not okay. Because, the truth is there's a really big part of me questioning whether or not I just threw my elbow on purpose with the intention of hurting Anna. But I can't possibly tell Harley that. He already thinks I'm a complete psycho.

Dressed in my pajamas, I relax on the sofa with a mug of herbal tea and the television remote. After a day like today I need some time to myself. Just me, my pajamas, and Netflix. But, of course, just as I get comfortable, my moment of peace is interrupted by an unexpected knock on the front door. Rolling my eyes, I groan in protest, feeling the day's earlier football match in every one of my aching muscles as I hobble through to the hallway, stopping to open the door. When I see Nash standing on my porch, my eyebrows knit together in confusion.

"Hey," is all I can say, stepping aside and holding the door open for him in silent invitation.

With his head bowed, Nash walks inside, coming to stop awkwardly in the small entry.

"Is everything okay?" I ask, closing the door to stop the night breeze from blowing inside.

"I just wanted to stop by and apologize for today," he starts, meeting my eyes with an apologetic look. "Anna's fine, and I didn't want you feeling bad. I shouldn't have yelled at you the way I did."

I immediately feel bad because what happened earlier hadn't actually crossed my mind since I'd returned home from Harley's. I mean, it's not like I maimed her or anything.

"Anna feels real bad for what happened today. How she acted," he continues. "She doesn't want things to be awkward between the two of you, and she's spoken to her friends and told them to back off, too."

I nod, looking down to my sock-covered feet so he can't see me roll my eyes. Yes, I'm relieved Anna's okay, but I really couldn't care less what she or her bitchy bridesmaids think of me.

"She wants to do dinner tomorrow night," Nash says, pulling me from my thoughts. "Just the four of us."

I look up again, my eyes wide.

"Sure." I shrug, managing a smile. "Sounds like fun," I lie.

"We're still on for the wedding cake testing tomorrow, right?"

I catch sight of his grin, his blue eyes dancing beneath the dim light of the hallway lamp. His gaze is so all-consuming, it's easy to become lost within it.

"Of course." I nod, snapping myself from my musings. "I baked the samples this morning. I just have to put the final touches on the frosting. I'll have everything ready by midday."

Nash's shoulders seem to sag in relief, and he steps forward, closing the distance between us, rendering me absolutely breathless when he wraps one of his arms around me, pulling me close. "You know I love you, right, Murph?" he whispers, his lips brushing against my temple.

I nod as my eyelashes flutter, my eyes closing as I breathe him in, basking in his embrace and the sentiment behind his words. And, in that moment, I'm almost certain I feel something pass between us, something unexpected, something I haven't felt in a long time.

Without so much as another word, he presses a kiss to the top of my head before turning and walking back outside through the door, leaving me breathless and unsteady on my feet as I grip the doorjamb in the hope that it will keep me from falling into a heap on the floor. I watch, waiting for him to get into his rental car, waving as he slowly pulls away from the curb before I close the door. Resting back against the wood, I can't hide the smug grin pulling at my lips as I consider what just happened. He still loves me.

75

Chapter 11

Monday is not only the start of a new week, it's the start of a new me. I have a newfound confidence, and a well-thought-out plan of attack. Normally, on any other Monday morning, I'd drag my sorry ass out of bed, shower, tie my damp hair into a knot on top of my head, brush my teeth, and throw on any old thing to wear to work to prepare for the week. Not today. Today I take my time in the shower, using my very best body scrub. I shave my legs. I moisturize every inch of my body. I brush my teeth while wearing an eight-minute eye mask that promises to help reduce dark circles and puffiness. I give myself a blowout. I apply primer, foundation, and I even contour, for Christ's sake. This morning I am somebody else.

Today isn't a day for jeans and an old T-shirt. Today I choose my prettiest floral skirt that twirls with every movement I make. I team it with a jean shirt tucked into the high waist, and a statement belt to help accentuate that I do, in fact, have a figure. With a pair of cute sandals, and my leopard print glasses, I'm ready to face the day and, more importantly, Anna and Nash.

It's a truth universally acknowledged that inside every woman is an inner-psycho, just waiting to be unleashed. Now, while I might never admit it out loud, I'm quite certain my inner-psycho reared her disheveled head the moment Nash Harris arrived in town to give me that damn invitation to his wedding. Ever since Friday, I've been doing things I can't even begin to explain, like lacing half the wedding cake testers with laxative …

I'm not even sure what I was hoping to get out of it. Maybe I was hoping Anna would get so sick, she wouldn't be able to make our dinner reservation. Then I could somehow convince Harley to stay away and I'd have Nash all to myself. But then what? Was I expecting Nash to come to his senses and realize I'm the one for him? I don't even know what it is, but it's as if I was an outsider looking in, unable to control my own actions. I'm on the verge of utterly certifiable, and I can't even stop myself at this point.

With a smile on my face, dressed in my pretty skirt, my hair bounces against my shoulders with every one of my steps as I walk into Reynolds' drug store. I have a casual conversation with Aubrey Reynolds over the great weather we've been spoiled with lately as she scans my box of overnight constipation relief. I then proceed back to my store with said laxatives in a brown paper bag, waving to Mr. Hanson as he walks by with his Labrador Retriever, before continuing to open up the shop as if I'm not about to do something completely unfathomable. I'm sure one day there will be a Netflix special written about me.

I watch the clock. It's after midday. I check my watch considering perhaps the clock is fast, or broken. But the clock is fine, and it's almost one o'clock. Standing at the counter, I tap my nails against the countertop, resting my chin on my other hand as I sigh, staring at the table I'd set up in the center of the small store. I'd gone all out. A pretty tablecloth. Two silver trays; one with Nash's samples, and of course, another 'special' batch destined only for Anna. I even decorated the table with a pretty mosaic vase full of fresh flowers, and a bottle of Pellegrino in a silver bucket of ice with two crystal champagne flutes. And, they're late. I quickly begin to grow impatient but, just like clockwork, my cell phone vibrates in the pocket of my skirt, and I pull it out to see a new text message from the one person I'd expected.

Nash: *Hey. Murph, I had to drive Anna to the city. There was a mix-up, and the designer couriered her wedding dress to their store in Atlanta! I'm so sorry, but I've asked Harley and Beth to stop by and test the cakes on our behalf. I hope that's okay x*

I read the message at least ten times, and it takes every ounce of my self-control not to have a complete meltdown. Such a great plan gone to waste. But, before I can think of an alternate, the bell above the entrance chimes and I look up from my phone to see Harley holding the door open for Beth, the two entering the store together. Harley looks excited for cake. Beth looks like she's ready to sacrifice her unborn child. I swallow the lump at the back of my throat.

"Hey, you guys," I chirp brightly, walking around the counter.

Beth offers me a cold, bored glance, clutching her expensive-looking handbag tightly as she stands on the spot, looking around with an unimpressed glower.

"Hey, *babe*." Harley smiles, rolling his eyes at me when Beth isn't looking before leaning down and placing a kiss on my cheek.

An unexpected flutter causes my belly to twist from his closeness and the scent of him, but I ignore it, forcing my smile to remain as I pour two glasses of sparkling water, handing one to Beth, which she snatches from me before taking a seat at the table.

After receiving the text from Nash, I had considered disposing of the tray of tainted cake samples. I thought maybe his text had been some kind of a sign. I couldn't poison Anna. What if she'd been allergic to something in the laxative? She could have died, and I'd have been charged with murder. Nash would have hated me forever and I'd have been confined to a federal prison. Then I look at the perma-scowl etched into Beth's hard face as she glares at me, and I silence my subconscious.

"Here, Beth." I push the tainted tray closer to her. "This batch has … less sugar," I say on the spot, knowing a girl like Beth would most certainly be the type to count her calories.

"Oh." She cringes, suspiciously eyeing the cakes. "I'm not here to eat cake. I'm dairy free, gluten free, and I don't eat carbs." She pushes the tray away with a disgusted look on her face.

I roll my eyes to myself and move to pick up the tray, but before I can get to it, Harley shrugs, murmuring with his mouth full, "All the more for me" as his hand reaches over the flowers, taking one of the red velvet samples.

"Harley, no!" I yell without thinking, but it's too late. He's already shoved the whole thing in his mouth, looking up at me in confusion, mid-chew.

"Wha—?" He guffaws with a mouthful, cake crumbs spluttering from his mouth.

Slapping my hands against my cheeks in exasperation, I know there's nothing I can do now, so I just choose to play dumb with a casual shrug.

"These are real good, Murph," he manages once he's swallowed. "I prefer this one over that lemon one."

I nod, my eyes widening momentarily when he takes yet another cake sample laced with laxative. Forcing myself to look away, I bite back the laughter threatening me. Of course it isn't funny but, at the same time, it kind of is. I'm a terrible person.

"So, you two are *actually* a couple?" Beth suddenly pipes up, tearing her focus away from her phone, which has been otherwise permanently attached to her hand.

Harley flashes me a look as he licks a dollop of chocolate ganache from his thumb.

"Yeah," I answer, turning away and busying myself with wiping down the glass front of the cake display cabinet.

"So weird …" Beth muses, and I can see a smirk pull at her lips in the reflection of the glass I'm cleaning.

At that, I turn, placing a hand on my hip. "What's *that* supposed to mean?"

She shrugs, casually continuing to scroll through her cell. "You just don't look like his type is all," she says with a conniving quirk of her brow, and I wonder if she actually expects me not to take offence to that.

She is right, though. I'm totally not Harley's type. In fact, we couldn't be more different. At six foot two, he's imposing, his arms and most of his chest covered in tattoos. He's the kind of guy who likes to be seen. The life of the party. And even though he'll never play football again, he's still a total jock, obsessed with sports. He's never been one to take life too seriously. And, of course, it goes without saying, he's a good-looking guy. Green eyes, unruly chestnut hair, and an infectious smile with the most adorable dimples. As Sarah kindly reminded me after news of mine and Harley's fake relationship hit social media, Harley Shaw is the most eligible bachelor in all of Graceville. All the girls love him.

Me? Well, I'm five foot three, with wide hips, pale skin, auburn hair, dark eyes, glasses. I've always been a total dork. I hate tattoos; I just don't see the point of permanently marking your skin just for the sake of it. And, unlike Harley who yearns for attention, I do everything I can to keep to myself most of the time. I fear attention. I'd rather stay in with a good book or a movie instead of going out just to be seen. I'm also the most serious person I know. I don't take anything lightly. I'm nothing like Harley Shaw, and I'm nothing like the kind of girl a guy like Harley Shaw would go for. We're best friends, not boyfriend and girlfriend.

I suppose Beth is right to question our so-called relationship. But, as I rack my brain with how to respond, Harley suddenly speaks up, surprising me. "You know what they say," he begins, offering me a conspiratorial wink. "Opposites attract."

I relax a little, releasing the breath I'd been holding, and I turn back to wipe the already spotless glass.

"Anyway ..." Beth stands from her chair, obviously finished

with the conversation, her handbag dangling from the crook of her elbow. "So, we've decided on the red velvet?" She looks to Harley who is still stuffing his face full of cake.

He nods.

"Well, actually, it'll be black velvet." I step forward, suddenly nervous for some reason. I don't know why. This is my business; it's what I do for a living. But Beth is intimidating, and I hate that girls like her have this effect on me. "I just have to perfect the color ratio."

"*Black* cake?" Beth looks at me in disgust, her already pinched face scrunched up even more.

I nod. "Yeah, it's something new I'm trying. Black velvet, black fondant with a gold leaf press, and a gold drip."

Harley looks unbothered, but Beth continues eyeing me, unconvinced. "Whatever." She finally shrugs. "I'm going to get a pedicure." And with that, she's gone, leaving an air of arrogance in her wake as the screen door slams shut with her hasty exit, causing the bell above to jingle violently.

"Ugh." I cringe, watching her walk past the store window with her chin held high in the air as if she's better than everyone. "What an asshole."

Harley suddenly chokes on a mouthful, punching his fist against his chest as he coughs and splutters before finally bringing up the morsel of dislodged cake from the back of his throat. Immediately, the awkward silence of the store is inundated by his roaring laughter, and I look at him incredulously. I don't normally cuss, and I've never been known to cuss anyone out, but that girl gets to me in a way I've never felt before. "There really is no other way to describe a person like that." I shrug, turning and walking through to the kitchen.

He continues chuckling as I tidy the countertop.

"Do you mind if I take the rest of this cake back to the bar to give to the staff?" Harley calls from the front. "They love your baking, Murph."

81

I stop, freezing on the spot. "The laxative!" I hiss under my breath as if I've somehow forgotten about the ill-fated cake in just a matter of minutes. My jaw drops and I cover my gaping mouth with a hand, shaking my head. Poor Harley. He's had at least half of it.

"Um …" I consider his question out loud. "Actually, no. I n-need it to—" I panic a moment as I try to think of an excuse. "I need to keep it so I can see how it sits overnight," I lie as convincingly as I can on the spot. "You can take the éclairs from the front window, if you want."

"I won't say no to that," Harley says cheerfully and I hear the legs of his chair screech across the tile before silence ensues and I just know he's piling a cardboard tray full of the sweets from the cabinet. "I've gotta get back to the bar to sign for a liquor order." His head appears in the cut-out wall between the kitchen and the counter. "I'll see you tonight?"

I turn, trying to remain casual, as if he hasn't just consumed almost an entire box of overnight constipation relief.

"Do you want me to pick you up on the way?" he asks. "It might be a bit more believable if we actually show up together this time."

I nod with a forced smile, and Harley leaves with a wave, none the wiser, his tray of éclairs placed gently in his arms like his firstborn son. Somehow, I seriously doubt I'll be seeing him tonight. Poor Harley.

Chapter 12

I choose a plain black dress for dinner, teamed with a pair of leopard print flats that match my glasses. I pull my hair back into a sleek bun, and I add no more than a sweeping of nude lipstick. I'm surprisingly happy with the finished result when I catch a glimpse of myself in the mirror on the wall as I head down the stairs. Tonight is the night I know I need to look my best. Put-together. Collected. Nothing like a woman who just doused wedding cake samples with laxative in the hope of poisoning the bride-to-be.

I sit at the kitchen island, tapping my fingers against the countertop to an imaginary beat, checking the time on the clock. I'm not sure why I'm even waiting around. Harley isn't coming. He's likely stuck on a toilet somewhere. Of course I hope he's okay. I'm seriously regretting what I've done. I poisoned him. And now, as payback, I'll be forced to sit through dinner alone with Anna and Nash who will probably spend the entire night looking at one another like a couple of love-sick teenagers. I'm sick to the stomach at the thought as I force myself to my feet, grabbing my purse on my way out. I wish I was stuck on a toilet and unable to go to dinner.

Continuing toward the front door, I collect my car keys and

my jean jacket from the coat hook in the entryway before opening the door.

"Hey!"

I almost scream, but I manage to collect myself, more than shocked to see Harley standing right there on my front porch. My brows pull together as I look him up and down incredulously. "What are you do—" I stop myself, snapping my mouth shut, not wanting to give anything away.

Harley looks down to the car keys in my hand. "I thought we were going together?"

He doesn't even look sick. In fact, sick is the farthest thing he looks. Dressed in a pair of jeans that fit him impossibly well, and a gray Henley that shows off his toned upper body, he actually looks handsome. His hair falls forward, the wayward curls flopping down over his forehead, and I just know he'll spend all night pushing it back and out of his face. His emerald eyes glisten bright beneath the dull light of the porch lamp. His skin seems to be illuminated from the inside as if he's just had a five-step facial.

Seriously, what the hell is with this guy? He's just consumed at least half a box of laxative, and he looks like he's stepped straight off the cover of *GQ* magazine. He smiles down at me—oblivious to my confusion—his dimples pulling into his cheeks, and I wonder if perhaps laxative loses its effect if you cook it at 350 degrees.

"You're late." I look up at him before turning to lock the front door. I tuck my keys into my purse, flashing him another unimpressed once-over. "I'd given up on you."

"I know. I'm sorry." Harley sighs, and I can almost hear him roll his eyes from behind me. "I got stuck waiting for Conrad to start his shift. He was late. *Again*." He continues talking about his sub-standard staff member, but I'm not really listening as we continue across the yard to his truck parked at the curb.

* * *

84

Pane E Vino is, hands down, the nicest restaurant in all of town. It's at the fancy end of Main Street. The end with the expensive salon I've never been able to afford to go to, and the florist owned by Margot Winton, the wife of Harrington's club pro. The stores on that side of Main Street cater for the wealthy Harrington Country Club crowd, the elite who flock to their holiday homes in Graceville in droves over the summer months because of its idyllic peacefulness, and small-town charm, far enough away from the hustle and bustle of the city where they earn their millions at their important jobs in the offices tucked away high in the sky-scraping buildings.

I've only ever come to Pane E Vino once before, on a terrible first date with a guy named Tom who I was only using to try to get over my breakup with Nash. It was a horrible experience. He spent the entire night comparing me to his ex-girlfriend who, by the way, I clearly didn't come close to comparing to. Then he proceeded to show me her Instagram page, and suddenly began—very loudly—cussing her out for posting a photo of her and her new boyfriend, so much so, the entire restaurant was privy to his bitterness. Tom was clearly not over his ex, and now, two years later, here I am walking into the same damn restaurant to see my ex-boyfriend, with my fake boyfriend, and I've never related to anyone more.

Harley and I walk into the restaurant where the hostess greets us.

"Reservation under Nash Harris." Harley smiles down at the young girl, and I almost laugh out loud when she openly swoons, gaping up at him as if he's some sort of god. But that's just it. In a town like Graceville, where almost everyone is obsessed with high school football, I suppose Harley Shaw is a god of sorts. He'll always be the nation's number-one high school quarterback, always be the varsity footballer who passed over four and a half thousand yards in his senior year, the player who broke the twenty-year county record for the forty-yard dash by almost two seconds.

He flashes me a smug grin over his shoulder as the girl squeaks something unintelligible before leading the way. I shake my head, rolling my eyes and pushing him forward, which only makes him even more proud of himself. But, much to my surprise, he stops and reaches for my hand, linking his fingers through mine as he pulls me with him, and I can't help but blush at the feel of all eyes on us as we snake our way through the crowded restaurant, hand in hand. It's not every day Harley Shaw is seen holding hands with a woman in public, especially not a woman like me.

Anna and Nash are seated out on the patio overlooking the Chelmer River. Their table is illuminated by the fairy lights decorating the space, hanging overhead, and little lanterns glowing in the center of the table, and it's beautiful, magical almost. Despite the beauty, I try so hard to mentally prepare myself for the onslaught of their sickening public affection but, when we reach the table, Harley steps aside and my brow furrows, not expecting to see Nash frowning while Anna hisses something in his ear, anger obviously radiating from her.

"Hey." I wave with an uncertain, tentative smile, looking between the two.

Harley stands next to me still holding my hand, and the awkwardness in the air around us is rife.

"Hey, guys." Nash's smile is tight as he flashes Anna a warning glance before standing from his seat to greet us, which is when his eyes flit down to mine and Harley's conjoined hands. I quickly let go, instinctively stepping away from my make-believe boyfriend just as Nash wraps his arms around me, pressing a chaste kiss to my cheek. Despite his smile, the tension in his body is evident.

"Is everything okay?" I ask quietly.

"Nash is being a little bitch," Anna scoffs, taking a big gulp from her glass.

My eyes widen in shock at her words, but I try so hard to pretend as if I didn't hear what she clearly just said, loud enough, in fact, that the table across from us heard.

Nash stiffens, and I can see his Adam's apple bob in his throat as he swallows hard. He nods at me, pressing his lips together in the semblance of a smile, otherwise ignoring my question before moving to greet Harley. Anna hesitates a moment before standing with a smile of her own that doesn't even come close to reflecting the somewhat menacing look in her eyes that just screams drunk. She moves around the table to give me a hug that, quite frankly, feels a little forced. And it's at that moment I notice the light smattering of purple lining her right eye that she's clearly tried to cover with concealer.

"Oh my God, Anna. Your eye!" I gasp, taking a closer look, feeling an overwhelming sense of guilt. "I'm *so* sorry."

It takes her a moment to realize what I'm apologizing for but, when she does, thankfully she just shrugs it off with a dismissive wave of her hand. "It's nothing. It was worse this morning, so hopefully it should be gone in a day or two."

"Still." I shake my head. "I feel terrible."

"It's fine!" She cuts me off and, despite her smile, her voice is hard and a little gruff, causing me to quickly shut my mouth.

I take my seat, looking at Nash as he sits back down, his shoulders tight and his jaw clenched. Anna joins him, exhaling before smiling between Harley and me. She finishes what's left of her wine, holding the empty glass in the air and beckoning the waiter. If she isn't drunk already, she sure is on a mission to get as wasted as possible. I flash Harley a sideways glance, but he remains oblivious as he studies the menu. Something is wrong. Between Nash's obvious tension, and Anna calling him a little bitch, could there be some sort of trouble in paradise? I can't help but grin to myself as I look down at my own menu, my mind working overtime with thoughts I certainly shouldn't be thinking.

Halfway through our dinner, Anna is already onto her third glass of wine.

I'm certainly not one to judge. I've been known to knock back a sixer of beer in one sitting. But, there's just something so glaringly obvious within her normally flawless demeanor, something hinting at the fact that she isn't drinking just to get a buzz on. She's drinking to get drunk.

"Anna, babe," Nash says. "Let me top up your water." He stands, reaching for the bottle of sparkling and leaning across to fill her glass.

"Thanks," Anna says with a smile, her teeth gritting together. "But I would really like another glass of wine."

"That will be your *fourth*." Nash smiles just as tight. "And you didn't eat lunch."

She looks at him, blinking once, her silence speaking volumes I'm sure she means only him to understand.

"Remember what happened last time?" he hisses, leaning in closer.

I quickly avert my eyes when Anna turns, her gaze flashing to mine momentarily before searching the patio for a waiter.

"So." I clear my throat, squaring my shoulders and pretending as if I'm not uncomfortable as all hell. I smile. "How did everything go in the city? Did you get the dress?"

Anna doesn't answer. I'm not sure she even heard me.

"Yeah." Nash nods, casting a glance at his fiancée who is no longer paying attention to anything other than the whereabouts of the waiter with the wine bottle. "We collected it from the designer's store," he adds before shoving a forkful of food into his mouth.

"That's good." I'm unsure what else I should say. Small talk really isn't working. I decide in that moment that I would actually rather the two of them to be sucking face than this unbearable tension they've got going on. I look down at my plate, no longer hungry, thinking how this night is actually worse than my ill-fated date with Tom. I glance at Harley, realizing how quiet he's being. I'm so relieved that he showed up. There's no way I could've handled this on my own, but he isn't even talking. He's doing little to help the situation. But when I take him in, noticing the beads of sweat collecting on his brow, the way he's breathing a little heavier than necessary, that's when it hits me. Oh no ...

"For you, miss?"

I jump in my chair, turning to see the waiter refilling Anna's glass before holding the bottle out for me.

I shake my head, covering my glass with my hand. "Oh, um, no thanks," I stammer, suddenly far too concerned with Harley to bother about the wine.

"Harley?" Anna looks up, hiccupping after a mouthful of red. "Are you okay?" she asks with an unnecessary giggle.

Nash looks up from his dinner, brows knitting together when he catches sight of his best friend across from him, shifting uncomfortably beside me. "You okay, man?"

"Is it hot out here?" Harley asks, pulling a little at his shirt and looking around for what, I'm not sure.

"No," I whisper, leaning in closer. The cool night air is beautiful.

"I'm cold." Anna pulls her silk kimono together for effect before finishing the rest of glass number four.

"You don't look so well." Nash notes from across the table.

It's at that moment an alien-like gurgle erupts from Harley's gut. He shifts again as if he's in an immense amount of pain, taking a few deep breaths. The look in his eye is one of pure panic. "Um—" He glances around, his eyes darting furtively. "W-where's the bathroom?"

"I think it's inside, past the kitchen." Nash cranes his neck, looking in through the windows, his eyes flitting once again to his best friend. "You good?"

Shaking his head quickly, Harley tosses his napkin onto his half-finished plate of crispy pork belly, clearing his throat. He wipes at his damp brow with the sleeve of his shirt, flashing me an imploring look as if he desperately needs my help. But all I can do is gape at him, at a total loss of what I can possibly do for him. Normally the whole situation would be hilarious, but not tonight. We're at Pane E Vino, for Christ's sake. The fanciest restaurant in the whole damn town. Everybody who's anyone comes to this place just to be seen, and here's Harley Shaw—the Football God of Graceville—about to crap his pants. I feel terrible. This is all my fault.

"E-excuse me," Harley hisses, his voice strained as he stands, clutching at his belly and turning so fast, he almost trips over his own two feet.

"I hope he's okay. He barely touched his dinner." Nash points his fork at Harley's plate of food.

"It must have been something he ate." I shrug casually as I watch Harley hurry through the maze of tables inside the restaurant.

"I hope it wasn't the wedding cake samples you made." Anna laughs between hiccups.

My eyes bulge at her remark, my cheeks heating. I know she's only joking, but I try to keep an impassive face, sinking a little lower in my seat. And I realize at that very moment that there's no maybe about it; I'm going straight to hell.

Chapter 13

"Shit," Harley hisses from the passenger seat, groaning quietly to himself as he shifts from side to side.

I keep a tight grip on the steering wheel, navigating his big truck through the dark streets of Graceville. With one eye on the road ahead, and one eye on him, I know I shouldn't be laughing, but I honestly can't help myself.

"Are you okay?" I chuckle, biting back my smile as best I can.

"No!" he groans. "And stop laughing. It's *not* funny!"

I press my lips together. He's right. It isn't funny, and I honestly do feel terrible. He barely made it to the bathroom in time back at the restaurant, and he was stuck in the stall for a good twenty minutes before he finally emerged long enough to tell me he needed to leave immediately.

"Do you want me to pull over? There's a restroom at the Wendy's—"

"I'm not gonna *shit* in a damn Wendy's, Murph!" Harley huffs, his voice gruff and a little strained.

"Well." I shrug. "When ya gotta go, ya gotta go."

I can feel his eyes on me like daggers, and I stifle the smile threatening me yet again, choosing to stay silent. As Harley protests every slight bump in the road, keeling over in pain when his gut begins contracting once again, I keep my mouth shut. Driving as fast as I can along the winding dark back roads that lead outside of town, I silently pray that we don't have any accidents until we make it safely to his house. And thankfully, by the time I maneuver the big F-250 into his drive, Harley has managed to keep his bowels under control. But before I even shut off the roaring engine, he pushes open his door, jumps out, and runs inside as quickly as he can while so obviously clenching his cheeks together. Left alone in the truck, I finally release the laughter I've been holding in, burying my face into my forearms as I continue gripping the steering wheel to keep me from breaking apart into a fit of hysterics.

Poor Harley. He's never going to live this one down.

I collect my composure and contain my own laughter as I invite myself inside Harley's house, stopping in the living room. I take a moment to look around at the place I know so well, and I can't help but smile. Harley's high school football jersey that was retired after his last senior game with the Graceville Bears is mounted in a big frame hanging on the wall. Beside it, a few other football memories hang proudly; the life-size banner of him that used to hang in the school corridors; a photo from his signing day with State; his *Sportscene* magazine cover. It's all up there on the walls, displayed like some kind of shrine, and I wonder for a moment if it's doing more harm than good. This is a guy who lost everything with one unfortunate tackle. I have no doubt that the memories on the walls are fond, but I can't help wondering if perhaps he keeps them there only to remind him of everything he could've had, everything he lost, and at that thought my heart aches a little for Harley Shaw. I know all too well what it's like to lose something you love.

Harley always wanted to play football. Nothing else ever interested him. It was what he loved ever since he got his very first football for Christmas when he was still just a little kid who believed in Santa Claus. Even if it was pouring rain outside, he would be on my porch, or at Nash's front door, jumping up and down in excitement, waiting impatiently for us to go out and toss the ball around with him. It was his one true love, but there was a sadness behind his love.

Harley's father had been quarterback for the Graceville Bears back in his day. But he never made it to college. When he was forced to get a real job at the steel mill after graduation because his girlfriend, Harley's mom, fell pregnant, Mr. Shaw resented his unborn son. Throughout his childhood, Harley was constantly reminded every day that he was the reason his daddy had amounted to nothing more than a drunk. That he was the reason his momma left to marry someone new. Harley tried so hard to make his daddy proud with football, but it just made everything so much worse. His father resented him for ruining his life, and being good at football only made matters worse.

So, one day, Harley gave up trying to please his daddy, and he spent every waking minute out of that house. He spent his days at the park, the empty lot behind the Wendy's, the field, my front yard, the woods behind our house, anywhere he could throw the ball around and practice his passes was where you would find him, doing what he loved, what he'd always dreamed of doing. But, football wasn't just his one true love; it was his savior, his escape, his one-way ticket out of Graceville and far away from his daddy.

I step forward as something on the mantel catches my eye. I lean in closer to take a look at the framed photos, and one in particular instantly brings a smile to curl at my lips. Harley, Nash and I stare back from within the frame. We're not much older than 12, maybe 13. The two boys are dressed in football jerseys brandishing their favorite team's name and mascot, while I'm wearing a Justin Timberlake T-shirt. Nash has Harley in a head-lock, both boys smiling for the camera and, for some reason, I'm holding their beloved football, with a grin so bright it emanates from the photo.

I pick up the frame, smiling down at the picture, and my heart begins to swell in my chest. We were so young, naive. We had no idea what the future held for us, but that was okay, because we had each other. Before high school football took Harley away, our Friday nights were spent camping in my living room with Momma bringing us snacks while we hid under our sleeping bags from horror movie villains playing out on the television screen. We were just kids back then, but we'd been through so much together. Those days were hard, but I miss them. Without Nash and Harley, I know one thing's for sure—I would never know true friendship, and I am so thankful Harley saved me from Billy Connor all those years ago.

I hear the downstairs toilet flush, and I turn, waiting for Harley. After a few moments, he steps through from the kitchen, a sheepish look in his eyes as he wipes his damp hands on the back of his jeans.

"Are you okay?" I ask, looking him up and down.

His enviable glow has been snatched from him, replaced by a pale, almost gray tinge to his skin. His eyes are glassy, red-rimmed, and his skin has an unhealthy sheen to it. He does not look okay; I don't even know why I asked.

"I don't know what the hell's wrong with me," he groans, burying his face in his hands as he flops down on the old leather couch.

I stand on the spot, looking down at him, trying not to let on how guilty I feel.

"I barely touched dinner," he continues with a shake of his head. "All I had today was a bowl of Cheerios, some deep-fried pickles, and those wedding cake samples."

I cringe at the combination, but at the mention of my tainted cake I force myself to look away, afraid he might see the truth in my eyes.

"Maybe it was the pickles," Harley murmurs, more to himself than for my benefit.

"You need water." I hurry through to the kitchen, quickly busying myself and taking the opportunity to get the hell away from him to avoid giving anything away.

"Shit. Not again!" I hear him yell from the next room. Seconds later, Harley runs past me, through the doorway that leads to the laundry, and I jump when the door to the downstairs bathroom slams shut. With a glass of water in hand, I stand awkwardly in the kitchen, wondering if I should just call an Uber and leave, but before I can do anything, my cell phone chimes from my purse, and I retrieve it to see the screen illuminated with a text message notification, and I can't help but smile as I enter my passcode.

Nash: *Did y'all get home okay??*

Yes, we only just made it … I reply.

The device vibrates in my hand with an almost immediate response.

Nash: *LOL. Is he okay?*

I leave the water in the kitchen and move back through to the living room, kicking off my shoes and taking a seat on the couch. I pull my feet up beneath me as I start my reply. *Well, he's currently in the bathroom for the second time since we got back to his house. You're the med student. You tell me, Dr. Harris!*

Nash: *Make sure he has plenty of water, and if he develops a fever, go straight to the hospital.*

Will do, I reply, although I know it's just a matter of time before the effects of the laxative wear off; unless, of course, Harley becomes dehydrated. Then, I don't know what I'll do. If I take him to the hospital, they'll find out he's somehow overdosed on laxatives. Harley will know what I did. He'll hate me. Everyone will hate me. I manage somehow to shake those thoughts from my head, focusing on the now and the fact that I have Nash's full text attention. I swallow the guilt and the anxiety as I quickly send off a follow-up text message in an attempt to keep the conversation going. *Did you and Anna get back to the hotel okay?*

Nash: *Yeah.*

His response is short, perhaps a little curt, and piques my interest immediately. I stare at his one-word answer, contemplating what's behind it. I could say goodnight and leave it at that, or I could do what I do best and pry. I chew on the inside of my cheek as I reread his text a few more times.

Was everything okay with you two tonight? I tap into my phone. I hesitate momentarily, wondering if I might be overstepping some kind of invisible boundary. Is it my place to ask Nash how he and his fiancée are doing? But then my curiosity gets the better of me and I press send.

After a few excruciatingly long moments where I begin to think the worst, those three dots appear in our text window for at least a few minutes. I wonder what he can possibly be replying with that is taking him so long. Then the dots disappear and my shoulders slump. The dots quickly reappear, and my heart picks up a few paces as I idly chew on my thumbnail, staring at the screen while waiting with bated breath. But just as I'm preparing myself to read his essay of a text message, my phone chimes in my hand, and my anticipation dissolves the moment I see his response.

Nash: *Yeah. We're fine.*

Well that response certainly wouldn't have taken two and a half minutes to write. What was he going to say? Maybe he was going to tell me the truth, because from what I saw earlier tonight things are most certainly not fine. I hate that he feels as if he can't be honest with me—we're best friends—but I decide to let it go. He clearly isn't in the mood for talking, and I feel ridiculous for allowing a few dots in a text window to get the better of me.

Okay. Goodnight x, I send back, huffing out a sigh of frustration as I sink back into the cushy leather of the couch. I roll my eyes at my own disappointment. I'm not sure what I was expecting. Did I really think he was going to tell me that everything between him and Anna is falling apart? That he's beginning to realize he isn't in love with her anymore? That he no longer wants to marry her because he's still head over heels in love with me? No, I didn't. Well, not really. First and foremost, before love got in the way and ruined everything, Nash Harris was my very best friend. We used to tell each other everything. I just want that Nash back, the one who isn't afraid to tell me the truth. The one who would write an essay text message, and expect an essay in return. The one I love more than life itself. I miss that Nash.

Just as I'm beginning to give up all hope on my plan to win Nash back because, let's face it, he really does seem to be well and truly over me, my phone vibrates from the couch cushion beside me. With a furrowed brow of confusion, I pick it up to see another text message.

Nash: *I miss you.*

I gasp out loud and, even as I stare at it, I don't actually believe my own eyes. But there it is right in front of me. Black and white. Illuminated in the dim light of the room. Glaring at me like the blinding light of a beacon. My jaw drops, and everything seems to come to a standstill, my heart thumping wildly in what feels like the very back of my throat.

He misses me?

I read the text message at least a thousand times, trying so hard to analyze those three tiny words. Does he miss me, Murph, his old friend? Or does he miss me, Murph, his ex-girlfriend? The one he shared so much with from our first kiss, to our first time? Those three words are so simple to misconstrue, and while my heart is beating unbelievably fast in my chest it feels as if it's about to explode, I know I can't let myself get too carried away. Nash misses me. I desperately try to collect what little composure I have left as I stare at the three tiny words on the screen. Three tiny words with so much meaning. Three tiny words that have the power to change absolutely everything.

Contemplating my reply, I consider whether or not to return

the sentiment, but before I can do anything, my phone buzzes in my hand once again.

Nash: *Goodnight, Murph.*

I exhale a trembling breath, staring at his final message, but I don't bother with a reply. Instead, I lock my phone and place it face down in my lap.

"Holy crap," I whisper under my breath as I relax back against the couch, shaking my head as a million conflicting thoughts race through my mind.

"Holy crap, what?"

I startle, turning quickly to see Harley hobbling through the doorway, clutching at his side. He's changed into a pair of sweats and a Bulldogs' T-shirt, and he looks like death warmed up as he flops down onto the couch beside me, relaxing back and closing his eyes.

"Nothing." I wave a hand in the air, dismissing his question, tucking my phone into my purse as I try to convince myself not to overthink Nash's cryptic text message. "I'll get you that glass of water." I stand, hurrying back into the kitchen to avoid any further questions from him. But when I return with the icy glass in my hand, I stop just shy of the couch. In the minute it took me to refill the glass with fresh cold water from the fridge, Harley somehow managed to fall into a sound sleep. I guess excessive pooping could knock anyone out for the night.

As I watch him snoring quietly for a moment, looking peaceful, I catch myself smiling at just how adorable he looks. His mouth is slightly open, his chin resting on his chest. Unruly hair sticks up every which way, the longer locks falling down over his forehead. Long lashes fan over his cheeks, and a slight furrow pulls between his brows as if, even in his sleep, he's overthinking something.

The longer I watch him, the more something I've not felt before pulls low in my belly, and I know right at that moment that I should leave, but I can't. I owe it to him to stick around.

He might become dehydrated through the night. If he did and I wasn't here and something happened, I'd never forgive myself.

So, placing the glass of water onto the lamp table within his reach, I sit beside him and tug at the afghan throw from the back the couch. Tucking the blanket over us, I nestle slightly closer to Harley, and I close my eyes, smiling at the thought of Nash Harris missing me.

Chapter 14

My eyelashes flutter to the sound of a crow squawking loudly from outside. Encased in an unfamiliar yet welcoming, all-consuming warmth, I nestle a little closer, slowly drifting back to sleep. But that's when it hits me. I freeze, stiffening completely. Squeezing my eyes closed, I don't dare breathe. I take a moment to comprehend what the hell is going on, where the hell I am, and why the hell I'm there, before I nervously open one eye. Peering through my lashes, I see Harley beside me, his arm wrapped around my shoulders as he continues sleeping soundly.

What in the actual heck?

Why the hell am I asleep with Harley's arm around me?

I begin finding it difficult to breathe, and yet he's completely oblivious to me and the current state of my mini-meltdown. I find some relief in the fact that we're both fully clothed—thank God—the two of us covered by a crochet blanket. Hell, there's even a throw cushion squeezed in between us. From what I can tell, nothing untoward has occurred. And suddenly I remember last night—the past twenty-four hours, in fact—and it all comes back to me.

The laxatives.

The cake.

Harley's diarrhea.

Drunk Anna.

Nash.

I miss you ...

I close my eyes tight again, resting my head against the back of the couch. Pushing my tangled hair out of my face and adjusting my lopsided glasses, I release a heavy sigh, and consider everything that's happened. Everything that's changed with that one text message. But then, I cast a sideways glance at Harley, my mind reeling. Why the hell is he so close to me? I become distracted and, for a moment, I find myself watching him sleep. His lips are pursed together, causing his dimples to pull into his cheeks, and his long eyelashes flutter ever so slightly as the hint of a grin begins to ghost over those same lips as if he's dreaming the most unimaginable of dreams. And, for the first time in the fifteen years I've known him, he looks innocent, angelic almost. I can't help but smile at the sight before me. He really is a beautiful specimen of a man.

When I sleep I'm almost certain I look like one of those furry cats with the out-turned eyes: my tongue hanging out the side of my mouth, drool trailing down my chin, the occasional snort. But Harley, he's beautiful, and the longer I watch him, the more I regret being woken up by that damn crow. With his arm wrapped around me, I haven't slept so peacefully in a long time.

Wait. What the hell am I even thinking? I quickly shake my head at my own thoughts, silently chastising my subconscious before forcing myself to unravel from the warmth provided by Harley's embrace, careful not to wake him. I stand, collecting my shoes and purse from the floor before tiptoeing out of the living room. But then I find myself pausing in the doorway, glancing back over my shoulder, and my eyes travel to Harley, to where I notice his arm is now clutching the throw cushion, as if in my absence he desperately needs something to hold on to, as if he's afraid to sleep alone, and at that thought an unexpected emotion comes over me, one I've never felt before, one I never expected to feel when it comes to Harley Shaw.

I spend almost twenty minutes in the shower when I get home. The hot water rolling over my tense muscles feels like heaven. The steam works wonders on my skin. But nothing helps to ease the conflicted thoughts racing through my mind. My mind keeps flashing back to last night. From Nash's confusing, heart-stopping text message, to the way Harley's arm felt when it was wrapped around me so warm and protectively, to the way his intoxicating scent invaded every one of my senses.

I shake my head at that last thought. I can't be thinking of Harley like this. I need to get my head back in the game, and it takes all I have to focus on those three words still burning a hole in my heart.

I miss you ...

I'd been trying to pry into Nash's relationship with Anna, and I thought maybe I'd pushed too hard, especially after his curt responses. But then, out of the blue, he tells me he misses me? I've never been so confused. I desperately want to ask him what he meant by that message, but I simply cannot bring myself to do it. I sure as hell don't want him to know that I've been over-thinking it, and, to be honest, I'm terrified what he might say.

After coming out of the bathroom, I walk into my bedroom to see my cell phone ringing from where it's charging on the bedside table. I don't know the number flashing on the screen, so I answer with my most polite voice in case it's a customer.

"Hello, Alice Murphy speaking," I answer with a smile.

"Murph?" A female voice comes through. "Murph, it's me. Anna."

And at that, my eyes bulge and instinctively I clutch at the towel I'm wearing as if I'm sinking and it's my only lifeline. My stomach drops at the thought that she knows something's up. Has she seen the text message Nash sent me? I sure as hell wouldn't

102

be too happy if my fiancé was messaging his ex, telling her how he misses her.

"Hello?" Anna's high-pitched voice rings through the phone.

"Um, yeah." I clear my throat. "Sorry. Hey, Anna …?"

"I'm so sorry to just call you out of the blue," she begins, and I breathe a sigh of relief when I hear the distinct smile in her voice. "I was wondering if you could meet me at the club?"

My brow furrows at her request, which actually sounds more like a polite demand.

"They're beginning to set up the ballroom for Saturday and I really want your opinion where to put the cake table. I want to make sure everyone sees your masterpiece, and I want to get the best possible photos when Nash and I cut it."

On one hand I'm relieved she obviously knows nothing about mine and Nash's text message conversation. But my relief is short-lived. Nothing has changed. The wedding is still on. They're not breaking up. It's not as if I expected to get a call today to tell me the wedding's been canceled, but I expected something. Nash misses me. Me! Or had I read too much into it? I know it wasn't my imagination—he really did send it, I saw it in my messages this morning—but maybe he didn't mean it like I'm thinking he meant it. I can't help noticing the way in which my shoulders fall at the realization that Nash and Anna are still getting married.

"Sure," I say, trying to sound cheerful while swallowing the lump at the back of my throat. "I can meet you there in an hour. Is that okay?"

"Oh, thank you, Murph," Anna gushes through the phone. "This means the world to me."

"No problem," I reply through gritted teeth, rolling my eyes as I end the call.

Great. I shake my head, taking a moment to look around at my surrounds. Now I'm being forced to see Anna, and Anna alone, and in the place she and Nash are getting married, no less.

I don't even have Harley as a buffer. I groan in frustration before flopping backward onto my bed. Throwing an arm over my eyes, I really could scream.

An hour later I'm walking through the main entrance of Harrington Country Club, yet again. Only this time, it's a Tuesday morning, and the elegant dining guests dressed in their finest evening wear have been replaced with wealthy retirees wearing polo shirts and tennis shoes. Housewives dripping in pearls and diamonds are dressed in designer activewear as if they're going to do anything more than sit out on the patio sipping mimosas before noon. Graceville's elite, who have enough money not to worry about holding down a day job, carry tennis rackets and golf clubs, and to-go cups.

I have to say I feel more than a little out of place wearing my blue jean dungarees and scuffed old Converse, but I'm only stopping in on my way to the bakery. It's not as if I'm here to pledge as a member. But as I wander aimlessly through the lobby, with no idea where I'm going, I fear I might be asked to leave.

"Murph!"

I turn to see Anna hurrying through the marble lobby toward me and, for a moment, I'm slightly taken aback by her appearance. She looks different. Normally she comes across as so put-together, so flawless. But today she looks tired, hungover, on edge, and a little disheveled. Maybe the wine at dinner last night has taken its toll. She closes the distance between us with her arms outstretched. I wasn't expecting an embrace, yet here she is wrapping her skinny arms around me as if she's known me for years.

"Oh my goodness!" She gasps a little breathlessly, pulling away and smiling at me, her eyes wide. "Thank you *so* much for coming on such short notice. You're a *lifesaver*."

I nod, looking around. It's not as if I have much else going on—I blocked out most of my calendar this week to make their wedding cake—but I wasn't about to let her know that, in case she expected me to be at her beck and call between now and Saturday.

Anna takes my hand, leading the way. "I think my wedding planner is going to *kill* me." She laughs nervously, glancing back at me over her shoulder. "I've told her three different places where I want the cake table, but I keep changing my mind."

I force a smile onto my face. "It's really not a big deal," I assure her, because it isn't. Quite frankly I'm confused she's even making it an issue. It's a cake table, for Christ's sake. "The cake can go wherever you—" I stop talking when we step through the double doors and into the grand ballroom, and I'm momentarily rendered speechless by the sheer beauty and opulence laid out before me.

Black silk hangs from the beams high up in the ceiling, draping overhead with a million twinkling fairy lights scattered in the darkness, giving the illusion of a clear night sky in the middle of the day. Strategically placed tables are dressed in stark white tablecloths accented by black and white striped table runners. Crystals hang from centerpiece vases, shimmering like diamonds as they catch the light. It really is quite magnificent. A little gaudy for my liking, definitely not something I would want, but still spectacular.

"Okay." Anna drops my hand, turning to me as she begins walking backward toward the black and white tiled dance floor in the center of the expansive room. "I was thinking of having the cake here." She indicates a space right beside the bridal table, looking to me with a tentative smile.

I shake my head. "No. Not a good idea. Someone is gonna get drunk, make a fool of themselves on that there dance floor. They'll probably end up going head first into the damn thing."

Anna looks from the dance floor, to where she was thinking of placing the cake, and back again. "You're right." She nods, cursing once under breath, and she actually looks disappointed in herself. "I don't know why I didn't think of that."

"How about here?" I move to the left of the stage where I presume a band will be set up. "Everyone will see it, but it'll be out of the way," I continue. "And the beautiful fairy light backdrop will show in the photos when you're cutting it." I point to where a man is standing on a ladder, draping a waterfall of twinkling lights behind the stage.

Anna nods, pursing her lips as she seems to consider my suggestion, but before she can say anything, her phone begins ringing in her hand. I watch as she looks down at the screen, and a small crease pulls between her brows. A heavy sigh causes her shoulders to fall. "Can you please excuse me, Murph?"

"Yeah, sure." I shrug, waving her off to answer the call as I turn, taking in the beauty surrounding me.

I walk to the demo table already set up in all its glory, and I trail a finger over the delicate gold flower petals immaculately presented in the centerpiece vase, smiling in wonderment at the sheer magnificence of it all. But then it gets me thinking about my own wedding. I wouldn't want it in some stuffy country club ballroom. I want to get married outside, maybe by the lake off Old Mill Road, with a reception under the stars. As I touch one of the delicate orchids beautifully arranged within the extravagant vase, my smile falls, because at that moment I realize how unlikely a wedding of my own actually is. The man I always wanted to marry is getting married to someone else, right here in this over-the-top ballroom, to a woman who is everything I'm not, and there's nothing I can do about it.

"I don't care!"

I startle, pulled from my thoughts by the shrill voice coming from the other side of the room. I turn to see Anna standing by the floor-to-ceiling windows, her hand waving in the air animatedly as she continues her obviously heated discussion over the phone.

"You know what?" she hisses, her voice low but still clear. "Don't bother!" She ends the call so forcefully, I'm surprised her

French tip didn't smash straight through the screen. Even from across the room I can see she's upset. She isn't crying or anything, but she's shaking her head and glaring down at her cell phone. The air around her is obviously tense, and I don't know if I should approach her or give her a moment. I decide on the latter and I give her some time as I take a seat at one of tables and begin scrolling through my phone.

"Sorry about that." Anna approaches me after a few minutes, taking a seat next to me.

"That's okay." I smile awkwardly, tucking my phone into the pocket of my pinafore. When I meet her eyes, I notice there's something there, something unexpected. She's no longer the confident woman I met that first night. She looks sad, defeated, and maybe even a little broken.

"Is e-everything okay?" I ask, despite myself.

I don't want to care. I wish I could just ignore her emotion, turn and leave with my head held high. But unfortunately, Momma taught me better than that.

Anna exhales a big dramatic sigh, shaking her head before burying her face in her hands. "No," she wails into her palms.

My eyes widen as I watched her fall apart right in front of me. I didn't actually expect her to open up to me of all people. I've literally known her for three and a half days.

"I need to be honest with you, Murph." She looks up at me. "I didn't invite you here to go over the placement of the cake table."

I blink at her, sufficiently confused.

"Oh, everything is *terrible*, Murph." She meets my gaze with a combination of fear and horror in her chocolate brown eyes. "Just *horrible*."

Oh, great, here we go. Time for some ridiculous sob story. I wonder what it is now: the wrong color peonies, maybe? Perhaps her hairstylist can't make it from New York on time to do her hair for the wedding? Poor, *poor* Anna. My shoulders sag in resignation at the fact that I'm stuck here now with her first-world problems, when I would, in fact, rather be anywhere but here.

"I'm so scared, Murph," she continues with a sniffle.

I duck my head in an attempt to hide my exasperation.

"I think Nash and I might be making a mistake with this whole wedding," she wails. "I'm considering calling the whole thing off!"

And at that, I look up so fast, my eyes bulge. "I'm sorry, but—" I push my glasses up my nose. "What?"

Chapter 15

Maybe I'm more supportive than I realized. Maybe I actually care more than I even knew I could care. Maybe I just feel sorry for her. Or, maybe, in my own messed-up way, I'm simply pretending to care so I can get some intel for my own benefit. Whatever the reason, I'm currently stuck listening to Anna bitch and moan while finishing her third glass of Sauvignon Blanc, as we sit out on the patio overlooking the pristine swimming pool of Harrington Country Club.

"My father isn't even coming to the wedding," Anna sobs through a sniffle as I search for the waiter, wondering where our food is. "He's paying fifty thousand dollars for the damn thing, but he refuses to attend because"— she hiccups through another sob —"he thinks I can do better than Nash."

At the mention of Nash, my ears prick, and I momentarily forget about my grumbling stomach. Meeting Anna's tearful eyes, my own widen before narrowing as anger flashes through me. "Why?" I ask abruptly, my brows pulling together of their own accord. "What's wrong with Nash?"

"Nothing!" Anna gapes at me, her face serious. "I love him. He's *perfect*." She sighs. "My father is old money from the Upper East Side. A real New Yorker. He always wanted me to marry a man from his firm, but then I met Nash. I knew I was falling in love with him, but Father did everything he could to try to convince me otherwise."

Anna's father sounds like a real jerk.

"But this week without him here, knowing he won't be walking me down the aisle …" She pauses to sniffle again. "It's been really hard, and I don't know if I can do it without his blessing."

I nod, because I can somewhat relate. I dread my own wedding. I won't have anyone walking me down the aisle, either. No father, not even my mom.

"Is your mother gonna be here?" I ask, taking a sip of water.

A small smile pulls at Anna's lips, despite the sad look in her eyes, and she nods. "Yes, thank goodness. She arrives on Friday morning. But the thing is, Nash really can't stand my mother."

My brow furrows in confusion at that. It doesn't seem right. I've never known Nash to dislike someone. Unlike me, who can barely tolerate most people, Nash actually likes everyone. There has to be a reason he can't stand Anna's mother.

"Why?"

"She once told him he needed to dress more appropriately, that sneakers aren't acceptable outside of the gym. One time, when we were going to have dinner at my father's members-only club, she made it so uncomfortably obvious that she didn't like his outfit, he went all the way back downtown to his dorm to change, and then came all the way back uptown to meet us at the club. He was just trying to make a good impression, but even then she chastised him for not ironing his shirt." She pauses with a shrug. "He says she's too controlling, and overbearing," Anna explains with a slight roll of her eyes. "And she is. Both my parents are, but they're my *parents*. I can't help how they are."

Finally, the server appears with our food, placing an assortment of starters in the center of our table and stopping to top off our respective wine glasses. I take a sip of my rosé, watching as Anna

110

almost gulps her Sav, and I know there's a lot more to her frustrations.

"But you do *love* Nash, right?" I ask, selecting a shrimp chopstick from one of the plates.

"Yes, of course I do. Nash is everything I've ever wanted in a man. He's my whole world ..." She giggles, her eyes glazing over a little before suddenly snapping out of her Nash-induced daze. "But we're fighting more than we ever have before." She shakes her head, stuffing a bacon-wrapped scallop in her mouth. "It's like he's been different since coming back here," she manages through a mouthful. "His whole attitude has shifted!" She splutters, morsels of food spraying from the corner of her mouth.

I press my lips together as my mind begins to wander. Could Nash's shift in attitude have something to do with me?

"I'm just beginning to worry that perhaps we've rushed into this," Anna continues before wiping her mouth with a napkin. "I mean, we've only known each other a few months. And we're getting *married*!" Her eyes are wide with incredulity as she takes another unladylike gulp of her wine. "Nash hasn't even finished medical school, yet. What if he doesn't want to stay in New York after he graduates? Or, what if he gets a residency someplace else and has to move?"

I stare at her, blinking once, wondering if she realizes the core requirement for a marriage is compromise.

"My home and my heart are in New York City, and I know he *hates* it there," she scoffs. "He's always going on and on about his *beloved* Graceville, but there's no way in hell I could live in a place like *this*." She shakes her head with another roll of her eyes before looking away for a moment and pressing her lips together. I can tell she's regretting what she just said, but she brushes it off with a wave of her hand. I try not to feel offended, but I can't help it. The disdain in her voice is like a slap to the face. As if those south of the Mason-Dixon Line are nothing but low-class.

111

"What should I do, Murph?"

I look up from my wine glass, surprised by her question. She's actually asking me what to do? Oh, if only you knew, honey. I bite back my smug smirk, offering a noncommittal shrug of my left shoulder as I throw back the rest of my wine.

"You're his best friend." She looks at me, her eyes imploring. "*And* you're a girl. You *have* to help me!"

I take the moment to look at her, studying her from her red-rimmed eyes, to her pale cheeks slightly hollowed as if she's not been eating enough, and I have to say I do feel a little sorry for her. I mean, does she even know Nash and I used to be together? Does she know Nash is the man I was hoping to one day marry? She seems so clueless. So desperate and hopeless, and a little pathetic.

But my traitorous heart tugs in my chest, reminding me that deep down I am, in fact, human. I don't know if the woman across the table from me is honestly in love with Nash, but I can tell she's obviously terrified of losing him and, with that, I can most certainly relate. And right at that moment I realize something: perhaps Anna and I aren't so different after all. Just two women hopelessly devoted to the same man.

Struggling with a grunt and a groan, my back aches in objection as I try and maneuver Anna's lanky body off the elevator. For a skinny girl no bigger than a size two, she sure weighs a hell of a lot.

"Come on, Anna," I hiss, pulling her awkwardly. "This way."

"Oh look!" She lunges forward, taking me with her, stopping by the ice machine in the corner of the hall. She giggles to herself, pushing the flap open and sticking almost her whole head inside. "Wow, Murph. It really is cold in here!"

"Yeah, it's an ice machine," I murmur, grabbing her hand and trying to turn her. "Come on." I wrap my arm around her tiny waist, forcing her with me.

After lunch, Anna had forced me to go with her to the bar out by the swimming pool where she consumed enough cocktails to take down a full-grown man. She'd been so embarrassing and obnoxious; we'd actually been asked to leave before the dinner rush started to arrive at the club. The moment she began yelling, "Don't you *know* who my father is?" I took that as our cue to leave, and practically dragged her skinny butt out of there before she made even bigger fools of the both of us.

The key she handed me after we'd been kicked out of the bar read three-sixteen. Holding on to Anna as best as I can while she stumbles and sways, I follow the signs on the walls until we come to a stop outside the door to her suite.

"Whose house is this?" Anna asks, looking around dazed and confused.

"Oh Lord," I hiss under my breath as I slide the keycard into the lock. She really is trashed. I can only hope that Nash isn't back from his fitting with Harley and the guys, yet. That way, I can put her to bed, leave, and pretend as if this afternoon never even happened. But before I can even reach for the handle, the door suddenly swings open. Anna loses what little balance she had, crashing into me, and I would have fallen face first over the threshold if it wasn't for the strong pair of hands gripping my shoulders and holding me upright.

"What the *hell*?"

I look up, collecting myself and Anna, my eyes widening at the sight of Nash standing there. His eyes glower in the muted light, looking at the both of us before focusing on Anna who's still giggling like an obnoxious teenager. With a frustrated sigh and a muttered curse, he wraps his arms around his fiancée, effortlessly picking her up, and I watch from the doorway as he carries her through the small living area, continuing to curse under his breath the entire time. They disappear through a doorway to what I assume is the bedroom, and my eyes move to the coffee table, finding it covered in silver room service trays.

And it is at that moment that I notice the candles scattered all over, their flickering flames illuminating the otherwise darkened suite.

Oh no. I immediately feel terrible and really awkward but, just as I consider an exit strategy, Nash returns, his eyes wide as he gapes at me incredulously. "What the hell, Murph?"

I hold my hands up in defense. "Hey, don't look at me!" I shake my head. "This was all *her* idea. I barely even had two glasses of wine. She was the one drinking like it was Spring Break at Panama City Beach!"

Sighing in defeat, Nash shakes his head, looking back over his shoulder in the direction of the bedroom as if in deep thought.

"You had plans?" I ask rhetorically, indicating the obviously romantic set-up.

He looks at me before glancing out over his handiwork. "Yeah," he scoffs. "We had a fight earlier. I *was* trying to make it up to her ..." He shakes his head again. "What a waste of time."

"I'm sorry." I look down to the floor a moment, feeling guilty even though this is completely Anna's fault and none of my doing whatsoever.

"It's not your fault, Murph," Nash relents, and I look up to see his face soften as his eyes meet mine. With a shrug, he waves his hand in the direction of the coffee table. "Wanna come in for a glass of overpriced champagne and some chocolate-covered strawberries?" He laughs humorlessly, rolling his eyes.

I consider his invitation, my eyes flitting to the bedroom door left slightly ajar, where Anna is inside, likely passed out. "I should probably get home." I point back in the direction I came.

"Just one drink," he counters with a hopeful raise of his brows. "I've already opened the bottle. It's gonna get tipped down the sink, otherwise."

"Okay." I hesitate, stepping in from the foyer. "Just one glass." I close the front door behind me, lingering in the entry as I watch

114

Nash walk into the living area. He pours two glasses, holding one out for me, and I don't miss the flash of a smile in his eyes. But it's that smile, and the fact that his wife-to-be is snoring obliviously from the next room, that makes me realize this night can only end badly.

Chapter 16

"So, what the hell happened to her?" Nash asks as I take the proffered glass of sparkling wine from him.

We continue out onto the balcony, overlooking the golf course, and I take a seat on one of the patio chairs, releasing a heavy breath. "She asked me to meet her so we could discuss where to place the wedding cake." Even as it comes out of my own mouth it sounds like a ridiculous excuse. Nash is watching me with a crease of confusion etched between his brows, so I think it's best to leave out the part where Anna only really asked me here so she could pick my brain about him and their relationship, and whether or not they should be getting married. "Then, I don't know." I shrug. "I guess I could just tell she didn't look very happy, so I asked her what was wrong, and she told me—" I stop, snapping my mouth shut. I can't tell him what she told me. It's not that I care about protecting Anna, but I don't want Nash to feel betrayed.

"She told you *what*?" he presses, staring at me with an imploring expression.

I shift uncomfortably in my chair, looking out at the view. The sun has disappeared deep into the horizon, and the sky is a spectacular shade of amethyst, with streaks of gold and mauve. It really is beyond beautiful. "Wow! Look at the sky …"

"Murph?" Nash warns. "Don't try to change the subject."

I sigh, turning to look at him, finding his eyes watching me, waiting. "She just told me about her dad, and her mom," I continue. "And that ... you guys have been arguing since being here in town." I shake my head dismissively, with a casual shrug. "No big deal."

Nash takes a deep breath, and I watch as he looks out over the crystal lake, all the way to the woods in the distance. His mind seems to be working overtime, his jaw clenching tight. I can tell he's trying to hold in whatever emotion he's feeling, and I don't want to push him, so I stay silent. I sip on my wine, enjoying the peacefulness of the evening despite the obvious tension radiating from Nash. But then he suddenly turns to me. His eyes narrow as he hesitates with whatever he is going to say—whatever he's trying to say—and, for a moment, he seems to be considering what to say.

"What is it?" I encourage him.

"It's just being back here. In this place." He shakes his head, hunched over, his elbows resting upon his knees as he looks down at his glass. "There's something about this damn place. I hate it so much because it reminds me of all the bad, but ..." He stops, finally looking up at me, his bottom lip clamped between his teeth, and there's something in his eyes, something in the way that he's looking at me.

"B-but what?" I ask so quietly my voice is almost swept away in the soft evening breeze.

"This place has a hold on me." He sighs heavily, breaking our heavy gaze and looking back out over the view before us. "Being here, it's as if I'm right back where I was, before New York, before college, before Anna." His eyes flit to mine at the mention of her, and I press my lips together, because I think I know what he's saying. "As much as I hate this place, I miss it like crazy when I'm back."

I swallow hard, looking down at my own glass.

"I guess I just didn't know how it would feel having my new life and my old life collide like this. Having Anna here, in my home, where so much happened that she'll never even begin to understand. Coming back to you and Harley suddenly together. Everything's changed, and … I don't know. It's just giving me all these confusing feelings."

I look at him. Really look at him. I notice just how torn he really does look, and, for the first time, I think I understand why, because I feel the same way. "A lot has changed, Nash," I say. "And, I get it. You went away, and your whole life is different, now. Hell, you've changed, whether you want to admit it or not. And, you expected to come back to the same old place, but—" I shrug. "It's not the same old place. Sure, the streets might look the same, but while you've been away, we've all changed. Harley has the bar. I'm running Momma's bakery. I've given up a hell of a lot, staying here, but I wouldn't want it any other way."

I nod, and as I'm saying the words, it's as if I'm just realizing how much I truly do love my life here. Sure, I could've gone back to New York after Momma passed. And I could have lived the life I'd always dreamed of: college and then some big, fancy job in the city. But I'm here now, and I've made this life for myself that might not be big-city glamorous, but it's mine, and I'm happy here, even without Nash.

"That's the problem." He laughs to himself, but his laugh is derisive. "I don't know if I like all these changes. I miss the old days …" He flashes me a guilty look, and I suddenly feel very awkward as the air between us shifts, the meaning behind his words not so hidden. "Can I ask you a question?"

I nod, reluctantly.

"Do you love Harley?" he asks with little to no emotion, the look in his eyes the only thing giving away how desperate he is to know the answer. His question knocks the wind out of me, rendering me breathless, and I find myself unable to move, just staring at him, not even blinking. But then he chuckles softly, shaking his head at me. "Do you want another drink?" he asks, changing the topic of conversation before finishing his glassful with one big mouthful, hopping up from his chair.

I've barely even touched my glass of champagne, and I had planned on heading home, and after his question, I probably should, but I don't. "Yeah." I manage a smile. "But, can I have a beer, instead?" I ask, holding my glass out for him to take. "This tastes like pee."

"Yeah. You're right." Nash chuckles, taking my glass and carelessly tossing the contents over the balcony railing before heading back inside.

Somehow, time manages to get away from us. Before I know it, we're three beers in, talking and laughing together about some of the stupid things we did when we were kids. The heaviness of our earlier conversation is otherwise forgotten, and it's just the two of us again. Nash and Murph. And, for the moment, I look beyond the button-down shirt, and the neatly pressed khakis, and I see my best friend.

Nash's hyena-like laughter dwindles to a small chuckle, trailing off as he looks down to the can of beer in his hand. "Do you remember that night? Summer before senior year, when Harley made us go with him to that field party and you got drunk for the first time?"

I catch sight of the knowing grin ghosting over his lips, and immediately I can feel my cheeks flush.

"Remember?" he teases, nudging me with his elbow. "We were drinking these." He holds his can up in the air as if to prove a point, but there's no point to be made. I know exactly what night he's referring to. My eyes glaze over at the memory, and my skin heats from the base of my neck, upward to my cheeks. I duck my head in an attempt to hide my traitorous smile. But, from the way his eyes are watching me, to the hint of a smirk pulling at the corners of his mouth, I know he knows exactly what he's doing to me reminding me of that night.

*   *   *

"I shouldn't be here," I hissed, ducking beneath the low-hanging branches of the overgrown willow trees scattered throughout the darkness. Nash held my hand tight, leading the way. He glanced over his shoulder, flashing me a lopsided grin in response to my protest. "Nash, if Momma finds out I'm drunk in a field somewhere, instead of at the movies like I told her, she's g-gonna kill m-me," I hiccupped.

"Shh," Nash hissed with a chuckle, pulling me with him through the wispy long grass that came up to our chests. "We're almost there."

The sound of the field party we'd snuck away off from was now nothing more than a murmured whisper caught in the gentle night breeze. We were alone. Just me, Nash and the crickets chirping in the wild grass surrounding us.

"Here it is," Nash said, his voice hushed so as not to disturb the peaceful still of the night surrounding us.

I looked up just as we made it to the clearing and, as he had promised me in his ploy to get me out here, I was left speechless. The beautiful vision laid out before me was awe-inspiring, like nothing I'd ever seen before. The inky night sky was brilliant as it loomed high above, making the stars seem as if they went on forever. The clearing was surrounded by the darkened woods, the tall pines illuminated by the fireflies flickering in the darkness.

"Wow," I whispered, fearing my voice might take away from the breathtaking sight. Looking around with wide eyes and a gaping mouth, I tried to take it all in at once, but it was overwhelming to say the least.

Feeling Nash's eyes on me, I turned to look at him with a smile. "You were right. This is beautiful."

He nodded. "Whenever I wanna be alone, or if I just need time to think," he began, "this is where I come."

"It feels as if we're a million miles away from the rest of the world." I looked up to the sky. It was so big, so expansive, it made me dizzy, and I almost lost my balance, but Nash steadied me, moving behind me. I could feel his warmth as he closed the distance between us. His chest pressed against my back, his arms coming around my waist. Resting his chin on my shoulder, his soft breath fanned over the skin at the base of my neck causing me to shiver despite the warm night air. My skin erupted in goose bumps, and I knew Nash could tell because his breathing changed and his hands gripped my hips a little tighter.

"You make me so happy, Murph," he whispered, his lips barely grazing the shell of my ear. "I'm the luckiest guy in the world."

My eyelashes fluttered, my eyes closing involuntarily, and I basked a little in the wake of his words, smiling when he pressed a lingering kiss to my shoulder.

"Hey, look at me."

Turning in his arms, I stumbled a little, silently cursing the beers I'd consumed against my better judgment. I was drunk. Or at least, I had been only a moment ago. But there, looking into Nash's imploring eyes, I became lost within his gaze. I saw something I'd never seen before, and a soberness came over me. It was as if my mind was trying to tell me that I was going to want to remember this moment.

Nash smiled, his eyes moving between mine, zeroing in on my mouth before capturing my gaze once again. He lifted his hand, tucking my hair behind my ear so tenderly, his touch alone burning into my skin. "I need to tell you something," he said, the tip of his tongue gliding out just enough to dampen his lips, and my heart stammered in my chest, watching him, waiting.

"What is it?" I asked, my brows pulling together in a combination of anticipation and confusion. I wanted to know, desperately, but I was also afraid of what he might say, because I knew, no matter what, his words were about to change everything.

He took a deep, shuddering breath. "I love you."

In that instant, it felt as if all the air had been stolen from my lungs. I was breathless in a way I'd never been breathless before. From the sincere and slightly frightened look in his eyes, to the sentiment of his declaration, I was absolutely beside myself as a *plethora of emotion consumed me from the inside out. I had been in love with Nash Harris for years. Maybe even since we were 9 years old. He was my first love. I'd given him everything: my first kiss, my virginity, my heart and soul. I loved him more than I ever knew it was possible to love another person. And now, he loved me, too. He'd said so himself. My smile got the better of me. As did the tears pricking at the backs of my eyes.*

"Are you crying?" he chuckled, nudging me playfully.

I ducked my head, burying my face into the crook of his neck, feeling his laughter as it rumbled through him, causing his chest to vibrate against mine. With a fortifying breath, I forced myself to look up, meeting his eyes, and he offered a small, knowing smile before leaning in and pressing a kiss to my forehead. I wrapped my arms around his neck, my fingers raking their way up into his hair so I could guide him closer, our foreheads touching. For a moment we just stood there, in the center of the clearing, with nothing but the crickets and the fireflies keeping us company. Just us beneath a blanket of stars. It was a perfect moment. The best moment.

"I love you, too," I whispered, breathing him in and looking deep into his eyes, searching them. "But I have a feeling you knew that a long time ago."

He smiled, ducking in closer until his lips finally brushed against mine in a kiss so all-consuming, I knew I would remember it for the rest of my life.

I look up from the beer can in my hands. The memory of that night alone brings a faraway smile to my face, butterflies swarming low in my belly. But when I find Nash watching me intently, his blue eyes a little dazed, something passes between us. The air around us shifts, thick with a tension that isn't awkward or uncomfortable, just obvious and quite possibly a little inappropriate. My heart stammers in the center of my chest, and I'm almost sure he can hear it.

"I'll never forget that night," Nash says in a whisper so soft I almost miss it.

And it's right at that moment that I realize just how much closer we've become in the last few minutes. He's leaning into me and I into him, the distance that had been between us is long gone, and we're in dangerous territory. My eyes flit between his, watching them darken right before me, and I'm completely overwhelmed by everything. The beer. The memories. The scent of his cologne which, even after all these years, remains the same. It's as if we're right back in that clearing, just the two of us, and it feels as if everything is about to change, and my stomach clenches.

"Yes," I find myself whispering without even realizing.

Nash's brows knit together as his eyes move between mine, ducking down to my lips and back again. "Yes, what?" he asks, his voice broken and hushed.

I inhale a stammering breath, my tongue dipping out to wet my suddenly dry lips.

"Yes what, Murph?" he presses, inching even closer.

And, at that, I pull back enough to break myself free of the hold I know he has on me, coming to my senses as best as I can, knowing this is the only way to stop whatever the hell it is we're about to do. "Yes." I nod, clearing my throat free of the uncertainty that's wedged its way at the back. "Y-yes, I love Harley."

I watch as a sharp intake of breath causes his shoulders to stiffen, watching as he is so clearly taken aback by my words. And, for a long minute, we just sit there, staring at one another, neither of us breaking away, and it's almost like a moment of clarity, for the both of us, whether we like it or not.

"Nash?"

We both jump at the sound of Nash's name being called from inside. I pull away as far as my chair will allow, almost toppling sideways, my cheeks heating and my heart racing so fast as I try to regain what little composure I have left. Nash's eyes remain on me as he curses unintelligibly under his breath. He seems reluctant, deliberating within himself before finally pushing up from his chair, taking a moment to smooth down the front of his shirt. Raking his fingers through his hair, he huffs out an exasperated breath before stepping around me without so much as a second glance, disappearing inside.

"I threw up in the bed," Anna cries from inside, her voice raspy and a little desperate. "Where *were* you?"

"I'm s-sorry, baby," Nash stammers, but the loving tone in his voice makes my stomach drop and twist painfully. "I'm sorry I wasn't there to help you. Come on," he continues. "Let's go get you cleaned up."

I wait outside on the balcony, listening for a door to close before moving. Hurrying as quietly as I can, I tiptoe past the bedroom, through the suite, making a beeline for the door. Things just went from zero to one hundred real quick, and I can't even deal with it right now. I need to get the hell out of here. Not only does the future of Nash and Anna's relationship depend on it, but I have a feeling the entire future of mine and Nash's friendship depends on it, too.

Chapter 17

I didn't sleep well when I got home. In fact, I only slept about three hours. Every time I closed my eyes, I'd see Nash's face. His lips, right there, just as they had been, dangerously close, before Anna had woken up and interrupted whatever the hell it was we were about to do in that moment. My mind kept flashing back to that one instant, when Nash's lips had been less than a hair's breadth from my own. When he'd been looking at me in a way he shouldn't be looking at me. When I'd told him, point blank, that I do love Harley, just so I could put a stop to whatever it was that was about to happen between the two of us right at that moment.

But all I could wonder is if that's the only reason I'd said it. And, most confusing of all, when I did eventually drift off, I'd had a horrible dream. I was at a wedding. Not Nash and Anna's wedding, but mine and Harley's. I was dressed in a bright pink wedding dress with poufy sleeves, and just as we were about to kiss as husband and wife, Harley turned to me, pointed a finger at me and called me a whore. The wedding guests chased me out of the church, throwing wedding cake at me as I ran. I woke with a start. My skin was dripping with sweat, I was breathless like I'd just ran a half-marathon, and I was so consumed with confusion and guilt, I couldn't think straight as I tried so hard to make sense of everything.

Hours later, and it's still only four in the morning. The sun hasn't even begun to rise yet. I've been staring up at the ceiling, watching the shadows cast from the trees outside my bedroom dance around the room for what feels like forever. But I've lain here long enough, allowing myself to get carried away with the confusing and conflicting thoughts consuming my mind while tossing and turning, and it's driving me crazy. So, I force myself to get up, get showered and dressed, and get to the store super early.

I'm seriously behind with Nash and Anna's wedding cake, so the extra few hours should help kick my butt into gear. Normally I'm much more prepared, but my head has been all over the place the last few days, and last night spent reminiscing with Nash about the old days, remembering how in love with one another we truly were, and my dream about Harley haven't helped at all. Maybe a day spent locked in the kitchen is just what I need to help to take my mind off everything, even if I am making a cake for the love of my life's wedding to someone else.

As I wait for the oven to chime, I allow my mind to wander back to last night, to the moment Nash inched so incredibly close to me there was barely enough room between the two of us to allow for a breath. Would I have kissed him back if he'd tried? I'd like to think I wouldn't do that … that I have more respect for myself, and for Anna—but, after everything I've done this week so far, I'm seriously beginning to doubt my own integrity.

As I stand here watching the timer, deliberating with myself over whether or not I would have kissed a soon-to-be married man, my mind flashes to Harley and what feels like guilt begins to twist low in my belly, and I don't know why. What is wrong with me? I wanted Nash back. I *wanted* him to kiss me. I wanted to be the one he chose, then, when he almost does, I do a complete

126

one-eighty and I don't even know why. I feel physically sick as the timer on the oven dings, echoing through the kitchen and pulling me from my thoughts. But I force myself to forget about Nash for the time being, and I keep my traitorous mind busy while the cakes cool, whipping up buttercream frosting for the crumb coat, and a dark chocolate ganache for the filling.

I've just finished frosting the three layers when I look up, surprised to see that it's beginning to fall dark outside. I've been at it all day. In between the crucial stages of Nash and Anna's cake, I've kept myself busy making a whole batch of blue and pink cupcakes for a baby shower. I placed orders for supplies, paid a few bills, served my regular customers—I did just about anything to keep my mind occupied and off two particular men and the fact that I'm about to see both of them at The End Zone.

I've been dreading it all day for two reasons. I'm terrified to see Nash after our encounter last night because I know we really need to talk about everything that's going on between us. But, on the other hand, I rack my brain with what I might possibly say so as not to sound like a complete and utter idiot. I'm almost ninety-nine percent certain he was going to kiss me on the balcony. But, what if by that one percent chance I'm wrong? What if it had all been a figment of my imagination, made up in my slightly intoxicated mind?

I sigh heavily, checking the time on the clock as I remove my apron. I'm late. And, to top it all off, I look like crap and I don't even have time to go home and change. So, I freshen up as best as I can in the tiny bathroom I share with the Burt's Butcher next door. After twisting my hair up into a messy knot on top of my head, I wipe my face with a cleansing towelette before adding a sweeping of pink lip gloss and a few strokes of mascara to help brighten up the tired eyes beneath my glasses. Looking down at myself, I cringe. I'm wearing overalls, for God's sake. I could pass as a damn janitor. Cursing under my breath, I brush at the dusting of flour from down the front before shrugging in resignation. There isn't much more I can do about my current state and, besides, it's only The End Zone.

Securing the long strap of my purse over my shoulder, I cross the road and continue up the sidewalk until I come to a stop outside Harley's bar. For a Wednesday it's relatively busy. I walk up the few steps and head through the open saloon doors to see most of the tables occupied with all eyes intently glued to the baseball game playing on every one of the television screens. I linger in the entryway scanning the entire space, my eyes zeroing in on a familiar blonde standing by the pool tables toward the back. The same blonde who currently has Nash's hands all over her while she giggles like an obnoxious schoolgirl. Strangely enough, though, it doesn't bother me like I expect. It just frustrates me, and I have no idea what that's about.

"Great," I hiss under my breath nowhere near as mentally prepared for tonight as I need to be.

As I make my way to a booth occupied by Nash's groomsmen, Kevin and Seth, I pause, finding Anna's bridesmaids standing by the jukebox, eyeing me dubiously and sniggering between themselves. Of course, they're all dressed up as if they're headed to some exclusive New York City hotspot. Beth's dress is covered in sequins and barely conceals her butt. And here I am in overalls and my trusty old Converse. But we're in Graceville, Georgia. Not the Meatpacking District or some equally trendy Manhattan neighborhood.

"Hey, Murph."

I jump at the sound of the voice coming from behind me. A familiar voice that makes my eyes widen in fear as a cold shiver runs through me. Turning, I meet the piercing blue eyes of Emma, Harley's 'friend with benefits', for lack of a better description. I openly wince, feeling all the blood drain from my face.

Now, it's not that I don't like Emma. I do. She's nice enough and, in fact, over the years she and Harley have been doing their thing, she and I have become quite close. Under any other circumstance I'd love to see Emma standing in front of me. But the problem is she knows better than anyone that Harley and I are absolutely not a couple, because she hooked up with him only a few weeks ago when she was in town visiting her sister.

"Hi," I finally say, my voice suddenly hoarse with the nerves racking through my entire body.

My eyes flit to Nash and Anna who are still currently all over one another by the pool table, and panic begins to set in. Where the hell is Harley? Has he told her? Does she know our secret? What if she gives everything away with one innocent remark? My heart races thunderously in my chest.

"So," Emma starts, a mischievous grin curling her lips. "You and Harley, huh?" Her eyes sparkle as she waggles her brows up and down suggestively and, surprisingly, I don't detect even the slightest hint of phoniness in her tone. Maybe he did tell her. Maybe she's just playing along. Thank goodness. I really didn't want my humiliating lie to come out tonight of all nights, in front of everyone. I'd never be able to live it down.

"He didn't tell me until I got to town this afternoon," she continues. "But I, for one, think it's *great*."

Wait. What? I can't even try to conceal my confusion.

"Yeah!" She nods excitedly, clearly noticing the bewilderment in my eyes. "I've been rooting for y'all to get together *forever*!"

So, she really thinks we're together? Harley told her we were together, for real?

I'm shocked. For all the years I've known Harley Shaw, I've never once known him to forfeit casual sex. I'm more confused than ever now, but I try to act unaffected as I offer a casual shrug. "Yeah." I laugh once, swallowing hard. "It's no big deal." I brush it off with a wave of my hand before pulling my wallet from my purse. "I'm gonna go grab a beer," I announce to the table. "What's everyone drinking?"

"Miller Lite!" Kevin and Seth yell out over the music, holding an empty pitcher in the air. I roll my eyes, laughing at them as I take the jug with me, snaking my way through the crowd toward the bar.

And, that's when I spot him, behind the bar, serving a line of customers waiting at the counter. For a moment, I just stand there, on the spot, watching him. The way he moves so effortlessly, reaching for glasses up above, and bottles behind him, pouring shots like some professional mixologist as he laughs casually with his customers like they're his very best friends. I clamp my bottom lip between my teeth as I continue staring at him from across the bar.

He looks good tonight. His wayward curls are contained by a backward End Zone cap, his strong jaw shadowed with a smattering of stubble. His dimples pull into his cheeks as he laughs at something someone says to him, adding a hint of boyish charm to his already charming exterior. His Adam's apple bobs in his throat with every word he says, and the tattoos inked into the smooth skin over his forearms seem to dance with every movement of his strong hands and long fingers. I'm not normally attracted to tattoos, but the longer I find myself unable to look away from him, the more they taunt me, hypnotizing me. I have to force myself to snap my gaze away, my eyes widening at my own thoughts.

Oh no. Please no. This isn't right. It can't be. Despite the dread sitting at the bottom of my belly, I convince myself to continue ahead and, by the time I come to stop at the counter, I find Harley right there, smiling down at me with a grin that only causes his green eyes to sparkle deviously like he knows a secret, and that's literally the last thing I need to see right now. I shake my head in an attempt to push him and his beautiful eyes to the very back of my priorities.

"You told Emma?" I hiss over the counter, placing the empty pitcher on the bar.

"Yeah." He nods, looking at me with a crease of confusion

pulling between his brows. "Isn't that the point of this whole thing? To ... *tell* people?" He shrugs a shoulder.

"Yeah, I guess." I sigh, not realizing until this very moment just how soft and full his lips seem to be up close. Again, I shake my head at my own thoughts. "But Emma? She's your ... your *smash* buddy. You said so yourself."

He shrugs again, focusing on the beer tap in front of him as he fills a new pitcher. I take a seat at the bar in an attempt to catch my breath a moment, and when I glance back over my shoulder to see Anna and Nash kissing passionately for all to see, his hands groping her ass over the tiny satin slip she's wearing as a dress, it leaves a bad taste in my mouth. I can't stop my face from scrunching up in disgust. I guess it's safe to assume their differences from yesterday are forgotten. And, for a moment, I wonder if the same goes for mine and Nash's moment together on the balcony last night.

I know I should be relieved, but I'm not. If I kissed Nash last night, would it have all been some horrible mistake to him this morning? Would I have been made to look a fool right now, watching the two of them flaunt their love right in front of me? Because I sure as hell feel like a fool right now. I'm not sad. I'm pissed off.

"You okay?"

I jump a little at Harley's voice, low and raspy, right by my ear, his breath warm as it fans against my skin. Looking up, I see he's standing beside me with a pitcher of beer in each hand.

I swallow hard. "How much do I owe?" I ask, opening my wallet and rifling through for some cash.

"Murph, I'm not taking your money."

I glare at him, quickly shaking my head in dispute.

"Consider it a perk of *dating* the owner." He winks, nudging me playfully with his elbow. I deadpan, and he grins down at me. With an eye-roll, I throw a handful of dollars into the tip jar before following him through the crowded bar back toward our booth, holding on to the hem of his T-shirt as he leads the way so as not to lose him in the crowd.

We pass Nash and Anna, and I glance over to see them finally playing their game of pool. She's bending over the table, lining up her shot, and he's leaning over her almost indecently, pressing a kiss to her shoulder in a way so intimately familiar it makes me blush. But then his gaze lifts, and his blue eyes find mine, and in that flash of an instant, something passes between the two of us, something that makes me stumble over my own two feet.

"You all right?" Harley asks, steadying me as he hands me a glass.

I nod quickly, taking it from him and gulping back a few mouthfuls of beer. Glancing sideways, I watch Anna celebrate her shot, Nash wrapping his arms around her waist, holding her tight and pressing a kiss to her cheek. But then, once again, his eyes meet mine from across the way. Only this time I don't look away, finding something deep within his stare that causes my heart to feel as if it's stopped dead cold in my chest.

Forcing myself to look away, I turn to Harley, watching as he talks to Emma. And I can't help but notice how he's smiling at her, looking at her as if she's the only woman in the entire world. Captivated by her. He's hanging on to every one of her words, completely rapt in her. I can't mistake the twinge of something I can only describe as jealousy surge through me as it comes to bubble beneath the surface of my skin. And it's ridiculous. Me? Jealous of Emma? Jealous of any of the hundreds of other women Harley Shaw has been with over the years? It's absurd.

But then without even realizing, my eyes begin to betray me, slowly trailing Harley from his head to his feet, and back again, to the way his End Zone T-shirt hugs his lean muscles, to the trademark jeans he wears, the ones that fit him as if they've been molded to each of his strong thighs. With a suddenly dry, scratchy throat, I down the remainder of my beer before pouring myself another from the pitcher on the table.

Glancing back at Nash and Anna, finding them once again kissing unabashedly, their hands all over one another, I don't even care. But, when I find myself looking back at Harley, the hint of a smile pulling at my lips, I realize at that precise moment that I am in way over my head.

Chapter 18

I had it all worked out in my head. My plan was foolproof. At least, I'd thought it was. But with every ounce of beer that I consumed, the more the finer points of my shoddy plan began to blur into a pixelated haze I couldn't for the life of me remember the details of. It was simple. All I had to do was get drunk enough so I could forget about Nash, and try it on with Harley without being all conspicuous and awkward about it. I was going to test myself. To see if my feelings for him were real, or if it was just my mind playing tricks on me.

Easy, right? You'd think so, huh.

I wrap my arms around Harley's shoulders, standing on my tiptoes, and I crane my neck to place a kiss on his cheek. Of course, he shoots me a confused look, his brow furrowed as he tries to make sense of my unexpected act of affection. But, thankfully he goes along with it, ducking his head to reciprocate with a kiss on the very tip of my nose; a move so unlike him it renders me a little breathless, but I somehow pull myself together. I tug him closer and he wraps his arms around my waist, burying his face into the crook of my neck, and I breathe him in, quickly becoming lost within his embrace.

I blame the alcohol.

I close my eyes, breathing in his heady scent of cologne, mint and liquor, smiling in an unexpected yet contented bliss. I've never felt this before, this all-consuming warmth as it floods through my body. But, when I finally manage to open my heavily lidded eyes, pulling myself from my Harley-induced reverie, I find Nash standing by the jukebox, watching me intently with an unreadable expression on his face. His lips are twisted to the side and his jaw is working overtime, clenching and unclenching, ticking almost painfully. A deep crease is etched between his brows, and his eyes are glaring as he runs a hand through his hair, his shoulders rising and falling in a heavy sigh before he tears his gaze away. I can tell he's trying to remain unaffected, but I know him better than that. He's very much affected.

I should be smiling like the Cheshire cat that got the canary. But I'm not smiling. Hell, I'm not even happy about it. I'm indifferent. And I suddenly understand why. With Harley's arms still enveloping me, his big hands splayed against the small of my back, and that damned scent of his that's invaded its way into every one of my senses, I feel something I've been unprepared to feel up until this point. Nash's jealousy means nothing to me, because I am wholeheartedly consumed by everything Harley, and I like it. It's official—my dreaded suspicions are confirmed— I like Harley Shaw. I wish I could blame it on the alcohol, but this has nothing to do with how much I've had to drink. I'm in dangerous, confusing territory, and I have to get the hell out of here before I perish.

"I need to pee!" I yell, surprising not only myself but Harley, too. He pulls back just enough to gauge me with a wide-eyed look. "Sorry." My nervous laughter sounds strangled and nothing like myself as I move out of his embrace. I step backward, stumbling over my own feet and knocking into a table. But I collect myself enough to flash him a wavering smile before turning and practically running to the bathroom.

I splash some cold water on my face, desperate for some clarity

135

for my deeply conflicted mind. Resting my hands on the porcelain sink, I take the chance to collect myself, taking a few deep breaths in the hope it might sober me up enough to realize I need to get my shit together. Placing my glasses back on, I look up and catch sight of my reflection in the mirror, shaking my head at the girl staring back at me.

"Who *are* you?" I hiss, wiping at the mascara smudges beneath my eyes.

The old me would never have concocted such a devious plan as to fake a relationship with my best friend, to make my other best friend jealous. Yet, here I am, drunk on a Wednesday, losing myself in Harley's penetrating, all-consuming gaze. This whole thing is getting way out of hand. I'm becoming a victim of my scheme, tangled within my own web of lies.

"Oh, hey, Murph."

I watch Anna's reflection walk behind me in the mirror with a sweet smile on her flawless face before she disappears into the stall. I groan inwardly because I am just not in the mood for her right at the moment.

"I've barely had a chance to talk to you *all* night!" she calls through the door while peeing, and it's all very awkward, to be honest.

"Yeah, sorry." I look down at my chipped nail polish. "I've been a little—"

"Oh my *goodness*!" she interrupts with a dramatic gasp. "I'm *so* sorry about last night. I don't know *what* came over me. I passed out before I could even thank you for bringing me back to the suite."

"It's fine. Don't worry about it." I shake my head as guilt twists low in my belly.

"I'm so ashamed of myself and the way I acted," she continues. "Nash told me I was in quite a state. I definitely shouldn't drink during the day."

I nod although I know she can't see me.

"He told me you left pretty much straight after I fell asleep?"

I'm not sure why, but her question catches me off-guard. Nash told her I left? He didn't tell her that I stayed for at least two hours after she passed out, or that I helped him drink the champagne he'd ordered for their romantic night in? He didn't tell her we almost kissed? I feel something pull hard in my chest. Something I've never felt before. Guilt? Absolutely. But there's something else.

"Murph? You still there?"

The flush of the toilet pulls me from my thoughts and I snap my head up, clearing my throat. "Um, yeah, sorry. Yeah—" I stammer. "Yeah, I left … pretty much straight after you went to bed." Anna walks out of the stall, smiling at me. "I was so tired. I went home and I actually fell asleep on the couch," I add for effect.

Washing her hands, she watches me in the mirror's reflection before turning and resting against the sink, taking a moment to look down at me. The intensity within her gaze is enough to make my heart race. I don't even know why, but she just has this way of intimidating me with one look.

"You know," she begins, folding her arms over her chest, "I really like you, Murph."

Oh God. I take a deep breath, pressing my lips together in something that resembles a smile, grinding my teeth together almost painfully as I wait for her to continue. But she doesn't continue. My smile falters as she leans in, wrapping her arms around me in an unexpected embrace, and I remain frozen in place, my arms by my sides until she pulls away. And with one last smile, she turns and walks out of the bathroom, leaving me all alone.

I find myself in the mirror once more, and I can't help but glare at my own reflection.

I walk back through to the bar to see a lot fewer people than there had been before I hightailed it to the bathroom. Anna's bridesmaids are nowhere to be seen. Kevin is long gone. Emma is playing a game of pool with Seth. And the only other people left are a few die-hard regulars perched at the bar, and a guy and a girl who look to be on a first date, whispering sweet nothings to one another, in a booth by the front windows. Harley is sitting at the table, talking to Nash and Anna, and just as I consider making a swift exit without anyone noticing, he catches my eye from across the space. Lifting his chin in my direction, offering a small smile, they all turn to see me, and I know there's no escaping now.

Dammit.

I'm so confused, conflicted in every sense of the word. I need to go home and sleep it off. I definitely should not be associating with the reason for my discontent, especially not when I'm going to be stuck in a car with him tomorrow for three hours while we drive to Myrtle Beach for the dreaded bachelor party. But, with a heavy sigh I force myself to continue across the room, stopping at the booth. I press my lips together in a tight smile before sliding in beside Harley, reluctantly meeting both Nash's and Anna's eyes from across the table.

"You okay?" Nash asks, his voice void of any semblance of care whatsoever.

I shake my dizzy head. "I'm drunk."

"Well, serves you right for having all those tequila shots." Harley chuckles, nudging me playfully with his shoulder.

"Kevin made a bet that I couldn't keep up with him!" I say, defending my choices.

"Yeah." He nods with a knowing smirk, snaking his arm around my shoulders and pulling me in close. "But he's three times your size, and even he had to get his sorry ass carried out of here."

I roll my eyes with a shrug, trying not to give away the fact that his closeness is making me feel all sorts of things I shouldn't be feeling, his arm around me is like something I've never felt before. It feels just right, but so, so wrong.

"You two are so cute together." Anna giggles. I look at her, finding her watching us with a goofy smile as she nudges Nash. "Aren't they, babe?"

Nash offers an unintelligible murmur, his eyes suddenly focused intently on some sports news program playing without sound from the television screen across the way.

"How long have you been together?" Anna asks, looking between Harley and me.

Harley flashes me a nervous glance.

"Umm." I think to myself for a moment, swallowing hard. I am way too drunk for this. "About ... six weeks, or so."

Nash quickly turns his attention to me, his brow furrowed. "Six weeks?"

I nod, confused by his abrupt tone.

He looks to Harley. "But you told me you hooked up with that chick from Alabama a month ago!"

"Yeah." Harley shifts uncomfortably beside me, clearing his throat, flashing me another desperate glance.

"I forgave him," is all I can think to say, and I reluctantly meet Nash's eyes, wishing I hadn't. He looks suspicious as hell as he seems to overthink things.

"But you're together now?" Anna looks at me, quirking one of her brows with a devious giggle. "Like, *together* together?"

I nod, trying so hard to smile like a woman happily in love, but it's almost impossible. Yes, I might like Harley, but right now all I want to do is crawl into a hole and disappear. "So, anyway. What about you guys?" I start, in an attempt to shift the conversation away from my blatant lie. "How did Nash propose?"

I don't really care. In fact, it's the last thing I want to know. But it's the only way to get the focus off Harley and me. From the way Harley's breathing has increased beside me, I'm worried he's about to spontaneously combust under the scrutiny of his best friend's suspicious gaze from across the table.

"Well," Anna begins, her cheeks flushed as she flashes Nash a

139

sneaky sideways glance. "I came home from classes and he was at my apartment. He'd surprised me by cooking my favorite meal. There were fresh flowers everywhere. Candles …" She trails off, positively gushing as she recounts every detail. "It was very romantic."

I try to smile—I really do—but I can feel my face beginning to fall of its own accord, which is precisely when Harley's arm around my shoulders tightens a little in a show of support I didn't realize I needed up until that moment, and I know he knows exactly what I'm thinking.

"So, once I'd freshened up," Anna continues with a faraway look in her eyes, "I came out to find him on one knee, and the ring was glistening from the collar of my darling Scottish Fold, Sheba."

I can't help but wonder if this is some kind of sick joke: flowers, candles and a damn cat named Sheba. It takes all I have not to laugh out loud. If it wasn't so hilarious it would be nothing but ridiculous. All I can taste is the familiar bitterness of bile as it climbs its way up the back of my throat. I reach across and grab Harley's glass of whatever it is he's drinking, thankful that it's just Coke, taking a few unladylike gulps to stop myself from gagging.

"It was *so* beautiful!" Anna clasps her hands together beneath her chin, turning to Nash with an adoring look in her eyes, her thick eyelashes batting. Nash smiles, reaching out and tucking her blonde hair behind her ear, a move so innocently intimate, and I watch on, remembering all the times he tucked my hair behind my ear for me through the years.

Harley clears his throat once more, shifting beside me, pulling me from my thoughts. "You've changed, man." He chuckles, looking at Anna with a mischievous grin. "The Nash I know would've ordered a pizza, had a sixer of Miller Lite chillin' on ice, and asked you to marry him during the commercial break of a Falcons' game." He downs his glass of Coke while flashing me an apologetic glance, and I know he's just trying to stifle the awkwardness, trying to placate my overwhelming emotions, and I'm so appreciative, but it's all pointless.

"I *am* a changed man." Nash shrugs, leaning in and placing a kiss on Anna's cheek. "For the *better*." Unsurprisingly, his words are like a kick to my stomach, but he continues, despite my crippling pain, and the worst thing is, I have a bad feeling he knows exactly what his words are doing to me. "It took me a while, but I finally met the right girl for me."

My jaw actually drops, and I stiffen as every single muscle in my body goes numb. My heart races, my skin pricks, tears sting the backs of my eyes, and it almost feels as if I can't breathe, like some unseen force is suffocating me from the inside out, squeezing the life out of me.

"Aw, babe!" Anna cries, turning and wrapping her arms around his neck, brushing her nose against his as she murmurs something to him.

Harley's hand squeezes my shoulder, letting me know he's still here with me, and I turn slowly, looking up and meeting his eyes. "Will you take me home?"

His jaw is tight, but he manages a smile. "Yeah," he whispers. "Let's get the hell outta here."

I shuffle out of the booth with Harley close behind me and, with one last fleeting glance over my shoulder at Nash and Anna who are both oblivious to our departure, I don't even bother saying goodbye before walking away.

Chapter 19

The entire drive home, my mind keeps flashing back to Nash. His words reverberate through my head like a broken record. *A changed man? For the better? Finally met the right girl?* I'm still reeling. Those words were like a slap to my face, and I'm almost certain that's what he was aiming for. He once told me I was the *only* girl for him. That I made him the best version of himself. That there would never be anyone else for him. That I was it. Forever and always. So what? Was he lying back then, or is he lying now? Or has he always been a liar and I'm only just seeing him now for what he truly is?

"You okay?"

I startle from my thoughts, turning to see Harley watching me from the driver's seat. And it's at that moment I realize we've stopped. I glance out the window to see my house shrouded in darkness, and I exhale a heavy breath, grasping at my purse in my lap. "Thanks for the ride," I murmur, reaching for the door handle. But I stop mid-way, glancing back at him, and the words are out of my mouth before I even have a chance to consider them. "He really loves her, doesn't he?"

Harley seems to hesitate a moment, his eyes looking at me so intently they're almost looking through me. He pulls his bottom lip between his teeth, clearly stalling, but finally he nods, offering me a sad smile. "Yeah, he does." He shrugs. "But he still shouldn't have said what he said. There's a thing called tact, and unfortunately he just proved that he doesn't seem to have much of that left in him."

I huff out a defeated breath, pursing my lips as I stare straight ahead through the windshield. "I thought I was imagining it. Actually, I *hoped* I was imagining it. I didn't want to accept it. But he really has changed, huh."

"People change, Murph. There's nothing wrong with that," he says with a shrug of his shoulder while inspecting something closely on his steering wheel, and I don't miss the context within his words. A deep furrow is etched between his brows, his jaw tight as he focuses intently on the cracked leather, picking at it with his thumbnail. He's awkward. So am I. Things have changed between us, and I know I'm not the only one who feels it.

"Do you want to come in for some coffee?" My question surprises me just as much as it seems to surprise him.

He straightens, squaring his shoulders and turning to me, his eyebrows raised as he meets my eyes. I stare at him, waiting for a response, and when he moves to unfasten his seat belt, nodding once, my shoulders sag as I breathe a sigh of relief because I really need him right now.

I can't even begin to count the number of times Harley Shaw has been inside my house over the years. Thousands, probably. When we were kids, he and Nash were forever hanging around, rifling through the pantry, raiding the fridge and drinking straight out of the juice carton. But this is the first time Harley's been in my house when it's ever felt different. Suddenly, with my confusing, newfound feelings for him, his presence in my home is overwhelming, like he's almost too big for the small space. As we stand in the kitchen across the island from one another, I can hear every one of his breaths, feel his eyes on me as I idly stir the two mugs of hot tea. And it's at that precise moment I realize I need something a lot stronger than chamomile tea.

"Actually," I say, turning and tipping the contents of both mugs into the sink. "Can you please get me that bottle of Johnnie Walker from on top of the fridge?"

"Blue label?" Harley chuckles from behind me. "Livin' large, Murph?"

I place two glasses onto the counter, rolling my eyes at him. "It's the only one that doesn't give me heartburn."

Harley smirks, pouring us each a nip of liquor before replacing the cork in the bottle. "Cheers." He smiles, holding his glass in the air.

I nod in return, meeting his eyes momentarily before he tilts his head back and takes a generous sip of the scotch whiskey. His eyelashes flutter closed as he hums in appreciation, and the sound alone elicits goose bumps to prick all over my skin. It takes all I have not to outwardly swoon as I sip my own shot, forcing myself to look away. I can't stand to see the look of satisfaction on his face any longer. So, instead, I focus down at the small tiles on the countertop as if they're the most fascinating thing I've ever seen.

What am I doing? I don't actually know. I've never considered Harley this way. He's never had this effect on me. Where Nash was always the love of my life, Harley was the annoying background noise I just couldn't seem to turn off. He was that insolent older-brother type who once ripped a whole heap of pages from my diary when I used to write Justin Timberlake fan fiction in freshman year. He showed everyone at school, and all his jock football buddies made fun of me for weeks.

One time in sophomore year, after the school had installed vending machines in the boys' bathroom, he chased me through the halls laughing like a lunatic with a flapping condom flailing in the air. In fact, for most of my teenage life Harley Shaw was been the bane of my existence, until he became the best friend I never knew I needed when I had no one else. And now, all I can imagine is what his calloused finger might feel like brushing against the curve where my shoulder meets my neck. What his lips might be capable of doing to me with just one kiss.

"I should get going."

I shake my head free of my inappropriate thoughts, watching as Harley places his empty glass onto the counter, and my heart begins to race as panic dawns on me. My mind works overtime to think of something, anything to get him to stay. I don't know why, but I don't want him to leave just yet.

"Can you fix my washing machine?"

Harley offers me a double take, his brow furrowed, and I can tell he's just as confused by my spluttered question as I am.

"Um, I-I mean, it." I pause for a moment before I stammer an explanation. "It's making this really loud clunking noise. I think it's off-center, and I don't know how to fix it." It's a total lie, of course. It isn't off-center at all. And even if it was, I know how to fix it. I've had that washing machine for years. It was my mother's and the damn thing goes off-center at least once a week. But Harley doesn't know that.

"You want me to have a look at it *now*?"

I nod.

"Murph—" He stops, looking down at his watch. "It's after midnight."

I roll my eyes. "Yeah, but I have clothes I need to wash so I can pack for Myrtle Beach in the morning."

"You mean to tell me you, Alice Murphy, Miss Organization herself, didn't have your bag packed on Sunday when you found out about the damn bachelor party?" He quirks a dubious brow.

I shake my head, despite his assumption being eerily accurate. Of course I had my bag packed for Myrtle Beach days ago. I've repacked it three times since then. But he doesn't need to know that.

"Fine," he huffs, turning and heading for the laundry, and I follow him with a smug smirk, although right now I hate myself.

I lean against the doorjamb, watching Harley on his knees, his head halfway inside the washing machine drum. I'm immediately captivated by the way his tight jeans pull slightly lower, the band of his boxer briefs showing, as is a sliver of his tan, taut lower back, and I can't help but smile to myself like the cat that got the cream.

"That should do it," Harley grunts as his arm yanks at something deep in the machine and, much to my dismay, he's done far too quickly. But, short of asking him to mow the lawn in the backyard, and paint a recoat of oil over the front porch, there really is no other reason to keep him here. With a forlorn sigh, I watch as he pushes himself up from the floor, finding his feet and brushing his hands over the back of his jeans.

"All good?" he asks, his eyebrows slightly raised as he looks down at me.

I nod, biting down on the inside of my cheek as I rack my brain. I know what I need to do to get him to stay. I need to make a move. In fact, I really should tell him how I'm feeling. The problem is, I keep imagining a million humiliating scenarios in my head, and I'm far too chicken. I simply cannot risk it.

"Murph?"

I pull my eyes from the spot on the floor I've been catatonically focused on, looking up to find him watching me with the ghost of a smile tugging at his lips.

"Yeah?"

"Um ..." Harley shifts awkwardly, pointing behind me. "You wanna move outta the way so I can get past?"

I turn quickly, feeling my cheeks heat as I lead the way back through the kitchen. Harley follows close behind, and I can smell his intoxicating scent, feel his looming presence just over my shoulder. It overwhelms every one of my senses, and I blame it and the tequila for my embarrassing befuddlement.

146

"So, I'll stop by in the morning to pick you up?" Harley checks, standing in the kitchen doorway. "Eight o'clock on the dot."

I watch as he twirls the keys to his truck around his index finger, my eyes zeroing in on the tarnished old Stonemason ring he wears, left to him by his grandfather when he died a few years back.

"Murph?"

I jump, realizing once again that I've been staring at him like a total weirdo. Meeting his eyes, I nod again, swallowing hard. My throat is suddenly dry, and my tongue feels like sandpaper as I clear my throat, continuing regardless of the consequences. "You know, y-you could just stay ... If you w-want."

A crease etches its way in between his eyebrows as he processes my words. And, to be honest, I can't blame him for his obvious confusion. I'm just as confused as he seems to be, because what the hell am I even saying?

"What?"

"I mean, you can ... umm ..." I fumble with my words, looking down and picking at the tiny blue tiles covering the countertop. "I mean, instead of going home. It's late." I look to the clock before meeting his eyes once again. "And your house is on the way outta town." I shrug. "We could just stop by and grab your things on the way to Myrtle Beach in the morning," I ramble.

Harley continues watching me, that sharp crease still furrowed into his brow as the air between us suddenly grows thick with a palpable tension. Awkward as hell. The longer I look at him, the more I wish the floor to my house would open up and suck me deep down into the depths of the unknown, or at least the basement. My heart is thumping, wild and aggressive, each beat whooshing in my ears so loud, it's almost deafening. My palms are damp with perspiration. I can feel a prickly heat climbing its way up from the base of my neck, and I actually want to die. I think death would be less painful, right now.

"You ain't got no spare bed. And there's no way in hell I'll fit on your couch," he says, his voice a little raspier than usual.

I press my lips together to stifle the laughter threatening me. It's both embarrassing and frustrating, and if I don't laugh, I fear I might cry. I mean, do I need to spell it out to the guy? I take a deep breath. My feet are heavy, like they have weights tied to them. My knees wobble a little unsteadily. And I can't help wonder if it's my body's way of telling me to stop whatever the hell it is I'm about to do. But I ignore all the apparent warning signs, crossing the small distance, and coming to stop just a few inches shy of him. Harley's chest rises and falls in a heavy, trembling breath as he looks down at me, his shoulders tensing when I gently, hesitantly reach out, tugging at his T-shirt.

"Murph," he begins, his voice wavering. "W-what are you doing?"

Ignoring his hushed, stammered question, I swallow the lump of apprehension at the back of my throat, staring up into his green eyes that glisten beneath the overhead lamp. I stand on the tips of my toes, craning my neck and breathing him in as I inch closer and closer to his lips. His eyes turn a slightly darker shade, smoky and heavily hooded, his pupils dilating ever so slightly with every inch closer I move. I'm completely intoxicated by both the alcohol I've consumed and his heady scent, and I'd like to say I have no idea what I'm doing, but of course I do. I know exactly what I'm doing. Closing my eyes, my lips finally brush against his, shocking me through to my core, and it's everything I imagined it to be and more. His lips are warm and soft. They feel like home—something I hadn't been expecting—and I'm forced to stifle the contented murmur as it creeps its way up the back of my throat when his lips parts and the very tip of his tongue glides against my bottom lip.

But suddenly, like a cold, hard slap to my face, everything comes to a crashing halt when I almost fall flat to the floor with how quickly he moves away from me.

"What the *hell*, Murph?" he yells, his voice hoarse as it echoes throughout the stark silence of the kitchen. "What the hell are you doing?"

I gape at him as he steps even farther away, keeping a good few feet of distance between us. Anger is evident within his blazing eyes. His chest is heaving as if he's just run a mile. His cheeks are a deep shade of pink as he glares at me, his eyes almost threatening. "This is all bullshit, Murph," he hisses from between gritted teeth. "It isn't real! It's a *lie*. It's *your* lie. Remember?"

"I'm s-sorry, I just—" Lost for words, I grip the edge of the countertop behind me. I breathe hard as the world around me begins to spin. I want to die. But, maybe I'm already dead.

"This was all *your* idea. Your *stupid* idea," Harley continues, and he's so angry. Furious, even. But, to be honest, I'm not even really listening anymore.

"I didn't mean it. I—" I try to speak but I'm suddenly riddled with a humiliation I doubt I'll ever be able to overcome. An unexpected sob bubbles up the back of my throat. "I'm sorry," I cry out, violently swiping at the hot tears trailing down my cheeks before pushing past him and running upstairs to my bedroom, desperate to get away from him and my mortification. I close the door behind me, resting my forehead against the cold wood as I try to catch my breath. But it's no use. I'm a mess. I hear the front door open before slamming shut, and I turn, sliding down my door and falling into a heap on the floor. Burying my face in my hands, I continue crying uncontrollably.

I hadn't expected it to hurt this much. I hadn't expected Harley's rejection to feel like such a slap to the face. I know I'm not even close to being his type, but I still hadn't expected to feel such emotion. I'm embarrassed, humiliated and angry with myself, and I can't help but wonder what the hell I've just gone and done.

Chapter 20

I woke with a hangover. At least, I thought it was a hangover. Now as I stand under the hot water in the shower, the taste of regret is still lingering on my tongue like the taste of a bad pill. I'm almost certain this is what humiliation tastes like, and it doesn't seem to be going anywhere anytime soon. My treacherous mind keeps replaying the events of last night over and over again, torturing me, mocking me. All I see when I close my eyes is Harley's face when he pulled away from me, mid-kiss. The sheer look of horror in his wide eyes as if he couldn't for the life of him believe what I was doing. The way his nose scrunched up in disgust. The way his top lip curled in a way that is like a thousand knives stabbing me right in the heart.

I can't believe how stupid I am. I doubt I'll ever be able to look Harley in the eye again. And now, here I am, forced to spend the next three hours alone in a car with him. I curse under my breath, allowing my head to fall forward, my forehead resting against the tile of the shower recess. I bang my head a few times in the hope it might help knock some sense into me, but I'm just tormenting myself even further.

Showered, dressed and ready to go, I wait on the porch with my overnight bag by my feet, checking the clock on my phone for the hundredth time in the last five minutes. He's almost ten minutes late. Maybe he went on without me. Not that I would mind, or even blame him. I should never have said yes to this damn bachelor party in the first place, but it seemed like a good idea at the time. Plus, if I'd said no, then Anna was going to make me join the girls. And there is no way in hell I was going to put myself through that torture. But now, with these morning-after regrets swirling around in my belly, I'm seriously beginning to think this whole thing was a terrible idea. And, in fact, the more I think about it, the more I truly do hope Harley has ditched me and gone on to South Carolina without me.

But, of course, I could never have such luck. When the thunderous roar of a V8 engine rumbles through the otherwise silent morning, I glance up from my phone to see Harley's Ford pulling up to stop at the curb. I exhale a sigh of defeat and my heart jumps up into the back of my throat as I watch him climb out of the cab.

"Great," I murmur under my breath, taking my sunglasses from where I'd hooked them into the collar of my shirt and, removing my spectacles, I slide the tinted glasses over my tender eyes in a petty attempt to avoid making eye contact with him. Picking up my bag, I hesitantly walk down the steps, watching the ground as I cross the front yard.

"Morning," he offers, his voice gruff as he takes my carryall from me, placing it into the truck bed next to his duffel bag.

I could be the bigger person, apologize for my actions last night, and we could both move on and have a wonderful day. But I'm not the bigger person. I never have been. I'm as stubborn as a mule. And suddenly my maturity level is nonexistent as I say nothing, ignoring him with my chin held slightly higher in the air while I walk around to the passenger side.

Inside, the truck is silent as I struggle to get myself comfortable while composing what little dignity I have, quickly fastening my seat belt. But then Harley opens his door and climbs in, and

I'm immediately hit with that same insufferable scent as it inundates the confines of the tiny space, swirling around me, and it only helps in reminding me of last night. I roll my eyes beneath the tint of my sunglasses, shaking my head as my subconscious reminds me: three excruciating hours.

Without saying a word, Harley starts the engine, and I'm thankful for the sudden onslaught of music drowning out the painful silence. Even if it is Mötley Crüe.

Our first stop is unexpectedly only about thirty minutes out of town, and I glance up from my book, looking out the window at the gas station we're parked at in the middle of nowhere, confused as to why we've pulled over.

"What's wrong?" I ask, looking at Harley as he unfastens his seat belt. "Are we out of gas?"

"I need to piss," he grunts.

"Charming," I quip, quirking a brow.

Ignoring my comment, he opens his door and slides out, and I expect him to slam it shut in my face without so much as another word. But then he surprises me. "You want anything from inside?" he asks without looking at me.

This time I ignore him, looking back down at my book. The slamming door follows a heavy sigh and after a moment I slowly lift my head, watching as he hurries across the lot and disappears inside. I relax back in my seat, releasing what feels like the first breath I've taken since we left my house. For the last half-hour I've been pretending to read a damn book, when in actual fact I haven't even turned the first page. I've been far too consumed with Harley. From the dramatic sighs I'm almost certain are for my benefit only, to the way he's been obviously glancing at me every few minutes. His hands have been gripping the steering wheel so tight I'm surprised he hasn't lost feeling in his fingers.

I can tell he wants to talk to me, no doubt about what happened last night, but I'd rather jump out of this godforsaken truck at seventy miles an hour on the interstate than have that conversation. Last night does not need to be discussed. Ever. I got carried away and I made a damn fool of myself. That's it. Nothing more. I've accepted the fact that Nash is marrying Anna, and he's happy. Now I just need to accept the fact that guys like Harley Shaw will never go for girls like me and, when we kiss them, they will run a mile and never look back.

Am I little offended that he wouldn't even kiss me when he bangs almost anything with a vagina that walks into his bar? Yes. What woman wouldn't be? But I'm sure what happened last night is for the best. If he would've entertained my pass, taken me upstairs and given me the *Shaw Special* all the girls in senior year used to giggle about, no doubt things would be even more awkward than they already are right now. I mean, he did me a favor. End of story. Right? It has to be. End of.

I stiffen immediately when I see Harley walking back toward the truck, and I go straight back to my book, pretending once again to be so caught up in it I don't even notice his return.

"I got you a coffee." He places a to-go cup in the center holder before taking a sip of his own and humming in appreciation, causing me to inwardly cringe, because it only sparks memories from the night before, memories I'm trying so hard to forget.

"Thanks," I mumble, refusing to look up from my book. I don't want to accept his coffee, but after thirty solid minutes of listening to his terrible choice in music, I really could use a caffeine hit, and the smell of freshly roasted beans does cause me to salivate. But I hold out until we're back on the interstate before I reluctantly reach out for the cup. Taking a sheepish sip, I catch the smug smirk curling Harley's lips from the corner of my eye, and I turn away to focus on the fast-passing fields out the window to avoid him altogether.

"So," Harley begins, clearing his throat. "Are you ready to talk about what happened last night?"

I cower a little in my seat, gripping my coffee cup tight, my jaw clenching. He turns down the music playing through the cab until it's nothing but the hint of a tune, and it's just the two of us once again. I close my eyes behind my sunglasses, trying so hard to mentally prepare myself. With a big sigh, I squirm a little in my seat, forcing myself to look at him to see his gaze set intently on the road ahead, his face impassive. Yes, I could tell him the truth. But I don't even know what that truth is right now. So, of course, I do what any woman would do in this situation. I lie through my teeth.

"I was drunk," I say with a casual shrug, trying to act as if it isn't a big deal. "I'm sorry, but I don't even really remember anything from last night." My subconscious is laughing at me as I take another sip from my coffee, staring at the back of the semitrailer following the road in front of us.

"You don't *remember*?" Harley repeats as if he's trying to make sense of my outright lie, and there's something about his tone; he totally knows I'm lying.

I shrug again with a shake of my head when I feel his eyes on me.

"O-kay …" He trails off, and another awkward silence ensues.

Thankfully no more is said, but that doesn't make me feel any better. In fact, my mind is a mess by the time we eventually arrive at Myrtle Beach. You see, the problem is my feelings have done a complete one-eighty, without me even realizing until it's too late. What I wanted my whole life, I suddenly no longer want, and I'm starting to wonder whether I truly wanted it in the first place. What I never wanted is now all I can think about and, again, I can't help but wonder if I've secretly wanted it all along. But after last night I've realized what I want doesn't want me back. And that hurts like hell, more than I'd ever expected it to hurt. And I'm trying to remain unaffected—indifferent—but it's driving me completely insane.

"Y'all finally made it!"

Nash jogs down the front stairs of the beach house as Harley and I climb out of the truck, stretching after the long drive. The place is a mansion. Three stories. All windows. And, of course, right on the beach. The sheer size and grandeur leave me speechless as I crane my neck to take it all in.

"Yeah, we made it," Harley murmurs, stopping beside me and huffing out a sigh as he rests his hands on his hips, eyeing the house dubiously. When Nash glances at me, I nod, quickly looking away.

"You two are on the top floor. It's a little more *private* ..." Nash clears his throat, suddenly looking awkward as hell.

My shoulders fall in resignation when I realize I have to share a room with Harley, and I don't know why I'm surprised, really. Of course we're expected to share a room; we are head over heels in love with one another, after all. I can't help but shake my head at my own thoughts.

"Thanks, man." Harley flashes me a sideways glance and I'm forced to avert my eyes, looking down at the wayward stones by my feet.

"Don't look too excited." Nash chuckles, looking from Harley to me.

I snap my gaze up, meeting his eyes, and I force a smile onto my face. But then I see a slight furrow pull between his brows as he looks between the both of us again. "Is everything okay between you two?"

I swallow hard, nodding a little too quickly. "Yeah, we're fine."

Harley clears his throat from beside me, not saying a word as he moves to retrieve our bags from the back of the truck, and Nash nods, but I can tell he doesn't completely believe me. "Okay." He claps his hands together, forcing a smile. "Well, the bus will be here in an hour to take us to the Speedway."

"We'll just drop our bags off upstairs and get ready," Harley says with a curt nod for me to follow as he turns and leads the way carrying both our overnight bags.

"Y'all better get ready to eat my dust!" Nash yells from behind, more excited than a kid on Christmas Eve. And I laugh for what feels like the first time in forever, rolling my eyes at him. I know he's just excited to drive a real NASCAR stock car, but there's too much damn tension in the air between Harley and me. I can barely breathe it's so stifling. I hope we sort our issues out sooner rather than later, or else the whole bachelor party is going to be a living hell for everyone.

Inside the house, the foyer opens up to an expansive sunken living area with a wall of floor-to-ceiling glass doors leading out to a sprawling deck overlooking the ocean. Outside, I can see Kevin, Seth, and a few other guys I'm assuming are Nash's friends from New York, all taking in the view, and I can't blame them. It's spectacular. I want to say something about the unimaginable color of the sparkling azure ocean, but Harley doesn't bother stopping as he continues up the stairs, clearly not as taken aback as I am. We make it to the landing in an uncomfortable silence. To the right is a sitting room with a small balcony opening up to yet another view of the water, and to the left is a door, which I'm assuming is our designated sleeping quarters.

"I guess this is us." Harley breathes a little unsteadily, looking up at the door.

I nod, pushing the door open, and we're greeted by pale gray walls, navy drapes, and crisp white finishings. Across the space, the floor-to-ceiling windows and doors open to another small balcony overlooking the expansive Atlantic, and I'm still enamored by the view. It's a beautiful sight. But then my eyes move to the big bed in the center of the room, and my heart sinks into the depths of my belly.

"I'll sleep on this," Harley grunts as if he can read my mind, stepping around me and dumping his duffel bag onto the armchair sitting by the balcony doors.

I don't know if I should be offended or not. I mean, he couldn't have raced to the chair any quicker if he tried. I want to say something. I want to argue and tell him not to be stupid. We're adults. And there are plenty of pillows to stack between us as a makeshift barricade if we sleep in the bed together. But I don't say anything. I can't. I don't have time. Before I even have the chance, he disappears into the en-suite bathroom and all I can hear is the pipes as they come to life behind the wall, before the sound of the shower drowns out my thoughts.

Chapter 21

I've been standing in front of the windows just staring out at the ocean in some kind of a trance, watching the water dance beneath the sun. For so long, in fact, I don't even hear the door to the bathroom open.

"Your turn."

I startle from the sound of Harley's gravelly voice behind me, and I turn quickly, immediately wishing I hadn't. Surrounded by a plume of steam swirling around him as it escapes the bathroom, he's barely even covered by a towel wrapped around his waist, hanging so low on his hips my eyes are instantly drawn to the V-lines of his pelvis, to the light smattering of hair that leads from his belly button down into the depths of the great unknown. Water droplets drip from the lengths of his wet curls, gliding down over his taut skin, trailing over the peaks and valleys of his tattooed chest.

I do everything I can to force my eyes back up but, when I do, I can't help but notice the hint of a smirk playing on his lips as he watches me, and I know right at that moment that I've been caught outwardly ogling him. My cheeks immediately heat and I gasp when I realize I haven't taken a breath, coughing to disguise my obvious reaction. Turning quickly, I reach for my overnight bag and busy myself with rifling through its contents, grabbing what I need, fully aware of Harley watching me from the small space between the foot of the bed and the bathroom door. With a change of clothes under my arm and my bathroom caddy clutched within a death-like grip, I avoid his knowing gaze as I step past him, holding my breath as I brush against his warm, wet body.

And once I'm in the safety of the bathroom, I practically slam the door shut behind me, collecting myself as best I can as I take the moment I need.

I thought another shower might help wash away some of the confusion racking my mind and my body, but it does nothing of the sort. It does the opposite, actually. All I could think about while I stood beneath the warm flowing water was the fact that Harley's wet, naked body had been standing in the exact same spot only moments earlier. Then I began thinking all sorts of highly inappropriate things, so I got out of there as fast as I could without slipping on the wet tile and killing myself.

Now, as I stand here staring at myself in the slightly foggy mirror, dressed in my jean shorts and bra, I'm in a much worse state than I was before, if that's even possible.

Damn him and his perfect body. Damn those tattoos. Damn that look he gets in his eyes when it's as if he knows exactly what I'm thinking when I shouldn't be thinking anything of the sort. Damn Harley Shaw. And damn me. In fact, damn Nash. He should never have invited me on his damn bachelor party. I have no place being here. I absolutely should never have said yes. I should've just stayed at home, alone, where I belong. The whole party is going to end in disaster if I don't get my emotions in check. I swear, I'm like a 14-year-old girl, giddy and fumbling for no reason. I need to steer clear of Harley for the rest of the trip.

I release a sigh of relief when I finally come out of the bathroom to find the bedroom empty and no trace whatsoever of Harley except for the lingering hint of his cologne, hanging heavily in the air as if it's mocking me. But I shake my head, ridding every thought of him from my mind while I collect what I need and hurry the hell out of there before I search for that damn cologne bottle and spritz my pillow with it.

Downstairs, the guys are crowding the living area watching some baseball game on television, their eyes glued to the screen. I take the opportunity to slip out onto the back deck unnoticed. The minute the salt air hits me, a smile immediately claims my entire face. I grip the glass railing, closing my eyes as the midday sun lands on my face, warming my skin, and I listen to the rhythmic flow of the waves as they crash onto the shore, the seagulls squawking in the background. If heaven had a soundtrack, I'm sure this would be it.

"What'cha doin' out here?"

The calm that had been cleansing my body is torn from me as I startle from the sound of Nash's voice pulling me from my reverie. I turn to see him walking out onto the deck, smiling as he joins me at the railing. I manage a smile, turning back to the view of the water. "It's so nice here." I close my eyes once again, breathing in that same beach smell.

"Yeah," he says from beside me. "Anna sure did a good job finding this place."

I roll my eyes behind my eyelids at the mention of Anna. Of course, this was all her doing. It's perfect. Just like her. I swear the two of them are made for each other. And me? Well, I was just some stand-in for Nash until he found his perfect match. I'm the girl who will never be good enough for anyone.

"Hey, a-are you sure everything's okay with you and Harley?"

I force my self-loathing thoughts aside. My brows pull together as I open my eyes and look up at him. He avoids my eyes, but I watch as he lifts a tentative hand, nervously scratching at the back of his neck before finally meeting my gaze.

I swallow hard, forcing another smile to my lips. "We're fine."

He nods, looking down once more, and I can tell his mind is

working overtime when he meets my eyes once again. "It's just ... y'all seemed a little distant when you got here."

"We had a fight over the radio. You know how terrible his taste in music is." I shake my head with a nonchalant smile, waving off his concern. "We're fine."

"If you say so."

For some reason, his words piss me off and I don't even know why. *If you say so.* As if he has any idea. But I let it slide, ignoring his remark.

Nash looks down at me, his eyes scanning me from head to toe as a grin curls his lips. "T-shirt a bit big, huh?"

I look down at the embarrassingly obvious *Nash Harris Stag Party* T-shirt Kevin had made for everyone to wear for the trip. "Yeah." I chuckle. "I guess he didn't stop to think that I'm half the size of almost everyone else on this trip." My designated T-shirt, the one with *Murph* printed on the back, was swimming on me when I put it on. It fell to mid-thigh—even longer than my shorts—so I had to tie it up at the side, and cut off the sleeves, which came down to my elbows.

"It looks cute on you."

At that, my head snaps up and I meet Nash's eyes. He quickly looks away, pressing his lips together, and I watch as he closes his eyes briefly as if silently chastising himself. And it sucks. He should be able to say those kinds of things to me. He used to tell me all the time that I was cute, or something I did was cute. Even before we dated. It used to piss me off because I never wanted to be cute. I wanted to be sexy or beautiful. But then, the way he told me I was cute started to grow on me. And I was suddenly his *cute* girl. But now? Now cute is unacceptable. And it sucks that everything has changed.

Silence settles between us, and I hate these silences. It's like neither of us knows what to say or how to act around each other anymore. In the years we've known each other, we've never had to deal with uncomfortable silences, but now it seems that's all we have left: uncomfortable silences and awkwardly fleeting glances full of something neither of us has the guts to broach.

"We should get going," Nash finally says, looking at me with a smile that doesn't reach his eyes. "The bus will be here any minute."

I watch as he turns and walks back inside, and I exhale a heavy breath, looking out at the ocean one last time in the hope of some semblance of clarity. A horn sounds from out front, and I take a fortifying breath, forcing a smile onto my face as I walk inside to meet the rest of the guys as they excitedly make their way to the door. I follow the throng down the steep front steps and we come to a stop at a blacked-out bus idling in the long driveway, deep bass thrumming heavily from inside and seeping out into the otherwise peaceful afternoon.

"Good afternoon, gentlemen." A woman wearing what can only be described as lingerie smiles as she steps down from the bus. Her eyes meet me, and her smile falters momentarily before returning. "Oh, and *lady*."

I shake my head, waving a hand in the air at her correction. "Consider me one of the guys."

She giggles, looking at Nash's T-shirt, which clearly indicates that he's the groom, and she takes his hand without asking, leading him onto the bus first before we all follow. Inside, the place is like a nightclub. Bright flashing lights, loud music, and a fully stocked bar. I smirk knowingly at Nash as I pass him, trying not to laugh as he sits looking awkward as hell with the scantily clad woman perched right on his lap. I continue to the seat at the back, sliding in by the window while watching as the guys all pile in, all of them laughing at Nash and taking photos with their phones.

"Don't you dare post those on social media!" Nash yells. "Anna will kill me, slowly and painfully."

"Nash, it's your *bachelor* party!" I laugh. "You're gonna have nothing but tits and ass in your face at the strip club later tonight."

"No strip clubs." He shakes his head vehemently.

At the mention of no strip clubs Kevin gasps out loud, flashing me a wide-eyed look of horror and disbelief as if he's a 7-year-old kid who's just been told Santa Claus isn't real. I shake my head, dismissing his concern with a wink, which makes his shoulders sag in relief and his boyish grin reappears.

"Can I sit here?"

I look up to see Harley standing above me, pointing to the seat beside me. I meet his eyes, finding a knowing look within them, one that matches the hint of the smile pulling at his lips. Once again, I feel my cheeks heat of their own accord, and I roll my eyes at myself before sliding across the seat to allow room for him as he sits down. His body is so close, and I'm fully aware of his thigh brushing against mine. I chance a look at him and he offers me a smile that hints at his dimples, quirking one of his eyebrows. "Can we please put last night behind us and just have fun today?" he whispers close to my ear so no one can overhear him.

I swallow hard as the memory of last night's painful humiliation floods through me. It still hurts, but I manage a nod, pressing my lips together with the best smile I can offer. He holds his hand out, palm up, and I look down at it, my brow furrowed in confusion when I meet his eyes once again. He chuckles to himself. Rolling his eyes in exasperation, he reaches down and takes my hand in his, his fingers threading mine before resting our interlocked hands on his thigh.

I wish I had the ability to act cool, calm and collected in those moments where I'm anything but on the inside. But I'm so embarrassing. I always have been. And right now, I sit there frozen—stunned—staring down at our hands. I don't even breathe. Maybe it's the unexpected way in which my body is reacting to his touch. Maybe it's the smile still lingering on his lips. Or maybe, it's the fact that Harley Shaw is holding my hand despite the fact that we're seated in the back and no one can even see whether or not we're holding hands. I don't know what this is, but I know it isn't just for show; he wants to hold my hand, and I want him to want to hold my hand. I don't miss the obvious beats my heart skips as we sit together in an awkwardly companionable silence.

And in that very moment, with a million and one conflicting thoughts racing through my mind, all I can be sure of is one thing as I release the breath I've been holding on to. I don't just like Harley. I, Alice Murphy, am head over heels in love with the guy, and now I don't even know what to think.

Chapter 22

Dressed in a racing suit at least two sizes too big, I hesitantly walk out into the pit on the side of the track, meeting the guys as they stand around a shiny stock car. The sun is beaming down from high up in the sky, and I can feel beads of sweat trailing down my back as my heart thunders in my chest, slamming against my rib cage in protest as I stare out over the looming track. Swallowing hard, I try to psych myself up, but it's no use. To be honest, NASCAR isn't really my thing. I tried to act all excited about it with the guys, but now that I'm here faced with the prospect of crashing headfirst into a barricade and killing myself, that excitement I felt is nonexistent. I hate driving fast.

Actually, I don't even really like driving. I'm not the kind of person who likes to get in the car with the windows down and drive to get lost just for the sake of it. I drive only to get to where I need to be. I have enough trouble navigating the streets of Graceville in my trusty little Cruze. I don't need to complicate things by driving two hundred miles per hour in a NASCAR vehicle. But, this is what Nash wanted.

The instructor goes over the emergency procedures, which only increases my anxiety, and explains everything else we need to know in regard to safety. The fact that we'll be driving with a professional driver riding shotgun doesn't make me feel any better, but at least if I die, I'll take someone with me.

"You okay?"

I look up to see Harley watching me, his brow furrowed as he studies my face.

I manage a nod, barely.

"You look like you're about to pass out."

"I'm fine," I snap abruptly, my voice strangely high-pitched.

"You know you don't have to do this, Murph," he says quietly, gently touching my shoulder. "You can just sit and watch. Or you can ride shotgun while the driver takes you around in a pace car."

"Really?" My brows climb higher in hope at that last suggestion.

"Yeah." He chuckles, obviously witnessing the relief flood through me. "You don't *have* to go fast."

I look around, for what I'm not sure. The truth is I don't want everyone to think I'm too chicken. It's weird enough that I'm the only girl on a guys' bachelor party trip; the last thing I want is for anyone to pander to me or, worse, call me a *girl*. Because, let's face it, I could kick all their asses.

"Actually, to be honest"— Harley leans in closer, his voice even lower, pulling my attention straight back to him—"I'm not too keen on this, either. I'll ride with you, if you want …?"

I meet his eyes, gaping at him. "Are you serious?"

He smiles with a shrug. "We can even say it's me who's too chickenshit to drive …"

I don't hesitate. Immediately my hand is up in the air and the instructor stops mid-sentence, pointing to me with a smile.

"Um, my boyfriend's scared," I say as Harley guffaws from beside me while everyone laughs at his expense. "Can we ride together while one of y'all drives?"

"Of course." The instructor offers Harley a dubious once-over before making a note of something on his iPad.

166

"Thanks, Murph," Harley murmurs sarcastically from beside me, nudging me with his elbow. "I owe you one."

I smile, and he winks at me before focusing his attention back on the instructor.

I rub a hand over Harley's back while he leans over the trash can in the pit, bringing up whatever's left in his stomach. Kevin and Seth are in hysterics, laughing and pointing at him and almost falling into a heap on the gravel. I flash them each a warning glare as Harley continues to retch and groan with every contraction of his belly.

"Here's some water." Nash hurries over, holding out an icy cold bottle.

"Thanks." I take it from him as I continue patting Harley's strained back. "He'll be fine. I think it's just the heat," I lie, knowing full well his upset stomach has little to do with the heat and everything to do with the sharp corners we just endured in the flying stock car. And it's all my fault. I'm the one who was yelling at the driver to go faster once I got the taste for it after the first lap. All the while Harley was in the back seat, squealing like a 12-year-old girl.

Harley stands, wiping his mouth with the sleeve of his race suit before offering Nash a curt nod. Pushing his hair back from his sweat-beaded forehead, he flashes me a sheepish glance as soon as Nash leaves us. He takes the water from me. I smile knowingly, squeezing his arm before turning and heading back to the rest of the guys as they gather around the shiny race car for a group photo. I make sure to keep to the side of the group, but the moment I move next to Nash's friend, Jake, Nash turns, his eyes finding me, and he makes a scene, running from his place front and center to grab my hand and pull me with him.

"I don't want to be in the front!" I hiss, flashing the photographer an apologetic glance.

167

"You, me and Harley in the front." Nash waves Harley over. "My two best friends."

I watch as Harley jogs over, again pushing his hair back from his face, looking a little less gray. He moves to the other side of Nash, his eyes flitting to me a moment before he wraps his arm around his best friend's shoulders and looks straight ahead toward the camera, smiling with his trademark dimples on show. I reluctantly snake my arm around Nash's waist, but when he returns the action, I jump slightly at the feel of his hand resting so low on my hip, his pinkie finger in dangerous proximity to my butt. I try so hard to convince myself that it's just an innocent slip of his hand—just an accident—but he makes no effort to move his hand and, in fact, he goes so far as to squeeze my hip ever so slightly.

What the hell?

I cast a sideways glance, finding him smiling at the camera with a slightly smug grin, and I don't know what to think. Is he doing this on purpose? Or, does he have no idea? I should move. Step away from him, out of his reach. But, I don't. I don't want to cause a scene. So, instead of making a big deal out of it, I turn to face the camera with a smile I know doesn't even come close to reaching my eyes.

After the awkward encounter with Nash's hand practically groping my butt back at the Speedway, I've done my best to steer clear of him for most of the afternoon. Our party bus hostess, Amber, brought us to the Myrtle Beach boardwalk, and we've spent the afternoon going from bar to bar, downing pitchers of icy cold beer and more complimentary shots than I've been able to keep track of.

Somewhere between bars we've visited, I've somehow managed to lose one of my Converse and I had to buy a pair of kitschy flip-flops from one of the souvenir shops on the promenade. Needless to say, as I now sit perched on Harley's lap while we continue drinking at a rooftop bar overlooking the ocean, watching Kevin drink a concoction of mixed liquor straight from my one remaining Converse, I'm well on my way to a night of bad decision-making if my fingertips tracing the tattoos on Harley's arm is any indication.

"You're drunk, Murph." Harley chuckles, and an involuntary shudder runs through me as his soft breath fans gently against the shell of my ear.

I glance at him, meeting his knowing gaze, and I can see from his heavily hooded lids, to the way the whites of his eyes are slightly bloodshot, that I'm not the only one who's drunk. "Well, this is a bachelor party." I shrug. "We're supposed to be *smashed*, man."

He gapes at me, offering a somewhat mock look of shock. "What?"

"Did you just say we're supposed to *smash*?" he asks with a dramatic gasp.

I bite back my own smile, shaking my head at him. "*No.*"

He quirks one of his brows. "I think ya did ..." he says with a teasing lilt.

"Well, we could've smashed last night, but you—" I snap my mouth shut, realizing what I've just said, my cheeks flaming.

Harley watches me a moment, one eye narrowing as a crease pulls between his brows. "But I thought you said you don't remember anything about last night?"

At this point, I'm fully aware of his hand splayed against the small of my back. Fully aware of his other hand resting on my thigh. Fully aware of the fact that I'm practically sitting on his crotch. I press my lips together, pulling them between my teeth as I consider what he's said, racking my brain with what I can possibly say without giving myself away. But then I'm reminded of how many lemon drops I've consumed this afternoon, and hell, it's not the first time I've made a fool a myself.

"I lied." I shrug as if it's no big deal, turning back to the table

169

and reaching for my beer. I feel his eyes boring into me as I take a big swig in the hope of buying myself some time. But sadly, it seems Harley isn't nearly as drunk as me.

"Well then, should we talk about it?" he presses, whispering.

I release a sigh, looking up to the afternoon sky a moment before meeting his eyes once again. His face is full of a seriousness I wasn't expecting to see, one I definitely don't feel like dealing with right now, and it actually sobers me up ever so slightly.

"Murph, we should talk about what happened," he urges, offering me a knowing look.

I shrug again, shaking my head. "What's there to talk about? I made a move I shouldn't have. You swiftly turned me down. The end. No harm, no foul."

His face remains stoic as he processes my words.

"It was a stupid, drunken mistake, and I'm sorry." I take another drink from my beer, watching as his eyes seem to bore into mine, his gaze so penetrating I'm forced to look away so he can't see straight through my nonchalant façade to the painfully shameful truth. "Anyway. I need to go to the bathroom." I stand from his lap, feeling his hand fall from its place on my lower back, and immediately I feel an obvious void at the loss of contact.

Harley just continues watching me, his face expressionless.

"Do you want anything from the bar?" I ask.

He pushes his hair back from his face, and his hands come together behind his head, resting at his nape, which only makes his T-shirt ride up ever so slightly, flashing a hint of the taut skin just above the waistband of his shorts. I quickly avert my eyes, zeroing in on his gaze once again, raising one of my eyebrows expectantly.

"No, Murph. I'm good for now ..." He shakes his head, the slightest hint of a smile pulling at the corner of his lips, a smile I can't quite decipher, one that makes me suddenly nervous, but in a good way. I don't miss the hidden innuendo behind his words, but I turn away as quickly as I can, hurrying off in the direction of the stairs that lead down into the main bar.

I don't even need to go to the bathroom. I just need some kind of reprieve from Harley's intensity before the alcohol coursing through me causes me to do something embarrassing like, I don't know, trying to kiss him again.

Chapter 23

I successfully managed to avoid both Nash and Harley for the rest of the afternoon by playing a few games of pool with Seth in the main bar downstairs. My excuse was that it was too hot up on the rooftop, and my pale skin just doesn't fare well in such a heat, but that was only a half-truth. Now that we're back at the beach house getting ready for our night, I've been sitting on the floor of the shower beneath the cool running water for so long I'm shivering while I try to get myself to sober up.

So, Harley knows I was lying when I told him I didn't remember what happened last night? So what. I'm sure he can understand my need to avoid any further awkwardness. But from the look in his eye when I ditched him to play pool, I know for a fact he wants to talk about it. And if I think I'm going to get through the rest of this night avoiding him, then I'm just as stupid as I often think I might be. We're staying in the same room, for Christ's sake. I force myself out of the shower, doing what I can with my face and hair, opting for minimal makeup and a messy bun before coming out to the bedroom. I release a breath of relief to find the room empty, and I hurry to find my clothes for tonight.

I'm dressed and ready to go in just a few minutes, but that doesn't stop me from staring at my reflection in the full-length mirror on the inside of the closet door, my own eyes full of judgment as they rake over me from head to toe. Wearing a pair of sensible espadrille sandals I know I won't fall over in, I've paired them with a tight black tube skirt I'd never normally wear, pulling at the slinky material as it clings to my hips and thighs. Teamed with a blue jean shirt tied at the waist and a pair of clear-rimmed glasses, I begin zeroing in on every single part of my body I hate. With my hands on my hips, my fingers tapping in time to an imaginary beat, I sigh in defeat because I know it's not going to get any better.

Like most women, I wish I was a little taller, maybe thinner around the bottom half, and I'd love for my B cup to miraculously turn into a C overnight. I can't help but think if maybe I was all those things, maybe Harley wouldn't have turned me down last night. Maybe he wouldn't have run out on me as if his life depended on it. But, I know I am the way I am, and things aren't going to get any better, so I resolve to accept myself with a final shrug of resignation. Thankfully I'm saved from my own scrutiny by the sound of my name being called from downstairs, and I quickly touch up my red lipstick before hurrying out.

Downstairs, the guys are gathered by the front door, all drunk, all rowdy, and all completely oblivious to my arrival. All except one. I do everything I can to avoid his gaze from across the group, but it's no use, and I can feel him approach even as I stare down at the floor.

"You look good," Nash says, his voice oddly quiet as he lingers close by.

Biting hard on the inside of my cheek in an attempt at stifling the shudder threatening my composure, I force a tight smile onto my lips as I glance up at him, pushing my glasses up my nose. He's dressed in a slightly wrinkled button-down and a black neck tie loosely tied into a sorry excuse for an Oxford knot, his hair disheveled, complementing his untucked shirt and rolled-up sleeves, and I must say, the old me would've almost gone weak at the knees at the sheer sight of him. But now, he's far too close for my liking. I can smell the liquor on his breath, and the way his left eyelid droops. Yes, he's drunk. Of course he is. It's his bachelor party. But he's also nothing like my best friend of fifteen years. This Nash, the same one who had his hand resting inappropriately close to my butt is different. I'm not sure I like him so much.

"Thanks," I say with as genuine a smile as I can manage, trying hard not to look too obvious as I move what distance I can from him. "You look … drunk."

He chuckles, and in the process, he somehow loses his balance and uses the opportunity to reach out and grab my arm to steady himself. His touch is soft, but there's a contradicting roughness to it and, when he doesn't let me go despite the fact he's clearly regained his balance, I can't help but look down to where his hand is wrapped around my elbow, almost possessively.

"We had a shotgun competition while you were getting ready," Nash explains, his words evidently slurred. "I lost."

I don't miss the hiccup he tries to conceal. Again, my eyes look down to where he's still holding me, and I wish he'd take the hint and move a few feet away. It isn't right that he's touching me again. It isn't necessary, nor is the way his gaze is lingering resolutely on my lips.

"Have you heard from Anna? Is she having fun at the retreat?" I ask, hoping the mention of Anna might remind him that he's engaged to be married in just a couple of days, and he most certainly shouldn't be looking at me the way he is.

He shakes his head, and much to my disappointment he actually moves closer instead of moving away, his hand trailing from my elbow to my waist as he leans in. "Did you and Harley sort everything out?" he whispers so close to my ear I can feel his lips brush against the shell.

Involuntarily I snap back, away from him, my face stark when I meet his red-rimmed eyes. I want to push him away, tell him

174

to back the hell up, but before I have the chance to say anything, I'm stopped by a strong pair of hands snaking around my waist from behind, effectively forcing Nash away from me. I turn my head to see Harley looking down at me with a playful grin despite the furrow between his brow and the knowing look in his eyes as he casts Nash a furtive once-over.

"Where were you?" I find myself asking as I turn in his arms, cowering slightly closer in an attempt to get farther away from Nash.

"I was getting ready in the downstairs bathroom because you were taking forever," he says, his eyes fleeting momentarily to Nash who seems to have otherwise forgotten about his advances toward me and is suddenly joking and laughing with the guys.

I exhale a harsh breath, my shoulders sagging in relief at his distance, but then I meet Harley's eyes to find a confused look within them as he studies me. "What?"

"A-are you okay?" he asks, nodding his chin in Nash's direction.

I manage a smile and a shrug. "Yeah. He's just drunk."

"He is …" Harley nods, but his eyes are still shrouded in confusion, and I'm fully aware of his arms still protectively wrapped around my waist, holding me close.

I find myself trapped beneath the weight of his stare, and I swallow hard because I think I know exactly what he's thinking. A few days ago, if I was in this situation with a handsy, drunk Nash, I would have been over the moon, and planning exactly how to seal the deal with him tonight. But everything has changed now. I'm almost positive Harley feels it, too. His arms around me and the heaviness within his gaze are surely proof that it isn't just me.

But, before I can think too much into it, before my heart beats right out of my chest, I'm literally saved by the bell at the sound of the bus horn honking from outside, and I thank whatever god

175

is above as I turn and follow the guys. As we make our way out through the front door and down the steep steps, I don't miss the way my heart is thumping a lot faster than it was only moments earlier.

I'm not surprised when we get asked to leave the steakhouse swiftly after we've barely finished our main course. Seth has his shirt completely unbuttoned while singing the chorus of a Guns N' Roses song to a group of middle-aged women at the next table over. Nash has a breadbasket on his head, and is standing on his chair while reciting all fifty states in reverse alphabetical order because someone bet him ten bucks he couldn't. I hastily finish what's left of my beer before wrangling the guys, while Harley picks up the check.

Outside, I lead the way back to the bus with the rag-tag team of drunks behind me, and I glance back over my shoulder to see Harley practically carrying Nash who still has the damn breadbasket on his head.

"Let's go to the strip club!" Kevin shouts with a defiant fist in the air as he staggers past me toward the bus.

"I don't know if that's such a good idea," I begin cautiously.

"Aw, c'mon, Murph. Don't go all *girly* on us, now!" Seth laughs, nudging me playfully with his elbow on his way past.

I place my hands on my hips, glaring at the both of them. "Don't call me a *girl*!" I yell, causing them to chuckle. I roll my eyes at them as I continue, "Nash is wasted." I look back to where Harley is clearly struggling with Nash. "I doubt he'll even get let in!"

"Buzzkill!" Seth groans.

"We could still go," Kevin suggests with a shrug. "He can just stay on the bus and sleep it off."

I laugh, shaking my head at the both of them as they pile onto the bus, and I move to help Harley as he and Nash approach the steps.

"Murph!" Nash yells, his dazed eyes seemingly lighting up as if he's just noticed I'm here. "*My* Murph!"

I know he's just drunk, but I'm momentarily taken aback by his words. *My* Murph? He stumbles forward, shrugging out of Harley's grip and I'm not prepared when he launches for me, wrapping his arms around me so tight I fall back into the side of the bus as I try to carry his unexpected weight.

"Careful of my girl, man!" Harley chuckles, moving in to pull Nash away from me, but suddenly the energy shifts and an overwhelming tension settles unevenly.

"Yeah, *right*!" Nash scoffs, turning on his unsteady feet. "She was my girl, *first*," he mutters through gritted teeth with an angry look in his hazy eyes as he tries to push Harley away from him with everything he has, which barely even causes Harley to budge.

Shocked at something I never for the life of me thought I'd ever be witness to, I remain against the side of the bus, frozen at the instant change in Nash's normally carefree demeanor, watching as Harley collects himself, calmly smoothing his hair back from his face. His eyes dart from Nash to me, and back again, and he looks to consider his options a moment, before nodding at his best friend, holding his hands up in the air in some semblance of surrender. Though I'm not sure why, it hurts me, and I can't help but wonder if it ever came down to it, whether Harley would ever be the guy to fight for me.

"C'mon y'all, let's go!" I finally find my voice, clapping my hands together in an attempt to attract the attention of Nash who looks just about ready to fight his very best friend. My eyes flit to Harley who is watching me intently, and I offer him an apologetic glance before moving to Nash and taking a hold of his hand to help him so he doesn't fall and break his damn neck.

"Murph!" He laughs, gripping my hand so tight as I carefully lead him up the stairs. "I just knew you'd choose me."

I try to ignore his obnoxious words. He's just drunk. Cursing deep down on the inside, I continue steadying him with each step before finally directing him to the first available seat on the bus. I watch as he falls asleep almost immediately, and I hesitate a moment, looking from him, to the rest of the guys already seated who are completely unaware of the tension that just transpired outside.

"Let's go!" Harley calls through to the driver on his way up into the bus. He stops to look down at me, an unreadable emotion flashing within his eyes as he looks at Nash before moving past and taking one of the seats in the back. And I want to go to him. I want to be with him. But Nash is in a real state, and he needs me. I just hope Harley understands.

Chapter 24

"Are you sure you don't wanna stay with the rest of the guys?"

Harley glances back at the flickering neon lights of The Pink Palace, an aptly named strip club on the outskirts of Myrtle Beach with an interesting collection of cars, trucks, and motorcycles parked in the gravel lot. He turns back to me with a tight smile, his jaw tense as he shakes his head, glancing over my shoulder to where Nash is barely conscious, resting up against a streetlight. And, to be honest, I'm glad he doesn't want to stay with the guys. Not only do I not feel like dealing with drunk Nash on my own, but I also know the two of us need some time together to try and talk about everything.

We say our goodbyes to the rest of the boys before they disappear into the strip club, and the bus stays parked in the lot while we struggle with getting a barely conscious Nash into the waiting Uber.

By the time we arrive back at the beach house, Nash is snoring loudly from the back seat. I look back to see his head flopped against Harley's shoulder, his mouth hanging open, and I release a sigh of frustration, rolling my eyes. He ruined his own bachelor party by getting plastered, and now Harley and I have to sort him out. Surprisingly, considering how drunk we each are, we somehow manage to successfully get him up two flights of stairs and into his bed without too much damage. I'm pretty sure at one point we may have connected a railing with his head, but he can deal with the pain tomorrow when he wakes up. Something tells me a bump on the head will be the least of his worries.

I sit on the edge of the mattress, removing Nash's shoes while Harley places the small trash can from the en-suite bathroom onto the floor by the bed, just in case he wakes up through the night to be sick. As I sit there, I take Nash in, from his mess of hair to the wrinkled shirt he's still wearing, down to his oddly socked feet, and an unexpected sadness comes over me.

I'm not sure what it is, but my mind drifts back to all the nights I used to sit up and watch him sleep beside me. When I'd sneak him past Momma and into my bedroom. When I would stay in his dorm with him when we were at college together, because my roommate was horribly mean to me. All the times I would watch him sleep because it was such a beautiful sight to see. I loved watching his eyelashes flutter with every rapid movement of his eyes; I imagined he was dreaming of something so spectacular, and I envied whatever it was he was imagining in those moments. I loved watching the way his lips would curve up ever so slightly, as if he was privy to a secret he would never tell. But now as I watch him, passed out and almost lifeless, all I feel is a sense of emptiness, because the boy I used to watch sleep is gone.

It's taken me until tonight to realize that my Nash is gone. Sure, there's the occasional glimpse here and there of the boy I used to know and love but, for the most part, he's a changed man and that's fine because, like Harley said, people change. And I'm trying so hard to convince myself that Nash has changed for the better, that he's happy and content. But I keep thinking back to the way his hands were on me earlier, to the look so unlike him in his eyes. I'm worried he isn't happy, and that he might do something he'll regret, but I quickly blink those thoughts away, reminding myself that despite his change, he's still Nash Harris. No matter what, he'll always be the boy who captured my heart all those years ago, and I'll always love him, even when he's a drunk jerk.

With a sad smile, I reach forward and gently smooth his sandy blond hair back from his face. Leaning in, I press a chaste kiss to his forehead before standing and walking toward the door, which is when my eyes find Harley's watching me with a slight furrow in his brow, one that quickly disappears as he squares his broad shoulders. "I'm gonna go down and have a drink out on the deck," he says quietly, rubbing at a spot on the back of his neck. "Are you going to bed, or …?"

"I'll join you." I shrug. "I could use a drink after *this* experience," I say with a chuckle, pointing back at an obliviously sleeping Nash.

Harley nods, managing a tight smile before turning and leading the way out of the room. I follow closely as we make our way downstairs to the kitchen where the counter is still laden with liquor bottles from earlier. I kick off my sandals and sit on a stool at the island, watching as Harley begins making something for us to drink. I smile to myself as he pours a mixture of different liquors into a metal shaker, shaking it like a professional bartender. He flashes me another tight-lipped smile before pouring the concoction into two Solo cups, sliding one across to me as he raises his in the air in silent cheers.

"What's this?" I ask, lifting the cup to my nose and taking a sniff. I pull back in horror, wincing as the scent alone feels as if it burns the small hairs in my nostrils.

"It's kind of like a Long Island Iced Tea." Harley chuckles to himself, taking a sip from his cup. "Without the rum. Because I know you can't drink rum after that one time at Kevin's graduation party."

Wait. What? I gape at him, sufficiently surprised by the mention of that night. A night I tried so hard to forget all about. A night so long ago. A night I can't believe Harley, of all people, remembers.

I was in a complete panic. On the verge of tears. My heart was racing, my head spinning. I didn't know what to do. I'd been drinking the punch all night and, somehow, I was drunk as hell. Had someone spiked my drink? Was someone trying to date-rape me? My heart thundered painfully as I began imagining the most horrible scenarios playing out in my hazy mind.

At some point during the night I'd lost Nash. He said he was going to help John Portman fix the dead battery in his truck, but that was at least forty minutes ago. I went in search of him, but somehow, I ended up outside in the backyard with no recollection of how I'd gotten there. I was so drunk and so sick, and so embarrassed to be in such a state. I was Alice Murphy, and Alice Murphy didn't get drunk at parties like everyone else. Alice Murphy was a good girl. A nice girl. A sweet girl. Being obliterated was not how I wanted my classmates to remember me.

Oh yeah, Alice Murphy? I remember her. She's the girl who was drunk as sin, out of her goddamn mind on the night of graduation.

No thanks. There was no way in hell I was going to wind up being that girl. So, I hid in the furthermost corner of the yard and stuck my fingers down my throat in an attempt to make myself sick, in the hope it would help sober me up.

"Murph?"

I snapped my head up, mid-retch, my eyes wide at the sound of the familiar voice coming from over my shoulder, his knowing chuckle echoing through my throbbing head.

"Is that you?"

"Crap," I groaned under my breath.

Wiping at the corners of my mouth, I turned slowly to see Harley standing there, looking down at me with a concerned look on his face, despite the hint of a smirk pulling at the corner of his mouth.

"Hey." I managed the best smile I could, sniffling once.

"Um …" Harley hesitantly pointed a finger at me. "You have … ah … some um, spew in your hair."

I jumped so high, tearing at the lengths of my hair, but I lost my balance and ended up falling back into the bushes, crying out in horror when I landed in my very own vomit.

"Are you okay?" Harley chuckled, and I could tell he was trying so hard not to laugh out loud, not that I could really blame him for finding this funny. The state I was in was one predicament I'd never imagined myself to be in, and I guess it was kind of funny, in a weird, unfair, completely messed-up way.

Harley crouched down, holding a hand out for me, and I took it, allowing him to help me back up to my unsteady feet only for me to sway once more. "Whoa!" He steadied me, his hands gripping my shoulders, and then I watched as he leaned in a little closer, narrowing one of his eyes. "A-are you drunk, Murph?"

I shook my head, and then I nodded, but then I started to get dizzy from all the rapid head movements. "I don't know. I think I am." I shrugged, clutching at the side of my spinning head. "But I don't know how! I didn't have any of the liquor from the kitchen. I didn't have a beer from the keg. I think someone spiked my drink, Harley."

Harley's eyes widened, his jaw tight as his cheeks flushed red and he gripped my shoulders slightly tighter, protectively. "What the hell?"

"Well, yeah …" I shrugged. "All I've been drinking is the punch. There's no way I—"

At that, Harley's hold on me loosened a little, his face deadpanning as he stared at me before a smile slowly began to creep onto his face, stopping me mid-sentence.

"What?"

"Kevin's punch?"

I nodded.

Suddenly, he threw his head back and laughed out loud, still holding on to my shoulders.

"What is so funny?" I glared at him, quirking a brow, which was a lot harder to do when I could barely feel my own face.

"Murph!" He managed to collect himself just enough, chuckling once more as he looked down at me, his eyes still smiling so brightly beneath the dull light of the garden lights. "That shit's at least three-quarters rum!"

"Rum?" I shrieked, my nose crunching up in disgust. I didn't even know what rum was, but suddenly my belly twisted again, and acid burned its way up the back of my throat. I slapped a hand over my mouth and turned away from Harley, bending over and retching once more into the already soiled bush.

"Where's Nash?" Harley asked from over my shoulder as he smoothed an awkwardly tentative hand over my back in a show of support.

I finished bringing up whatever the hell was even left inside of me, and I turned to him, scrubbing my hands over my face and smoothing my hair back from my clammy forehead. I took a few deep breaths. "I don't even know." I shook my head. "He left a while ago to help John Portman fix his truck."

"He just left you?"

I nodded, looking down at the vomit stains splattered down the front of my dress.

Harley cursed once under his breath. "Here."

I looked up, watching as he unbuttoned the flannel shirt he was wearing, shrugging out of it before handing it to me. I took it from him, looking him up and down left in only his jeans and T-shirt.

"You can put that on to cover your dress." He nodded to the shirt before glancing out over the backyard, checking for what I wasn't sure. I shrugged his shirt on, thankful that it covered most of the sick that had splattered on my dress. After tying my hair up into a knot on top of my head, I folded my arms around myself, shivering as the cool night breeze whipped through the air.

"C'mon." He held a hand out for me. "I've only had one beer. I'll take you home."

I hesitated a moment before giving him my hand, feeling something unfamiliar flutter low in my belly when our skin touched. But I ignored whatever the hell that was, and I allowed him to lead the way through the dimly lit yard and around the side of the house, until we came to his beat-up old truck parked at the end of a long line of beat-up old trucks in the driveway. Harley stopped to unlock the passenger door with his key, opening it for me. But I hesitated once again, gripping his arm and offering him a wide-eyed look.

"What's wrong?" he asked, his brow furrowed.

"I can't go home like this." I shook my head. "Momma will kill me!"

He rolled his eyes, shaking his head with a laugh.

"It's not like your house. I can't come and go as I please, and I certainly can't be drunk and covered in my own spew," I continued, gripping his arm even tighter. "Momma will kill me, then she'll kill you. And if Nash ever reappears from wherever the hell he disappeared to, she'll kill him, too!"

"It's okay, Murph. You can just crash at my place."

I sighed heavily in resignation, knowing there was no other option as I climbed up into the truck as best I could manage. And as Harley and I drove through the quiet streets of Graceville in the middle of the night, I cursed two things that night. I cursed Nash Harris for leaving me, his girlfriend and apparent love of his life, at that stupid party. And I cursed rum, all rums, vowing never to touch the stuff ever again for the rest my life.

As I think back to that night, I realize even to this day I still have no idea where Nash disappeared to. He just left me there, and it was Harley who rescued me. I remember being so angry about the fact that Nash wasn't there. I'd kept Harley awake all night drunkenly rambling on and on about my inconsiderate boyfriend, when I should have just been thankful for Harley saving my butt, for letting me sleep in his bed while he took the hardwood floor. It's funny how it can take years to see the truth for what it really is. I was always saving Nash, but it was Harley who kept saving me.

"What?"

I look up from my cup to see Harley's curious green eyes watching me, a small hint of a smile pulling at the corner of his lips as one of his brows quirks.

"I can't believe you even remember that night ..." I bite back my smile.

His eyes widen as if he's just realized something, as if he's just said something he shouldn't have, and I don't miss the hint of a pink tinge flushing his cheeks. But instead of saying anything, he takes a big swig of his drink and moves around the island. Stopping by the sound system, he pulls his phone from the back pocket of his jeans, plugging it into the dock. My heart is a flutter, and my mind is racing with a whole heap of confusing thoughts, but then the sound of a Florida Georgia Line song I love begins playing throughout the silence, interrupting my overwhelming thoughts. With a shake of my head in an attempt to snap myself out of my confusion, I turn to see Harley opening the big glass doors before disappearing outside onto the back deck.

"You gotta get out here and see this, Murph!"

With a steadying breath, I stand to my slightly shaky feet, walking outside with my drink, joining Harley on the deck, and immediately I'm rendered speechless by the sight laid out before me. The jet-black inky water glistens beneath the blanket of stars sitting high in the dark night sky, and it's breathtaking, like nothing I've ever seen before.

"Wow," I whisper under my breath, wholeheartedly captivated by the view.

Harley stands beside me at the railing as we stare out over the small waves crashing onto the shore, the beach illuminated only by the glow of the moon. I don't have any words. It's all too perfect, and my words would simply pale in comparison to what I'm truly feeling. It's pure bliss, like something you might see in

186

a painting in an art gallery. I'm simply existing in this space right now. Between the sounds and the smells of the ocean, the view, and Harley's warmth right beside me, I can't think of anywhere else I'd rather be, and I smile to myself as I take a sip from my pretend Long Island Iced Tea, basking in the moment.

"So, about last night …" Harley says unexpectedly, subsequently ruining the moment.

I almost choke on my mouthful of liquor before swallowing hard. Placing my cup onto the railing so I don't drop it, I close my eyes. Tight. I knew last night would be brought up again, especially after I admitted I lied about not remembering anything. But now? Seriously? Can't we just enjoy our companionable silence and the damn view?

I force my eyes open because I can feel Harley watching me. His presence and his stare are heavy. I turn my head to find him right there, his gaze set on me and the slightest hint of a smile pulling at his lips, as if he knows the agonizing torture I'm being put through right now. But I don't speak. I don't say anything. Instead I just huff out a heavy breath, cocking my head to the side, quirking a brow at him, waiting for him to say whatever it is he feels he needs to say right now.

"I just wanna know one thing …" he begins, pressing his lips together in an attempt to stifle the grin that is so obviously trying to claim his entire face.

"What?" I snap abruptly, casting him a look of indifference I don't really mean. It's a defense mechanism. I don't want to give myself away. But somehow, I think it's too late. He already knows. "What?" I ask again, with a slightly less harsh tone.

The lingering hint of a smile falls from his lips, and he suddenly appears so fragile, so nervous.

"Harley?"

"Can you kiss me? Again?"

My jaw drops at his question, so hushed, so pleading, so desperate.

He's playing me. He has to be. But as I stare at him searching for even a hint of sarcasm, I come up short. He's serious. He's actually freaking serious. "W-what?" I stammer, my voice suddenly broken.

"You heard me, Murph," he says with a knowing look in his eyes.

"Y-you want me to … what? To k-kiss you?" I clear the sudden bubble of doubt lodged in the back of my throat. I try to add a nonchalant laugh as if I'm not nearly as affected as I am, but it's impossible. I'm a mess, and judging by the look in his eyes, he knows it. Before I can say anything, or do anything to further give away how completely and utterly crazy he makes me, Harley reaches out, cupping my jaw with his hand, and just as my mind attempts to catch up with my racing heart, his lips crash against mine in a kiss so all-consuming, I'm as good as done for.

Chapter 25

Somewhere between the feel of Harley's tongue stroking mine, coaxing me so tentatively, so delicately it's almost adorable how hesitant he is, and the painful pinch as his fingers tangle themselves within the lengths of my hair, I begin to come to my senses. Barely. Placing my hands against his chest, I'm momentarily lost in the feel of the tight muscles clenching beneath the smooth taut skin underneath the soft shirt he's wearing, but I force myself to gently push him away with a little less conviction than I was hoping for.

Harley stumbles backward with a grunt of objection, and I look up at him through heavy lashes finding his cheeks flushed, his lips swollen, and his chest rising and falling with each heavy breath he fights to take. His eyes penetrate mine, looking at me incredulously.

"Harley," I manage through my own breathlessness. Placing a hand over my mouth, I close my eyes. I touch my lips, and beneath my fingertips I can still feel his lips on mine. I can still taste him. I still want him. But I shake my head, clearing those intoxicating thoughts from my painfully conflicted mind. "Harley, we can't do this. It's a lie. You said so yourself, last night."

Shut the hell up, Murph, my subconscious hisses at me. My

189

own words leave a terrible taste on my tongue, and I watch as Harley seems to battle with his words, opening his mouth only to close it again, over and over as if he's having some kind of silent war within himself. He presses his lips together in a firm line, looking up to the sky a moment, his hands fisting his hair. I stare at him, watching as he exhales a heavy breath of frustration before finally meeting my eyes again. But this time, there's no look of lust or want in them. They're blank. Indifferent. And I'd be lying if I said it doesn't sting.

"Harley, I—"

"Is this about *him*?" He cuts me off, and I snap my mouth shut, my eyes widening of their own accord.

"What?"

"Nash," he hisses, and he rakes his fingers through his hair, tearing at the longer lengths as he meets my eyes. "Is this all still about him, because … you're doing my fuckin' head in. One minute you're kissing me like I'm the only guy you want to be kissing, the next minute you're choosing him *over* me. *Again*. And, I can't—" He snaps his mouth shut, pressing his lips together and closing his eyes momentarily before turning to looking out over the ocean.

"Harley?" I take a step toward him, reaching out a tentative hand to touch his shoulder, but he quickly backs away from me, and I pull my hand away, flinching from his rejection.

Shaking his head, a small smile tugs at his lips, one that doesn't reach his eyes. Smoothing a hand over his wayward hair, he offers me a curt nod, grabbing his cup from the railing ledge before turning and staggering ever so slightly. "I'm gonna go to bed." He casts a fleeting glance over his shoulder, this time not meeting my eyes. Finishing what's left of his drink, he tosses the empty Solo cup to the ground, causing it to bounce upon the decking, and he disappears inside with a murmured, "Goodnight, Murph."

And just like that, I'm left all alone with nothing more than the memory of his lips on mine, the lingering hint of his intoxicating scent, the painful sting of his words, and the sound of the waves crashing against the shore, reminding me of a moment ago when everything was almost perfect.

A shiver runs through me, despite the mild night breeze blowing in from the ocean, and suddenly I'm stone-cold sober. I release the breath I've been holding, my shoulders sagging in defeat as I move to the railing. I stare out over the inky water, taking a sip from my drink, wincing at the suddenly bitter taste. Maybe it's the drink; maybe it's the vile aftertaste of what just occurred between the two of us. Closing my eyes, I down the whole thing in a few mouthfuls, cursing under my breath as the liquor burns the back of my throat.

Sometimes I find myself wondering just how I can be so damn stupid. I'm so scared to be myself; hell, I don't even know who I am, anymore. I'm so good at playing a part—the sarcastic tomboy I forced myself to be growing up because it was easier than being the slightly chubby dork no boy would ever want— I'm often shocked when glimpses of the real me show through. The girl who has a heart that's been broken for longer than a heart should be broken at my age. The girl who believes in love and wants it more than anything. The girl who desperately wants her happily ever after.

I'll never admit it out loud, but sometimes I think Nash broke me. I don't even know who I am without him. It was always him and me when we were growing up. Then it was the two of us when we were together. Then, after our breakup, it was just me, but I seemed to lose myself in the memory of what I had with Nash and, when I lost him, I'd lost the person I thought I was. Because of the love I felt for him for such a long time, it's almost as if I'm broken for any man who isn't him. Because of the way I fell so hard for him, I'm scared I'll never love again. Because of him, I can't even lose myself in a drunken kiss with Harley. I shake my head at the memory of the way he looked at me just

191

now before he disappeared inside. He seemed so incredulous, confused, and possibly even a little hurt.

Why? I have no idea. This is all a lie. He said so himself just last night when he was rejecting me in the most humiliating way possible. Yes, maybe my feelings have become confused somewhere along the line, but I can't let that get in the way of whatever the hell it is I'm doing. It's Harley Shaw, for Christ's sake. If I let my feelings become tangled within his infamous web, I'll only end up hurt.

But it's just a kiss, my subconscious argues. Yeah, and kissing leads to God knows what else. *Just one kiss,* she continues relentlessly, and I just know she's not going to give up without a fight. One kiss is all it takes. *But imagine how good his hands would feel caressing your skin …*

"Dammit!" I curse out loud. Damn my subconscious. She's always getting me into trouble. Making me do stupid, unimaginable things, like lacing an entire cake with laxative.

The memory of the feel of Harley's lips on mine comes flooding back to me, and I stifle the shiver threatening to run through me as I trace my lips with my fingers. I glance up at the house, to the big window on the right. Our room. And a million conflicting thoughts begin racing through me. He's probably naked up there. Is he in the armchair? Maybe he's in the bed. I wonder if he's thinking of me. Is he up there waiting for me? My heart is racing so fast I can feel the thrum of my heartbeat bang heavily against my eardrums. What's going to happen when I go up there to bed? What will he do? Will he pretend as if I don't exist? Will he offer one of his smug smirks, knowing I was going to eventually give in and go to him?

Suddenly, my skin pricks and I feel my cheeks flush as I imagine him lying in the bed, dressed only in his boxers, his hand dipping beneath the waistband … But at that thought I blink hard, shaking my head, realizing just how dry my mouth is when I try to swallow the ball of nerves pulsating in the back of my throat. God, I need to calm the hell down, or grow a set of proverbial balls and go the hell up there. Last night I was ready to jump his bones. Tonight, suddenly I'm too chickenshit. I'm just as drunk as I was last night. Maybe even more. So, what the hell has gotten into me?

I walk a little unsteadily back into the house, stopping in the kitchen, and I move to the island, gripping the marble counter with my hands. As I take a few deep breaths, trying to calm my racing heart, I notice my knuckles turning a stark shade of white. That's when I catch sight of the bottle of tequila, and I consider it for the briefest of moments.

"Sleep on the couch," I hiss under my breath, closing my eyes tight. "Or else you're gonna make a damn fool of yourself! Again!"

Opening my eyes, my hand moves of its own accord, grabbing the tequila. And as I take a swig straight from the bottle, it's like I'm an outsider looking in, and I have no control over my actions. At least, that's my story and I'm sticking to it.

With the bottle in one hand, I smooth my hair back from my face with the other, taking a deep breath as I turn and head toward the stairs. Climbing each step one at a time, I stop halfway to take another swig from my comfort tequila. I don't even wince at the burn as it trails down the back of my throat, and I'm worried I might be too far gone, further than I had originally anticipated. I pause at the landing, and in an unexpected moment of clarity, I look left to my bedroom door. A voice deep down at the back of my consciousness pleads for me to go back downstairs to the living room and sleep it off on the couch as far away from Harley as I can possibly get. But that voice is fleeting, fading into the background noise of my racing heart and heavy breaths.

I bite down hard on my bottom lip and continue to the bedroom door at the end of the corridor. Stopping momentarily, I stare at the wood, my mind a complete blank as I down yet another mouthful of tequila before that idle hand of mine does the Devil's work and reaches up, tentatively knocking against the pine.

I wait.

Nothing.

Chewing nervously on the inside of my cheek, I look down at the bottle in my hand before staring at the door once more. I knock again, this time slightly harder. But then as I continue to wait with no sound of life coming from the other side of the wall, the seconds begin to feel more like never-ending infinities as they tick by at a snail's pace. I swallow my nerves and reach out for the knob, turning it slowly before pushing the door open as quietly as I can.

As my eyes adjust to the darkness, I zero in on his form curled up lifelessly in the armchair, his legs stretched out with his feet resting upon his duffel bag, and my shoulders sag in resignation. He's asleep. In the armchair. I spent too long deliberating with my snarky subconscious and now he's passed out, and I'm standing here like a complete and utter fool. Thankfully, I'm the only one who will ever know about this particular humiliation.

I tiptoe inside, stepping over my randomly strewn clothes on the floor as steadily as I can in my state, continuing through to the bathroom. Closing the door behind me, I release a trembling breath, looking down to the bottle of tequila still in my hand. With a shrug, I console myself with one final swig before placing it onto the counter by the sink.

Talk about an anticlimax. But I know it's for the best. I mean, God knows what would happen if he'd been awake. Kissing is one thing, but would I actually have sex with him? What if I did, then what? I'm sure I would only wake up tomorrow morning with a serious case of regret and self-loathing. Maybe it would change everything. Surely, we couldn't remain friends after something as intimate as that. It's been bad enough looking him in the eye today after drunkenly kissing him last night, I can only imagine how awkward things would be after having drunk, mindless sex with him. There's no way we could be friends after that.

With another sigh, I move to the vanity, removing the elastic from my nest of hair and allowing the wayward curls to fall down around my shoulders. I untie my shirt, unfastening the buttons before pushing my skirt down over my hips, the material pooling at my feet before I kick it off into the corner. I top my toothbrush with some of Harley's toothpaste because I forgot mine, and I stare at myself in the mirror's reflection as I brush my teeth, thinking of all the things that could've happened tonight, realizing just how lucky I am that they didn't. I really dodged a bullet.

Harley and I can't have sex. It would be mortifying. I'm so not the type of woman Harley sleeps with, and I'm proud of that. I don't need to be another notch on his proverbial bedpost; that's for sure. It'd be awkward as hell. I can't help but laugh at what could have been as I spit and rinse, but just as I'm wiping my mouth with the hand towel, I startle when the door behind me suddenly swings open.

Shielding what I can of my barely dressed self with the tiny hand towel, I turn, swaying unsteadily thanks to all the tequila I've consumed, and my eyes bulge at the sight of Harley standing in the doorway.

"What the *hell*?" I try to yell, but my voice cracks at the end when my traitorous eyes trail down over his naked chest, taking in the tattoos inked into his smooth skin, moving down over the peaks and troughs of his abs to the shadowed V line of his pelvis dipping beneath the low-hanging waist of his boxer briefs. Swallowing hard, I force my eyes back up to his, ready to give him a piece of my mind, but I'm rendered speechless when I find his gaze focused intently on my body, slowly raking up and down my form as if he simply can't get enough of me. Me. Alice Murphy.

"W-what are you doing?" I stammer, cringing inwardly at my sudden inability to speak with even the slightest semblance of conviction.

195

Harley rests languidly against the doorjamb, folding his strong arms over his broad chest, which only emphasizes his tattooed biceps. The hint of a smile plays on his lips; a cocky smile that pulls at his dimples, and I actually feel my knees go weak, and again, I blame the tequila.

"Harley?" I press, trying so hard not to give away my breathlessness, but he just continues watching me, his eyes unabashedly taking me in.

I'm fully aware of my mismatched bra and panties, wishing I could go back to when I packed my bag three times for this trip. If I'd known I was going to be standing in front of Harley Shaw with little more than this on, I would have tossed in a lacy thong and matching bra. But I didn't, and instinctively I pull my gaping shirt together, covering myself as best I can as I continue standing my ground, silently wagering him with a hard look.

Harley chuckles to himself, scratching the back of his neck. For a moment he averts his eyes, looking away, and I can almost see him considering turning away. But then his eyes find mine again and that infuriating smirk falls from his lips the very second his green eyes begin to darken. And suddenly I'm being looked at in a way I've never been looked at before, and my heart starts to race almost violently in my chest. I take a step back until I bump into the vanity. Realizing I have nowhere to go, I grip the counter behind me tightly as I stare into his eyes that are so dark they're almost black.

Time seems to come to a standstill. The space around us is palpable and thick with an overwrought tension. The bathroom suddenly feels too small—the air stifling—and I almost can't breathe as I wait for him to say something. Anything.

"Fuck it," he suddenly grunts, pushing off from the doorjamb. And he launches at me, his hands grasping my face as his lips crash against mine in a kiss so full of desperation it's both sexy as hell and heartbreaking at the same time because he needs me

196

to kiss him, like he needs air, but I'm momentarily frozen, deliberating whether or not this is a terrible idea.

Of course it's a terrible idea—I can confirm that without a doubt—but before I can make yet another mistake and allow him to get away, I reach up and wrap my arms around his neck, pulling him even closer. Meeting his tongue with mine, I'm rewarded with a raw, animalistic groan, one that tumbles into our kiss and only turns me on even more than I am already. His hands move down, pushing my shirt off my shoulders before reaching my waist and grasping me low on my hips, his fingers digging into my flesh almost to the point of pain.

I gasp when he effortlessly lifts me up onto the vanity. Our toothbrushes, my makeup, his cologne, everything goes tumbling, crashing loudly to the tile, and I pull back from his kiss, startled by the sound as it echoes through the bathroom. I take the opportunity to try to catch my breath, meeting Harley's hooded eyes watching me so intently, his lips swollen, his cheeks flushed, and I actually can't believe this is happening.

"Is this okay?" he whispers, his fingers dancing over the waistband of my panties.

I don't know. Is this okay? Do I want this? It's now or never.

I graze my teeth over my bottom lip painfully, looking between his eyes and finding something in his gaze I hadn't been expecting, nor prepared to see in Harley Shaw. He's scared. Or nervous. I can't quite tell, but it's an emotion I've definitely never seen in him before. I watch as his shoulders rise and fall with every rushed breath, and I find myself reaching out, placing a hand over the pirate ship inked into the center of his chest, tracing the outline of the violent waves crashing around it with my fingertip. I'm shocked at the feel of his heart racing just as hard as mine, and for some reason I take some solace in that.

"Murph?"

I snap my gaze up, once again meeting his eyes, and I exhale the trembling breath I'd been holding, my hand still placed against his heart.

"Can you call me Alice? Please?" I whisper, hoping I don't sound as needy and pathetic as I think I sound.

The ghost of a familiar smile, one I haven't seen in a long time, tugs at his lips as he sighs my name in the most incredible way, like the soft tune of a beautiful melody. "Alice ..."

My eyelashes flutter closed as the pad of his thumb traces the curve of my bottom lip, and I sigh in contentment, never having felt this before. My name has never sounded better, and a small smile pulls at my lips at the sheer look of relief that seems to flood through him at the sight of my smile. And in an instant, his lips are on mine again. And while tomorrow morning's impending regrets flash through my mind like a warning sign, I'm inundated by everything Harley. Tomorrow can wait.

Chapter 26

I shiver as calloused fingers, rough and demanding, contradict the softness of his touch, burning my skin and bringing goose bumps to erupt all over from my head to the very tips of my toes. My back arches in response to his lips, warm, soft yet firm and unrelenting as they torture the sensitive skin at the base of my neck. At first his kisses are gentle, like the flutter of a butterfly's wings. But then they become urgent, needy, his lips almost bruising me as if to leave his mark so that I'm forever branded by him. Never before have I felt such desire, such inexplicable need and want. With each kiss, his lips creep closer and closer to mine. My hands find his hair, fingers tangling through his curls as he claims me completely.

"Harley!" I cry out, breathlessly, my voice raw and hoarse.

I startle, my eyes flying open, and I gasp when I'm met with nothing but silence and darkness. Confusion overwhelms me as my heart races and my chest heaves with every labored breath I try to take. Clutching the sheets, I lift my head and look around to find the room dimly lit from that almost nonexistent glow of morning, just before the sun rises, casting the space around me in a shade of gray so hazy it's like a smokescreen.

What the hell?

With trembling hands I scrub my face in the hope it will help to provide some semblance of clarity, help bring me back to the present, but nothing more than clouded, pixelated memories from the night before keep flashing through my mind, and I don't actually know what to think. A vision of Harley and me in the bathroom pops into my head, one where my nails are scratching down his back so hard blood is drawn to the surface.

I close my eyes tight, trying to rid myself of that image. But then I'm consumed by another explicit vision of the two of us in the shower and, at that thought, I begin choking on my own breath, coughing and spluttering. Pushing up from the pillows, I bang on my chest as I continue gasping for breath, which is precisely the moment I come to realize that I'm stark naked on top, with only a bed sheet draped over my just as naked bottom half.

Christ.

I grip the sheet tight, pulling it up to shield myself, and just as I finally catch my breath, my eyes adjust to the muted light enough to make out the outline of the very tattooed, very naked body lying on the bed next to me. My jaw drops as I grip the sheet even tighter, but I can't help but get a closer look at the man sleeping obliviously beside me. Face down, his pert backside barely covered by the mess of sheets, his head is turned to me, his eyes closed, eyelashes fanning over his cheeks. His pouted lips are slightly parted, his hair a chaotic mess of wayward curls sticking up in almost every direction.

I turn away quickly, searching the room for what, I'm not even sure. What the hell have I done? I've never felt so overwhelmingly full of remorse. We slept together. Drunk. Harley and I had drunk sex. The thought alone causes bile to rise up the back of my throat and I swallow hard in an attempt to stop myself from bringing up last night's tequila right here in the bed.

I slept with Harley Shaw because drunk me let her stupid

feelings get in the way. Can the earth just open up and swallow me whole? It would be so much easier. I had sex with Harley and, now, I want to die. It isn't that I regret it, per se. In fact, if the hazy memories are anything to go by, regret is the last thing I feel. But what if he regrets it? What if I see that look of regret in his eyes when he wakes and finds me naked in bed right beside him? I doubt my heart will be able to handle it. I will never be able to recover from a humiliation like that. I wish drunk me had listened to her sober thoughts last night.

Pulling my knees up, I bury my face and try to take a few calming breaths. Breathing in through my nose and out again, repeating as best as I can. But it's hopeless. I can't come back from this. And the worst part is I can't even remember it because of course I had to go and consume a quarter bottle of tequila before the fact, as if that was a good idea.

I'm on the verge of a full-blown panic attack when I feel a warm hand graze against my lower back, causing me to stiffen. The mattress shifts beside me and I close my eyes so tight, unable to risk seeing him and the look of regret in his eyes. I don't think my heart could handle that first thing this morning. But then, completely unexpectedly, the hand on my lower back trails up over my spine, smoothing circles over my skin, which warms me from the inside, and I'm forced to stifle the shiver threatening my composure. I feel lips press to the skin between my shoulder blades, lingering slightly longer than necessary. Slowly, I lift my head, staring straight ahead at nothing as his kisses continue covering my skin, his lips moving to my shoulder, to the curve of my neck, and my brows pull together in utter confusion as a swarm of butterflies is let loose in my belly to swarm rampantly.

I turn my head toward him, my senses overwhelmed by his scent as I breathe him in. Hesitating momentarily, I reach a trembling hand out, running my fingers through his hair, tilting my head sideways to give him better access to the one spot at the base of my neck that drives me absolutely wild. And suddenly, the regrets from last night are washed away as an overwrought need floods through me. I don't care about the consequences anymore. I don't care that this is all sorts of wrong. I don't care that we'll probably resent one another. All I want is him.

Forcing myself away from the assault of his lips on the one spot that will inevitably cause me to come undone, I grab him, cupping his stubbled jaw and taking a moment to look at him in the dim light. His face is pure sex. Or maybe he's just still drunk, or half-asleep. I can't tell. Either way, it's sexy as hell. Hooded eyes, a lazy smile, mussed hair. He's all kinds of beautiful, and my heart shifts suddenly in my chest as I take in his perfection.

"What are we doing?" I find myself asking in a whisper so soft I'm doubtful he even heard it.

Cupping my face, his hands are so tentative, soft and gentle as if I'm fragile, like I might break. His gaze penetrates mine in a look so intense I know he can see all of me, even the bits I've tried to hide my whole life. I'm open to him in a way I've never been open to anyone, and it's both terrifying and exciting.

"Who cares …?" he murmurs, inching closer and closer until his lips are a mere hair's breadth from my own.

Pulling him closer, I need his mouth like I need air to breathe, and he obliges without hesitation. His hands roam all over my body before finding their place in my hair, raking through the lengths as his tongue finds mine, producing a moan that only seems to encourage him. Pushing me back against the pillows, Harley nudges my knees apart with his thigh before settling in between my legs. As our tongues dance together, exploring one another, I smile into our kiss and I swear it takes everything I have not to outwardly giggle like a schoolgirl.

I'm having sex with Harley Shaw. Harley *freakin'* Shaw. I wonder if I pinch myself, would I wake up? Would I even want to wake up if this was a dream that could end so abruptly? Focus, Murph. Harley's lips move to pepper kisses over my jaw, my neck and shoulders, his hand trailing down my arm, to my waist, following the curve of my hips as desire pools low in my belly. My heart thunders in my chest as a comforting warmth floods through me. His lips claim me entirely.

And, in that moment, I realize that something has changed between us. This isn't just some drunken, forgettable thing we will inevitably regret. This is real. The feel of his lips hovering against the shell of my ear as he breathes heavily against my skin causes me to shiver, as do his long fingers as they dance over my skin. My head falls back into the pillows, and his lips find mine once more, his tongue invading my mouth desperately. When our touches, kisses and our animalistic sounds become all too much, Harley pulls away abruptly, his eyes glaring through the muted light as they search every inch of my face, his breathing labored and trembling as his gaze sets upon my own.

"Why do I feel like there's no going back after this?" he asks so softly I'm not sure he meant for me to hear.

I know what he's asking, what he's thinking, because I'm thinking it too, but I don't answer him because I don't know how. To be honest, I feel like we crossed that blurry line of ambiguity the night at his house when we fell asleep together on his couch. We've just been too ignorant to whatever the hell it is we've been doing ever since that night to admit the truth to ourselves. I reach up and grasp the back of his neck, pulling him closer. We're so incredibly close. Two souls joined as one. Our closeness is like nothing I've ever experienced with anyone before—not even Nash—and it's overwhelming to say the least, but nothing has ever felt so perfect, so right, so meant to be.

Neither of us so much as mutters another word. We don't have to. Somehow, it's as if we know exactly what the other wants and needs, and the silence between us only adds to the tension settling heavily in the air around us, ready to combust at any moment. I've never been so close to someone before this. Never been so consumed by one person. It's just the two of us, as if the rest of the world has faded away and we're all that remains.

With my arms wrapped around his neck to stop myself from crumbling, I feel tears prick at my eyes from the all-consuming emotion as Harley presses kisses to my jaw, trailing down my neck. It takes all of about twelve seconds until I'm falling apart in a way so spectacular, it's like nothing I've ever experienced. Crying out, gasping for breath, I feel my entire body tremble. Harley holds me even tighter as he stills, and everything around us comes to an abrupt stop. Nothing but the sound of our breaths rings through the silence of the bedroom.

A whimper falls from his lips as he presses his lips to my neck, stifling his sounds as he reaches his high, and this time, I hold him as tight as I can until we both collapse together, exhausted, breathless, sweaty and obliterated.

I finally collect myself as best as I can, coming back down to earth, and I turn my head, meeting Harley's heavily hooded eyes watching me, a sleepy smile pulling at his lips. He reaches out a trembling hand, tucking my hair behind my ear before gently sweeping the backs of his fingers over my flushed cheek, stopping at my lips. Tracing the curve of my Cupid's bow with the pad of his thumb, he smiles again, moving in closer to press a chaste kiss to the very corner of my mouth. Pulling me into his strong arms, he kisses me again, claiming me as if I am his.

In that moment, as I begin to drift off into a contented, blissful slumber, I know, after this, nothing between us will ever be the same.

Chapter 27

It's later in the morning when I wake again. The sunlight pours in through the open shutters, and I can hear the sound of seagulls squawking outside. Stretching languorously, I can't even begin to wipe the smug smile from my face as memories of what I'd spent most of last night and much of this morning doing with Harley play through my mind. We had sex. I, Alice Murphy, slept with Harley Shaw. Not once, but two times. And, if I'm being honest, I could probably do it over and over again. At that thought, I roll over and open my sleepy eyes, but confusion floods through me when I realize I'm all alone in the bed. I reach out and feel the space on the mattress beside me, finding the sheets cool to the touch and, for a moment, I wonder if it had all been a dream.

Sitting upright, my eyes squint involuntarily against the bright light of the sun shining in through the wall of windows as I search the room to find nothing. His overnight bag that was on the footrest by the armchair is gone. His boots that had been kicked off and were sitting haphazardly by the door are gone. His watch and wallet that were on the dresser are gone. In fact, the only memory of him is what's left of his scent lingering on the pillows, and the unmistakable residual feel of his lips on my skin.

"Where the hell did he go?" I ask the silence surrounding me.

Maybe he just got an early start on packing. Maybe he's cleaning up downstairs. Maybe he's cooking breakfast. I try so hard to reason with myself, but it's pointless because the self-doubt at the back of my mind causes my subconscious to rear her ugly head, and I know straight away he's gone.

It was all a joke, the mean girl in my mind taunts me. *You're a joke.*

Am I just another notch for him to carve into his bedpost? Another name to add to his little black book of bangs? I continue sitting there, looking at the space beside me in bed, the space he'd lain all night holding me in his strong arms, and I release a long sigh of resignation. I thought I'd felt something so real with him last night, but he's gone and left me here all alone. Harley regrets what we did, and I can't blame him. I knew he would. Hell, I thought I would regret it, but that's the problem, I don't. For some reason what we did means more to me than it should and, at that thought, my heart sinks low into the depths of my belly. If only I could regret last night, at least then maybe this wouldn't hurt so much.

After a painfully hot shower, I delay going downstairs for as long as I can. I pack and repack my bag a few times, carefully folding each item of clothing as if I work at The Gap. I strip the bed sheets. I even wipe down the bathroom vanity, and clean the mirror. But, I know it's inevitable and I can't stay up here forever. I have to face Harley sooner or later; hell, we're going home today and I'm going to be forced to sit with him in his truck for three hours.

"Murph!" I startle, looking up from my bag at the sound of my name being called from downstairs. "Breakfast is ready!"

With a fortifying breath, I collect my things and head out of the bedroom, albeit reluctantly.

Downstairs, the house is a flurry of excitement. Music is playing loudly, voices resonate throughout the open space, and the smell of bacon lingers low in the air causing my stomach to growl. I continue out onto the patio where everyone is sitting, but when I spot Harley sitting at the far end of the table, I come to an abrupt stop, my feet suddenly unable to move as I linger awkwardly in the doorway.

"Murph!" everyone cheers from around the table as they all look up at me. Well, everyone except Harley.

I try to smile and join in on their apparent excitement, but I can't stop my eyes from flashing in his direction, finding him with his cap pulled down low and a pair of sunglasses shielding his eyes. I swallow the painful lump of humiliation at the back of my throat and step out into the sun, taking a seat next to Kevin, as far away from Harley as I can possibly get.

"How was the strip club?" I ask, looking around at everyone, careful to avoid Harley's end of the table.

"Seth got us kicked out!" Kevin laughs loudly, his head thrown back in utter delight.

"Wait, what? Why? How?" I shake my head in confusion, laughing as I look across to Seth whose head is bowed sheepishly. He's normally the quiet, responsible one, especially compared to Kevin, and I can't help but laugh.

"You know when you're at a strip club, and a girl's shakin' her ass on stage, so you throw a few dollar bills on the stage?"

I nod, piling scrambled eggs I know I won't be able to eat onto my plate.

"Well, this idiot didn't have any dollar bills left," Kevin continues, nodding across the table at Seth. "So, he throws a fist full of damn coins onto the stage. One of the girls slipped on a stray quarter and almost broke her damn neck!"

My mouth falls open as I gape at Seth.

"I was drunk!" He holds his hands up in defense, staring down at his plate of untouched bacon.

I chuckle, shaking my head at the both of them, but then as I look at all the other guys around the table, my traitorous eyes

207

land on Harley again, only this time he's looking up. I can't tell if he's focused on me or not because his sunglasses are so darkly tinted, but I quickly avert my eyes not wanting to give myself away. He doesn't deserve to know how much he hurt me this morning. I'll take the pain of that humiliation with me to the grave.

"Hey, where's Nash?" I ask, looking around, suddenly realizing he isn't out here.

Everyone falls silent, looking awkwardly at one another, and I know something's up.

"Beach." Jake nods his head in the direction of the ocean.

At that, my brow furrows in confusion as I narrow my eyes to see through the glare, finding a lone figure sitting on the white sand staring out at the water, his shoulders slumped as if he has the weight of the world resting upon them.

"What's he doing out there?"

"I don't know," Kevin says with a mouthful of food. "He's been a pissy little bitch all morning. Especially after he and Har—"

"Kevin!" Harley suddenly pipes up, his booming voice echoing throughout the morning, causing everything to stop.

I gape at him but he doesn't say anything as he stands up from his chair, storming into the house. I look at the rest of the guys, seeking some semblance of an answer as to what the heck is even going on. But I get nothing more than a few awkward glances and a shrug from Seth before the guys begin talking more about last night, laughing and joking among themselves over something stupid one of them did, but I'm no longer listening. I try to eat my breakfast, at least what I can stomach of it, but my mind is elsewhere. I'm worried about Nash, and Harley, and I can't stop thinking about what I was stupid enough to do last night with Harley, only for him to leave me in the morning like some kind of sleazy one-night stand.

And, at that thought, my mind wanders back to my ex-boyfriend, the once love of my life, and I begin to think how he would never walk out on a girl the morning after a night like the one I had shared with Harley last night. I silently chastise myself at those thoughts, shaking my head to dismiss them.

After breakfast, which was really just me pretending to eat bacon while trying to laugh along with the guys, avoiding Harley's end of the table at all costs, I head down to the beach. Treading the hot sand, wincing as my feet burn, I stop just shy of Nash, looking down at him as he continues staring out at the waves.

"Hey."

He doesn't acknowledge me, but I take a seat beside him anyway, offering a sideways glance before looking out over the sparkling blue water.

"Is everything okay?"

Again, silence. I turn to him with a furrowed brow, shielding my eyes from the sun overhead, finding his face hard yet emotionless, and my confusion only grows. What the hell is up with him? I try not to roll my eyes at his mood.

"Hangover, or is it something more?" I press, nudging him playfully with my shoulder, and at that, I receive something similar to a scoff, and I expect him to be smiling, but instead he looks annoyed. I continue, despite his obvious attitude. "I know it's something," I begin. "You know you can talk to me."

"I'm *fine*!" He looks at me this time, but his eyes contain something I hadn't been expecting. He's pissed. With me.

"Nash, what's wrong?" I gape at him. "What did *I* do?"

He shakes his head, avoiding my eyes as he moves to get up. "Nothing, Murph," he grunts, brushing sand from the back of his shorts, which catches in the breeze and blows right into my face. "You and me, we're just *fine*." And, with that, he turns and leaves.

Bewildered, I watch him stalk back up the beach toward the house as I wipe the sand from my eyes, and a million confusing thoughts worry my mind. He's angry with me. Me. What the hell did I do? Maybe he's upset because I took him home early last night. Maybe I said something to him in my drunken state that I can't remember. In our fifteen years of friendship, I can't actually ever remember a time when Nash has been angry with me. Sure, we've had fights and arguments, but they were silly and quickly forgotten. Hell, even after we broke up he called me the next day to tell me about something hilarious that had happened to him on the subway.

I feel sick to my stomach. Pulling my knees up to my chest I press my lips together as I stare out over the water, and what was beautiful only moments ago now seems wild and dangerous, and threatening. The longer I watch the violent waves crashing to the shore, the more my heart sinks. I've never felt more alone. I just want to go home and pretend as if this stupid trip never happened.

I meet the guys back up at the house after collecting my emotions, but when I find my overnight bag dumped on the floor by the front door with the others, I can't help but notice Harley's absence.

"Where's Harley?" I ask Seth.

He turns to me with a confused look. "He left …"

He *what*? I feel my face fall and I assume he notices.

"Something about stopping in Atlanta for something for the bar …" He quirks a dubious brow, looking closer. "Y-you didn't know?"

I swallow the lump at the back of my throat, feeling tears prick my eyes. He left without me. He couldn't even stand the drive back to Graceville with me in his truck. I want to cry but, instead, I manage somehow to force a smile onto my face, nodding quickly. "Oh, yeah." I shrug. "I forgot all about that," I lie as convincingly as I can manage.

"You're riding with me in the Ferrari, Murph." Kevin walks up behind me and I turn to see him twirling his keys around his finger, giving me a cocky grin.

"You mean your beat-up old Dodge?" I scoff.

He chuckles and rolls his eyes at my correction before reaching down and picking up my bag. Although I can manage it myself, I don't bother stopping him. Instead, I follow him and Seth outside onto the front porch just in time to see Nash getting into his rental car without so much as a goodbye, and that only adds to the pain and suffering of the war of emotions stirring deep down inside of me.

"Shotgun!" Seth yells running down the steps toward Kevin's truck.

And all I can do is sigh at the thought of being stuck between the two of them the whole drive back home, while my mind is consumed by a million and one regrets.

Chapter 28

"Wow, that looks so good, Murph!" Sarah gushes from where she's sitting on the countertop, licking what's left of the frosting from a big metal bowl.

"Thanks," I say through a stifled yawn. My eyelids droop, my eyes burn, and my back is killing me, and it feels as if I haven't slept in five excruciatingly long years as I stare at the finished product that is Nash and Anna's wedding cake.

After enduring three hours of torture, wedged between Seth and Kevin while listening to Eminem's entire discography on the drive home from Myrtle Beach, I knew I wouldn't be able to wind down when they dropped me off at home. My mind was completely shot with emotion, and rampant thoughts raced through it, taunting me. All I could think about was how Harley just left me in South Carolina without so much as a second thought. But, at the same time, I racked my brain over why Nash was angry with me, as if I was the bad guy. The whole thing was doing my head in. When I got dropped off at home, the house just seemed even more empty than usual because at a time like this, all I want is my momma.

So, I left my bag by the front door, turned around, and came straight to the store, which is where I've been for hours working on the cake, which isn't what I'd originally planned.

Black buttercream with a light smattering of gold leaf haphazardly sponged into the sides. I decided to leave it simple without any unnecessary accents, just some simple white orchids strategically placed throughout, with a few sparkly gems hidden within the petals.

"Do you think it needs more rhinestones?" I ask Sarah while slowly assessing and silently critiquing every part of the cake.

"Nope." Sarah jumps down from the countertop, placing the dirty bowl into the sink before coming to stand beside me. "I think it looks perfect. You don't want to go over the top. This ain't no New York City." She laughs to herself.

She's right. I don't want it to look gaudy. It's perfect as it is. The longer I stare at it, the more I truly believe it may be my greatest work of art. I take my cell phone from my purse, and begin to snap some photos for my cake-dedicated social media account, but I stop when I can feel a heavy gaze set upon me, and I glance over my shoulder to see Sarah watching me.

"What?"

"Are you sure you're okay with all this?" she asks, waving a hand in the direction of the three-tier masterpiece in the center of the room.

"What?" My brows knit together in confusion. "The cake?"

"No!" She rolls her eyes indulgently, shaking her head at me with a wry smile. "With the whole wedding thing. I mean, you and Nash ..." She scoffs once. "If I recall correctly from Seth's yearbook ..." She pauses, glancing up toward the ceiling pensively. "I believe you two were voted most sickeningly in love couple of your class. Kids in my year still refer to you guys as 'couple goals,'" she scoffs, air-quoting with her fingers. "And now you're forced to make the damn cake for his wedding to some other woman!"

"Oh, pfft." I laugh, brushing off her concern with a wave of my hand. "I'm fine." And at that, I stop at my own words. *I'm fine.* A small smile plays on my lips, because I realize for the first time since Friday when Nash arrived unexpectedly to tell me he was getting married, I actually am fine. He's marrying another woman, and I'm fine with that. But he's mad at me, and I'm not fine with that. I don't know what I've done to make him mad, and almost immediately my smile falls.

"Huh," Sarah muses from beside me, pulling me from my thoughts and I cast her a slightly annoyed glance, quirking an eyebrow, knowing she has something she feels she needs to say. "So, it's Harley?"

"What's *Harley*?" I shake my head at her cryptic words strung together in half-assed sentences I can't understand. "What are you even talking about?"

"He's the reason you've spent the entire day looking like someone told you the Easter Bunny, Tooth Fairy *and* Santa Claus ain't real."

"What? No, I haven't!" I laugh indignantly, gaping at her, but I quickly look away, because I know she's right.

"What did he do?" she asks, and I can feel her eyes on me.

I desperately want to tell her. I need someone to confide in. But that would mean confessing my shameful and embarrassing secret, and of all the people I could possibly tell, Sarah is the last person I could ever trust. She's an 18-year-old gossip queen. I know at least half the entire town would know my lie within a few hours.

"What are you even still doing here?" I shake my head at her, deflecting the obvious. "Your shift finished hours ago. Don't you have homework to do? Or someone else to annoy? Seth's home. Why don't you go hang out with him?"

"I'm waiting for Tyler to pick me up!" she answers matter-of-factly, and I roll my eyes at her as she continues smiling self-righteously, but before I can tell her to stop, we're both startled by an unexpected knock coming from the glass door at the front of the store. It's past seven. We closed two hours ago.

My curiosity piques as I walk through the shop, but I stop suddenly, and my heart stammers heavily in my chest when I make out Harley standing at the door, looking in at me through the glass.

The stubborn part of me wants to ignore him, leave him standing out there on the sidewalk like he left me at Myrtle Beach. But I don't do that, because I'm a sucker for punishment and I really want to hear whatever sorry excuse he has for leaving me in another state.

I unlock the door but I don't open it; he can open the damn thing himself. Turning, I take a few steps as far away as I can get before turning when I hear the door click closed. And, with my arms defiantly crossed over my chest as if to shield myself from any further pain I know he is capable of inflicting, I cock one brow, watching him, waiting for him to speak. But before he gets the chance, we're interrupted by Sarah walking through the store, awkwardly glancing between the two of us.

"Sorry," she says through gritted teeth, flashing me an apologetic glance. "My ride's here." She stops at Harley, looking up at him and she slaps him a few times on his shoulder, looking back at me with a smug smile. "You better apologize. She is *pissed*!"

"*Goodnight*, Sarah!" I snap, my voice warning.

She giggles to herself on her way out, and I close my eyes a moment, making a mental note to fire her for the tenth time since she started with me only last year. With a sigh, I open my eyes to see Harley standing on the spot, looking to the ceiling, the floor, anywhere but in my general direction as he nervously scratches the back of his neck before shoving his hands deep into the pockets of his jeans. Shifting his weight from foot to foot, it's almost unbearable watching him avoiding me as awkwardly as possible. So, I cut him some slack and speak first. "I thought you had the rehearsal dinner tonight?"

"I couldn't make it," he says with a shrug. "Someone called in sick," he adds, not bothering to look at me.

"So, what are you doing *here*?"

He slowly lifts his head, removing his backward cap only to secure it on his head once more, looking from his feet to me, and although his face remains expressionless, the look in his eyes gives away the truth; he's conflicted. I soften a little, unfolding my arms and clasping my hands together at my front as I lower my cocked brow. In return, he seems to relax, and I can see his shoulders sag, dropping at least an inch.

"I'm sorry I left you," he says with a rushed breath, as if the words alone offer him some semblance of relief.

Without saying a word, I continue watching him, waiting, knowing there's more.

"What we did last night, it was … it was—" At an obvious loss for words, Harley averts his gaze, looking over my shoulder a moment as he obviously searches for a way to break it to me gently.

Again, I help by speaking for him and finishing his sentence so as to lessen the blow for myself. "It was a *mistake*."

His eyes dart to mine, a slight furrow pulling between his brows as he studies me a moment, and I capture something in his gaze, something that makes my stomach twist with an emotion I've never felt before. Raking his teeth over his bottom lip, he finally nods, shrugging his left shoulder.

"It's okay, Harley. Don't worry about it." I shake my head, looking down at my clasped hands a moment to consider my words. "We can just pretend it never happened." I cast a nervous glance at him, meeting his eyes with a hopefulness I hadn't been expecting until now as the thought of truly losing him for good crosses my mind. "Can't we?"

And I realize something in that moment. As much as I've tried to deny it, as much as I didn't want to believe it or admit the truth, as much as it pains me to admit how truly lonely I am, Harley Shaw really is all I have in this town. He's not only my best friend, he's my all. I can't possibly lose him; the thought alone terrifies me.

216

A heavy sigh falls from his lips, and a small smile tugs at the corner of his mouth as he nods once again. "Sure, Murph. We can forget all about it."

This time it's me sighing as I release the breath I've been holding, but I try and hide my relief as best as I can, not wanting to give myself away too easily. It's not that pretending as if last night didn't happen doesn't sting worse than I ever could have been prepared for, but losing Harley would hurt a hell of a lot more. So, pushing my pride aside, I'd much rather have him as my friend than nothing at all.

"I should get back to the bar."

I offer the most convincing smile I can, watching as he turns and reaches for the door. But then he pauses, looking at me over his shoulder. I raise my brows, waiting for whatever it is he has left to say, wondering just how much worse this whole thing can get.

"This thing you made up about you and me," he begins, looking me in the eye questioningly. "Our *fake* relationship," he adds so quietly I almost miss it.

Reluctantly I nod.

He hesitates a moment. "It wasn't *all* a lie, was it, Murph?"

My heart drops deep into my belly as I stare into his knowing eyes and all the air in my lungs seems to escape me. My cheeks heat and the skin at the back of neck pricks as my heart thunders in my chest. I have no words. No words that won't make me look like a total fool. So, I remain silent, momentarily looking down at my hands once again as I consider the fact that I really do have nothing left, and therefore, nothing left to lose. With a deep, shuddering breath, I meet his penetrating gaze, and all I can offer is a pathetic shrug of my shoulders and the semblance of a sheepish smile.

He stands there, studying me a moment, and if I'm not mistaken, I can almost see the battle of emotions warring against one another inside his head. But it doesn't last long before he nods once more with a tight-lipped smile before leaving, the glass door slamming heavily in his wake and echoing throughout the overwrought silence around me, reminding me just how empty I am.

With a stifled yawn I unfold myself from the car, slinging my purse over my shoulder as I follow the path to the house. But when I make it up onto the front porch, something catches my eye in the darkness, and I shriek, stumbling backward when the rickety old porch swing moves causing the rusted chains to clang together.

"Murph, it's just me!"

I narrow my eyes to see through the darkness of the night, and relief floods through me, calming my racing heart when Nash steps into the muted glow of the streetlight.

"Jesus!" I gasp, clutching at my heaving chest. "You scared me half to death." With a trembling hand, I unlock the front door and reach inside to flick the light switches, the porch illuminating immediately. But then I see the state Nash is in, his mussed hair, droopy eyes, and untucked Oxford, and even if he didn't have an open can of Miller Lite in one hand and the remaining five hanging from the plastic in the other, I'd know he was three sheets to the wind.

"You okay?" I ask, walking inside the house. "I thought you had the rehearsal dinner?"

"We did," is all he says, his voice hoarse.

I'm fully aware of him following so close behind me, his unsteady feet scuffing against the hardwood as I continue through to the kitchen. I don't know why, but something feels off. Why the hell is he even here? At my house. Drunk. Stopping at the island I take a deep breath before turning, but all the air is stolen from me when I come face-to-face with him right there, our chests almost touching.

"N-Nash, I—" Stumbling to find the right words, I instinctively place a hand against his chest, holding him at bay. But unfortunately, he seems to take that as an advance, and he only takes another step closer. "W-what the *hell* are you d-doing?" I hiss, pushing him away with as much strength as I can find.

He staggers ever so slightly, his sixer of beer falling to the floor with a heavy thud and a hissing fizz as one of the cans pops.

"Dammit!" I hurry to the sink for the dishcloth before dropping to the floor and mopping up what I can.

"I'm sorry."

"What are you even *doing* here?" I yell, gaping up at him as I clean up the mess.

With an almighty sigh, Nash collapses onto one of the stools, scrubbing a hand over his weary face. I can feel his dejection from across the room, and I pull myself up, tossing the exploded can and the dishcloth into the sink. Turning back to the island, I keep my distance as best as I can, watching him. And it's right now that I realize just how broken he looks, and I know something is seriously wrong. I'm going to need a stiff drink if I'm going to deal with this tonight. In seconds, I'm prepared with a glass in one hand and a bottle of Jack in the other, and I pour myself a generous shot, unable to chance another look at him until I'm well and truly sated with liquor.

"Nash, what's going on?" I ask after downing my shot, pouring myself another, and just as I tip my head to throw it back, his bloodshot eyes meet mine and, after an unnecessarily long pause he says something I couldn't have ever been prepared to hear.

"I want you back, Murph."

Chapter 29

Silence rings true, and it's one of those silences that makes your ears ring so loud it's almost deafening. But then suddenly, whiskey is exploding out of my mouth, spraying all over the island counter, and drenching Nash in the process.

"Y-you *what*?" I finally manage through a choked cough, my voice a few octaves higher than it normally is. My bulging eyes scan his face for some semblance of humor, because he has got to be joking. He has to be. But blue eyes stare at back me and, sadly, there is nothing but a somewhat innocent seriousness in them as they implore me with a look of hopeful desperation.

"Nash?" I try to laugh, try to make light of the situation, but it's awkward and uncomfortable, and I really just want it to be over. "What the hell are you even *talking* about?"

He continues watching me, and I close my eyes tight, shaking my head, trying to make sense of everything as I take another swig of liquor straight from the bottle this time. "You're getting married." I laugh incredulously, waving a flustered hand through the air. "*Tomorrow!*" I splutter, wiping whiskey droplets from my chin.

Nash buries his head in his hands, groaning as if he's in the most unimaginable, unbearable pain. "I know."

I watch his fingers tear painfully through his mop of hair as he shakes his head, murmuring a string of incomprehensible curse words, and something tells me there's a lot more to his ridiculous declaration of wanting me back. I hesitate a moment before walking around the island, and when I finally reach him, I place a tentative hand on his shoulder, not sure whether or not I might be overstepping a line. "Nash?"

Hesitating momentarily, he lifts his head to look at me.

"What's *really* going on?" I ask softly as I take a seat on the stool beside him.

"Everything is so shit, Murph," he says with a scowl as he glares down at his can of beer on the counter. "Nothing feels right anymore."

I watch him, waiting for him to continue as he picks at a tile on the countertop.

"It kills me to see you so happy with him. It kills me to see y'all so damn happy."

Him? Harley? At the mention of him and our apparent happiness, my heart sinks a little in my chest because if Nash really knew the truth then I'm not sure he'd even understand, let alone ever forgive me. So I remain silent.

"Hell," he says with a derisive scoff of disgust, "I even had a damn fight with him this morning because I heard y'all having sex last night and it drove me fuckin' *insane*."

My cheeks heat, but my embarrassment is fleeting and almost immediately forgotten when I realize what he's just said. "Wait. You had a *fight*? With *Harley*? This morning?"

Nash nods, closing his eyes tight, and I can see how full of regret he is. "I pushed him, and I would've knocked him out, but Kevin and Seth pulled us apart."

I almost laugh. Nash even thinking he might knock Harley out is hilarious. Harley has at least six inches over him and a good twenty pounds. But then I think back to this morning when Harley wouldn't even look at me and Nash was on the beach by himself, and any hint of laughter inside me fades. Harley and Nash fought while I was still blissfully asleep. I guess that explains why Harley left me in bed, left me in South Carolina. I'm angry, but I also feel responsible; it's all because of this godforsaken lie. My lie. And the worst part of all is that that stupid lie worked. I made Nash jealous enough that he's here on the eve of his wedding telling me he wants me back.

But my lie also caused two lifelong friends to fight, and I hate myself for causing that, and I just know I need to come clean. I know I need to be honest, but if I tell Nash the truth now, then he could hate Harley even more for lying to him. And he'll hate me. I've really become tangled within my own web of lies.

"Nash, can I ask you something?"

His eyes meet mine and he nods.

"Do you *love* Anna?"

Without even a moment's hesitation he nods again.

"And do you *want* to marry her?"

He nods again, a little slower this time, looking down at his empty beer can, twisting the ring pull until it pops off.

"So what's the problem?" I shrug when he looks at me. "Where do I come into it?"

He sighs an almighty sigh, his shoulders rising and falling so heavily as he buries his head in his hands once more. "It's just being back here. My home. Seeing you and Harley together, laughing. It just reminds me of everything I don't have no more. I miss it. I miss you. I miss Harley. I miss this damn place."

I press my lips together and, sigh with a small smile when it suddenly all starts to make sense. I gently squeeze his arm, causing him to look at me again with a slight furrow of confusion pulling between his brows. "Nash, you don't want *me* back." I shake my head with a small laugh, and he looks at me, studying my face for a long moment as he considers my words. "I just remind you of everything: the good, the bad, how things used to be. I remind you of home."

222

After a palpable silence, he releases a heavy breath, his shoulders sagging as relief seems to wash over him. A small, sheepish smile begins to tug at his lips as he looks down to where my hand is touching his forearm and, without meeting my eyes, he takes my hand in his, squeezing it tight. "You're right," he says, his hoarse voice hushed. "Ever since I've been back here I've been plagued by all these old memories. Of my dad. Of you and me. How you always were there for me. How you saved me. I thought everything would still be the same coming back here, but it's all different. And I miss it."

He turns my hand in his, his thumb tracing the emerald ring I've been wearing ever since my momma passed away. It was her grandmother's and, one day, maybe I'll have a daughter of my own to pass it on to.

"But you have your new life now, Nash." I smile. "You have Anna, and med school. Soon you're gonna be a doctor. You're gonna go off and do so many incredible things. I'll always be here. So will Harley. But, now ... Now it's time for us all to live our own lives. Wherever that might be."

"Is it weird if I say I think I'll always love you?" His voice quavers with a fragility I also feel deep down in the murkiness of the great unknown, settling in my belly.

I'm quick to shake my head. "I think it would be weird to say otherwise. You and me, we'll always have something special."

He squeezes my hand once again, but this time he lifts it to his lips and closes his eyes as he places a soft kiss to the back. And, with another stammered breath, he sits up a little straighter, letting go of my hand before looking down at himself. With a soft chuckle, he shakes his head, flashing me a mischievous smirk. "Do you think I could go clean up before I order an Uber to take me back to Harrington's?"

I look at the whiskey splatter marks staining the front of his white Oxford and I laugh with a nod. "Sure. You can go up and use my bathroom. Actually, I have an old T-shirt of yours in the second drawer of my dresser."

He goes to move before pausing, flashing me a sideways glance, one of his brows slightly quirked. "You kept my old T-shirt?"

I realize what I've said and again, my cheeks flush with embarrassment, but what's the point of lying now? I've already humiliated myself enough. "Yes. And I slept in it every night after we broke up."

His eyes widen momentarily, but then he laughs—a real honest-to-goodness laugh—unexpectedly pulling me into a warm embrace. His strong arms hold me tight and I wrap mine around his waist as I smile against his chest. And, for what feels like the first time in forever, I breathe him in.

Idly wiping the countertop while Nash is upstairs getting himself cleaned up, I find myself thinking back to what Harley had said on his way out of the store earlier. The look in his eyes deeply contradicted the nearly nonexistent smile on his face. He's always been a closed book. So hard to read. He never gives himself away. He'd asked if this week had all been a lie and I was honest with him. In not so many words I'd told him the truth. In fact, I think I was being honest with myself for the first time in a long while. This whole week hasn't been a complete lie. Maybe I should call him and try to explain myself a little better. Maybe he could stop by after he closes up the bar. I could finally talk to him. Tell him the whole truth. Tell him how I really feel. But what the hell would I say? Where on earth would I even start?

I'm pulled from my thoughts by a knock at the front door.

What the hell? I glance at the clock to see that it's almost eleven.

"Nash, did you order your Uber already?" I yell up in the direction of my bedroom as I pass the stairs on my way to the entry, but he doesn't answer me.

Expecting to see some angry Uber driver waiting impatiently on my porch, I reluctantly pull open the front door, but I'm caught off-guard at the sight of Harley standing there. With his head bowed down, his hands tucked deep into the front pockets of his jeans, he slowly looks up, his eyes finding mine through the dim light of the porch lamp.

"Harley?" I gasp, not believing my own eyes.

"Hey," he murmurs, pressing his lips together in the slightest hint of a smile.

"W-what are you doing here?"

Taking a tentative step closer, he takes a hand from his pocket, scratching the back of his neck, so obviously battling with his words. My eyes take him in from his head to his toes, but when I find him looking at me in a way I hadn't been expecting, my heart leaps in my chest, skipping at least a few beats. The way he's looking at me. I've never seen such an emotion in his eyes. And from the way he's looking at me now, to the memory of the way in which he looked at me back at the bakery, I know straight away, he feels it too, and I can't help but bite back the threatening smile, as my stomach somersaults deep inside of me.

"I-I um ..." He huffs out a frustrated breath. "I wanted to come by and tell you that I—" He pauses again, considering, and the anticipation of his words is positively killing me. I want to scream at him to just spit it out, or at least kiss me. But I don't. I just watch him, waiting.

After a few cleansing breaths, he meets my eyes with a small smile. "I wanted to tell you, I—" Stopping mid-sentence, his whole energy shifts so suddenly, and I watch as his gaze moves over my left shoulder, his smile falling, replaced by a deep crease pulling between his brows.

"What'd you say, Murph?"

I freeze, my heart flying up into the back of my throat at the sound of the voice coming from behind me.

Oh no.

Turning slowly, I watch as Nash staggers unsteadily down the stairs from the direction of my bedroom and, as if that's not bad enough, he finishes pulling that damn T-shirt down over his naked torso, the state of his ruffled hair only adding to the already compromising situation.

"Harley?" He stops halfway down the stairs, gripping the bannister as his wide eyes move from Harley, to me, and back again, the whole while my mind is racing a million miles a minute as to how to explain.

I turn back to Harley, my face stark like a deer caught in headlights despite trying my most nonchalant smile, but I'm met with a hardness in his eyes that cuts straight through me.

"Well ..." He balks in disgust, looking me up and down before meeting my eyes and continuing with such vitriol it just about slices me in half, "Looks like you got what you wanted after all."

And, with one last feeling look between Nash and I, he turns to leave, and my heart thunders in my chest as I stand there shocked and frozen, watching him stalk back toward to his truck parked at the curb and out of my life without so much as a second glance over his shoulder.

Chapter 30

Somehow, I manage to come to my senses before Harley reaches his Ford. And, snapping out of the shock-induced daze, I curse under my breath before running down the porch steps and chasing after him.

"Harley!"

He stops and turns. I can tell he's trying to act unaffected, trying his best at a bored, uninterested glance. But the hard crease furrowed into his brow is giving him away. I know he's pissed. And I know he cares, I can see it the way his jaw ticks. "What?" he hisses between gritted teeth, folding his arms across his chest.

I consider my words, glancing back toward the house. But when I find Nash standing in the open doorway, I shake my head at the situation. Of course it looks bad. I can't blame Harley for thinking what he's thinking. "*Nothing* happened, I swear. It's not what it looks like!"

He quirks a disbelieving brow at me but says nothing, and I smooth my hair back from my flustered face, stammering for the words I need. "He was here waiting for me when I got home." I shrug. "He was drunk, and confused. I just talked to him." I shake my head again, imploring his eyes with my own in the hope of seeing some semblance of understanding. But his eyes are empty. "We just *talked*. That's it."

"Talked?" He laughs a derisive laugh void of any humor. "Up in your bedroom? Half-naked?"

I shake my head vehemently. "No! I accidentally spilled liquor all over him." I purposely leave out the bit about Nash telling me he wants me back. "He was just cleaning up in the bathroom before ordering an Uber. And I had one of his old T-shirts up in my room." To be fair, it actually sounds worse coming out of my mouth, and I just wish I could shut the hell up.

Harley continues watching me for a long moment without saying a word. "That's all. I *swear*." I stare into his eyes, not once breaking the penetrating hold he has on me. For some reason, this feels like the make-or-break moment that I could potentially lose him forever, and I feel sick to my stomach.

"Harley, it isn't what it looks like, man!" At the sound of Nash's voice ringing through the silence of the night, I close my eyes in a combination of frustration and fear, wishing he'd just shut the hell up. But, of course not. He proceeds to make his way across the yard to join us, and I finally open my eyes to see him standing next to me in that damn T-shirt I once slept in for three weeks straight without washing it because it smelled like him.

"You two need to sort your damn shit out," Nash continues, looking between the both of us. "As much as it pains me to say …" He laughs once under his breath before continuing with all sincerity, "Y'all are *perfect* for one another." He turns, looking up at Harley. "Forget about what I said this morning. I was confused and hungover. I didn't mean what I said."

Harley flashes me a look I can't read, but before I can think too much into it, Nash continues. "I told her about the fight," he says. "I won't let y'all break up just because I'm a dickhead."

But something in Nash's words seems to cause Harley to stiffen, his broad shoulders tensing obviously as his stubbled jaw clenches, and my brow furrows in confusion as I witness a darkness cloud over his eyes, and it suddenly dawns on me.

No. Please, Harley. Please don't.

"It was all a *lie*," he finally murmurs, his raspy voice almost lost within the breeze rustling through the leaves of the elm tree hanging above us, and my stomach drops as I watch him, as his dark eyes intently focus on me.

"Huh?" Nash asks, sufficiently confused. "What was all a lie?"

After a few intense moments of silence, Harley tears his gaze from me, looking down at Nash in anger. "This whole damn thing was a *lie!*" He laughs another humorless laugh. "Me and *her*," he says, nodding his head in my direction and referring to me as if I'm a piece of shit, which actually hurts more than I ever could have imagined. "We're not *together*. We *never* were."

A lump of dread balls in the back of my throat, and I stare down at the grass because I can't bear to see the look on Nash's face when he learns of my vindictive scheme.

"*She* made it all up because ... Hell, I don't even *know* why. She wanted to make you jealous? She didn't want you to think she'd been sitting around all this time waiting on you to come running back to her? She didn't want you to be happy with anyone but *her*? Who fuckin' knows!"

Tears sting my eyes as I slowly lift my head, but when I find Nash looking at me with eyes full of confusion and an obvious hint of betrayal, Harley with the ghost of an '*I told you so*' smirk pulling at his lips, all I wish is that I could go back to the beginning of the week and change everything.

"Murph?" Nash finally speaks, his voice so quiet. "Is that true?"

All I can do is nod because it is true. All of it. And, while we're talking of the truth ... "And, I laced the wedding cake samples with laxative hoping Anna would eat them and get so sick she couldn't make dinner, because I wanted you all to myself that night."

Nash's eyes bulge.

Harley's jaw drops in realization.

But I ignore them both as I continue with a quiet, croaky voice full of emotion, "And I'm pretty sure I elbowed her in the face on purpose when we were playing flag football on Sunday." Both of them are gaping at me, clearly shocked by my confession, but I don't stop there. "I made it all up—Harley and me—because I wanted you back," I say, looking at Nash before turning and meeting Harley's steely glare. "And it *was* all a lie." Harley blinks hard, looking away. "Until Wednesday night when I realized that I—" I snap my mouth shut, contemplating my words when the reality of what I'm about to say crashes over me in a wave.

Harley snaps his head back, meeting my eyes again, both of them watching me but neither saying a word as they stare at me with stark faces. I glance down at my hands a moment, taking a few deep breaths. I know I need to be truthful, but the doubt is seriously starting to get the better of me. But, again, this is that moment. It's now or never. So, I lift my head, meeting Harley's eyes. "It was all a lie until Wednesday night when I realized something." I pause to swallow my nerves, exhaling a trembling breath full of self-doubt before continuing, "I'm actually in love with Harley. And I have been for a long time."

Silence ensues as my heart sways unsteadily from side to side in my chest, like a pendulum, literally hanging in the balance as I watch Harley, waiting for a response, or at least some kind of reaction. But he remains indifferent, not giving anything away, just staring at me, breathing hard.

"So, you *both* lied to me?" Nash breaks the silence, his eyes moving between Harley and me, flashing with an anger I naively hadn't been expecting. Of course he's angry. He has every damn right to be.

"I'm sorry, Nash. I—" I try, but he cuts me off.

"You mean to tell me," he yells, glaring at me while thumbing back toward the house, "you just let me say what I fuckin' *said* to you ... You let me *feel* what I felt all week ... You let me *doubt* my entire relationship with the woman I'm about to marry, and this whole time it was all a damn *lie*?"

I avert my eyes because the betrayal in his is far too painful to withstand. Swallowing the lump at the back of my throat, I nod once, looking down to the ground.

He scoffs to himself. "I don't even know you no more, Murph." At those cutting words, I look up, finding him shaking his head at me before turning to Harley and pointing a finger in his best friend's chest. "And *you*? You let a lie come between *us*?"

Harley exhales a hard breath, tearing his gaze from me, looking at Nash with a hard stare, not saying a word, his jaw clenching so tight.

"I can't *believe* you two!" Nash yells, looking at us both in exasperation before turning and storming toward the road.

"Nash, stop!" I yell pleadingly, taking a step toward him. "Where are you going?"

"I can't even stand to look at either of y'all!" he yells over his shoulder.

"Nash, man, wait," Harley yells. "I'll drive you back to Harrington's."

"I'd rather fuckin' walk!" he shoots back, his hoarse voice echoing throughout the quiet street.

Harley and I remain frozen on the front lawn, watching as Nash walks off into the darkness, his shadowy figure eventually disappearing around the corner and into the night. The air between us suddenly turns thick and palpable with an overwhelming tension, and as I turn to look at him I'm surprised to see he's already watching me with an unexpected and confusing emotion in his eyes. He lifts a hand, scratching the stubble shadowed over his jaw before pulling his bottom lip between his thumb and forefinger, staring at me the whole time in a look of deep deliberation.

Taking a step forward, I wring my hands together, at a loss of

231

what to say or do, but I know I need to say something. "Harley, I—"

"Don't." He stops me, holding a hand up to silence my stammered words. "Just don't, Murph. You've done *enough*."

Just when I think he's going to continue, going to tell me whatever is on his mind, he doesn't say anything at all. Instead, he simply shakes his head before turning and walking toward his truck. And I'm stuck in one place, unable to move as my emotions get the better of me. The roaring engine of his truck comes to life, echoing throughout the silence, causing me to jump. And, as a solitary tear slides down over my heated cheek, I watch as he pulls away from the curb, the rumbling of the V8 fading to nothing as he drives farther and farther away.

And, all alone right there on the front lawn, in the silence of the night, I come to a realization, one I wish I'd figured out a long, long time ago: Nash was never the one that got away because he was never the one. It's been Harley all along, and I think I might have just lost him.

Chapter 31

I took the cake to the country club early. So early, in fact, the sun hadn't even finished rising for the day. I didn't want to risk seeing anyone. Maybe I was being a coward, but I couldn't bear to show my face. Not after last night. And I'm so glad I succeeded in avoiding everyone, especially after the text message I received from Nash when I'd returned to the store.

Nash: *Don't bother coming to my wedding.*

I stared at the words on the illuminated screen for so long my eyes began to burn, blurring from the unshed tears pooling within them. But, I must say it didn't surprise me to receive such a message. I admitted to trying to poison his fiancée. I admitted to intentionally giving her a black eye. I admitted every last shameful detail of what I've done over the last week. He's right to not want me around. But that doesn't mean it hurts any less.

So, while I otherwise would've been arguing with my own reflection and doubting every single dress I owned, instead, I'm enjoying my second glass of Tito's and cranberry before noon while sitting on the island counter at the back of the bakery, all alone, staring at the wall straight ahead while trying so hard to push my own self-loathing thoughts to the back of my mind.

Trying so hard to dispel my own shame with another sip of vodka. But it's no use. All I keep thinking of is all the bad I've done.

Don't bother coming to my wedding.

I shake my head as Nash's words flash in my mind. I finish what's left of my cocktail, hoping somehow the alcohol will help to ease my self-inflicted pain. But it doesn't. Sure, it numbs it a little, but the pain and the shame is still there, taunting me.

I've really managed to screw everything up. Royally. I should get a damn award.

I'd like to thank the friends I've lost because I'm an asshole, and my family who are either dead, or dead to me ... I cringe at my makeshift acceptance speech while I top up my glass, but I'm stopped—rendered frozen—by the sound of the door to the store opening and closing.

"We're closed!" I yell, wondering how whoever it is managed to miss the glaringly obvious sign stuck to the window of the shop. But then an unexpected face appears in the cut-out wall, and my eyes widen, my heart coming to stop hard in my chest. "Anna?"

She continues through to the back, coming into the kitchen with an exasperated and dramatic sigh. Dressed in matching sweats that would look shocking on anyone other than her, her blonde hair in rollers, her beautiful face immaculately made-up complete with delicately winged liner and a crimson red lip, she takes a long look at me, folding her arms over her chest.

I push myself off the countertop, gaping at her in utter bewilderment. "W-what are you doing here?"

She cocks her head, quirking a brow as she eyes me. "I *know* what you did."

Oh damn.

"Nash told me *everything.*"

I blink once, frozen as I stare at her, holding my breath while accepting whatever it is my fate may be.

"You're a complete psychopath," she says with little to no emotion. "You know that, right?"

I look down at my hands, nodding once, wondering if she came here just to make me feel worse than I already do.

"But what kind of wife would I be if I didn't try everything I can to help mend my husband's broken heart?"

Surprised and confused by her words, I look up finding the slightest hint of a smile ghosting over her red lips.

"I know he'll *never* forgive himself if his Murph isn't at his wedding," she continues. "And I know he's miserable right now."

I swallow hard, watching as she closes the distance, stopping at the opposite countertop and taking a moment to gaze around at the shop with a faraway look in her eyes. "So, this is the bakery, huh?" She smiles, looking from the shiny turquoise KitchenAid, to the vintage jars that were my grandmother's, lined perfectly up against the pale pink wall. She picks up my apron from where it's sitting on the counter, the apron my mother made me as a graduation gift before I left for New York. She'd made it for me, making me promise that no matter what great, exciting things I go and do in my life, I'll never forget where I came from, that I will always come back.

Anna looks down at it, tracing a finger over the delicate lace, my name, Alice, embroidered over the front. She casts me a glance, her eyes full of an emotion I hadn't expected. "I'll admit when I first arrived in Graceville, I couldn't understand the hype about it. The way Nash went on and on about this place." She smiles, a thoughtful look of consideration in her eyes as she carefully places the apron back onto the counter as if she's afraid she might break it. And, with another smile, she nods. "Now I get it."

My brows knit together. "Get what?"

"I grew up in a city with eight million people." She laughs once, shaking her head. "And, don't get me wrong, I love New York, but this place ..." She sighs, looking around at my poky

235

little store with the pale pink walls, lace curtains and the gingerbread-man-printed drapes, black and white floor tiles with a million scuff marks. "This is Nash's home. You, Harley, Graceville, it's all home to him, and I get it, because it's something I've never had."

I press my lips together, pausing before finally speaking and breaking the silence that's settled between us. "You must *hate* me for what I did," I whisper, unsure if she even heard me or not.

Anna glances up toward the ceiling a moment, her lips twisting to the side in consideration before she flashes me a knowing look. "Actually ..." She shrugs. "It's *because* of what you did that I *don't* hate you."

My brow quirks in confusion of its own accord, and Anna laughs at my obvious reaction. She steps forward, moving around me and pulling herself up onto the counter. I tentatively follow suit, sitting on the very edge, right next to her, watching as she smiles to herself. "I owe you an apology, Murph."

"Huh?" I scoff. "You owe *me* an apology?" I gape at her, at a loss for words, and all I can do is continue to stare at her.

She flashes me a slightly guilty-looking smile. "When I met Nash he told me *all* about you. All about the girl from Graceville, Georgia. The girl who *owned* his heart. The girl who *saved* him. The girl he swore he'd *never* stop loving."

My heart jumps up into the back of my throat, causing me to choke on my own tongue. I cough, clearing my throat, gawping at her, not having expected that.

"Of course I was *insanely* jealous. Jealous of a girl I'd never even met, because I knew ... I'd never be able to compare to you. You shared so much with him. So much more than I will ever fully understand. You're everything I'm never going to be, Murph."

"M-me?" I laugh incredulously, pointing to myself before pushing my glasses up my nose.

She chuckles softly, gauging me, looking at me closely, and I can't help but cower beneath her scrutiny. I know I look a mess with my unruly curls all frizzy and wayward, wearing a tank top, sans bra, holding an empty glass of vodka at eleven o'clock in the damn morning. I place the glass onto the counter so I don't I drop it to smash against the floor.

"Yeah, *you*, Murph." She laughs at me with an incredulous look in her eyes. "I did *everything* I could do to try to convince him *I* was the one for him. Not you. I even … and I'm *so* sorry—" She pauses and I watch as she closes her eyes a moment, seeming to take a fortifying breath before swallowing hard and looking at me. "One night we were at a friend's birthday dinner, and Nash went to the bathroom. Well, he left his cell phone on the table and it lit up, and I saw a text message from you."

I watch as she so clearly battles with whatever it is she's about to say.

"I read the message. It said" — She closes her eyes, recounting word for word — "*I miss you. I'm so empty. I wish you were here. I need you.*"

I gasp, remembering that exact text message. It was a stupid mistake. I'd been drunk and lonely, and I'd been thinking about the night we spent together over New Year's. "He never responded …" I think out loud.

Anna's face tells me without words exactly why Nash never responded to me that night. She intercepted and she deleted the text before he even had a chance to see it. And I nod, not needing her to clarify any further. "You did some shitty things this week, Murph."

"I know," I whisper, bowing my head.

"But I get it." She smiles and, most unexpectedly, she reaches out and takes my hand in hers. I look down at our hands a moment before my eyes meet hers. "Don't worry about Nash. He'll get over it," she continues. "And I promise, no matter what, I'm *never* going to take him away from you. I might be his wife, but you'll always be his Murph."

I manage a smile, although it's difficult to smile when all you really want to do is cry. But I won't let her see me cry. It's her wedding day. She doesn't need to deal with my emotions, especially when I'm the one who's caused my own tears.

"Please consider coming today," Anna says as she pushes herself off the island counter. "It'll mean *more* than the world to Nash if you're there."

I exhale a sigh.

"It'll mean a lot to me, too." She smiles.

I don't commit to anything, instead I push off the countertop, and I lean in to return the hug she's pulling me into. With her arms around me, I can't help but feel as if this exchange between us is genuine and, for a moment, I become lost in our embrace.

"Now," Anna says with an exasperated huff as she pulls away. "I must get back. Mother will no doubt be *beside* herself when she realizes I'm not at the club getting ready." And, with an air kiss to each of my cheeks she turns back toward the doorway before pausing and looking at me over her shoulder. "Oh, and Murph? I bet Harley would like to see you there today." She flashes a knowing smile, and then she's gone almost as quickly and unexpectedly as she'd arrived.

And, in an instant, my heart is left stammering in my chest at the mere mention of Harley, and I glance across the room, to the framed photos hanging on the far wall. Photos of Momma and me. Photos of me and Nash. Photos of me, Nash and Harley. My life up on the wall in the one place where my heart lives.

But then my eyes move to a set of photobooth pictures, from a night I'd almost forgotten about. I walk across the kitchen to get a closer look. It was the night Harley surprised me for my twentieth birthday with tickets to the sold-out Taylor Swift show in Nashville. He knew how badly I wanted to go, and how bummed I'd been when I'd missed out. But then he showed up on my doorstep with two tickets, and drove me all the way to Nashville. I smile as I look at the two us in the photobooth that had been at the stadium, and I can't help but laugh at Harley wearing his

Taylor Swift tour T-shirt, smiling like a total dork. He's done so much for me over the years. I hate that I've wasted every opportunity to tell him how I feel because I've been so caught up on something that was never meant to be. Something that has been holding me back for far too long.

I consider Anna's words, biting down on my thumbnail.

Would Harley really want to see me? After everything I've done, I have no doubt that he hates me. But he owns my heart, and I can't give up on my heart. This could be my only chance to truly tell him how I feel. I have to try. I can't lose him without at least trying, first.

Taking a deep breath, I feel more conflicted than ever.

I stare at my reflection for what feels like forever.

Considering I'd raced home and gotten ready in less than an hour, the mirror presents an image I don't immediately hate. Dressed in a tea-length, red satin dress with a full skirt, teamed with royal blue heels and a matching clutch purse, I somehow managed to wrangle my wayward hair into a messy bun that contradicts the perfection of the dress but seems to work. With my makeup left to a minimum, I didn't want to take away from the striking dress I'd been keeping in the back of my closet for a moment like this. And, as I look at the girl in the mirror's glass, I still can't believe I'm about to watch on as Nash marries a woman who isn't me.

And, in that moment, my mind flashes back through the years, and our most precious memories play through my head. I remember the first time I heard him laugh. Really laugh. He'd been covered in bruises his horrible father had given him; a black eye, a split lip, he was in so much pain both inside and out. But I'd said something—I can't even remember what it was—I don't even think I meant for it to be funny but, for whatever reason, he found it to be the funniest thing he'd ever heard, and he roared with laughter. It was a sound like nothing I'd ever heard before:

throaty yet high-pitched, not dissimilar to a hyena. And I smiled, watching his head fall back in hysterics, knowing that it was me who'd just made him laugh like that when he was clearly in so much physical and emotional pain, and I knew it was a sound I'd cherish for the rest of my life.

I remember the first time he'd looked at me in a way I'd never been looked at before. The way it made my heart feel as if it had actually skipped a beat. The way he'd stolen my breath away with just one look. The way he'd made me feel like I was the only other person in the entire world. I remember our first hug, our first kiss, our first everything, and I'm so thankful I got to experience so many firsts with him.

But those memories, they're past. And I know now that Nash isn't my future, and I'm okay with that. Exhaling a shaky breath, I manage a smile despite the raw emotion overwhelming me. It's time to let go. I'm the luckiest woman to have had Nash in my life, but it's time to move on from what was, time to say goodbye to what will never be again.

Chapter 32

By the time I finally force myself to leave the house, of course I'm late to Harrington Country Club. Most of the wedding guests are already seated by the time I walk through the doors of the chapel, but I stop in the entrance, my jaw dropping. I'm struck, taken aback by the sheer beauty inside. A string quartet is playing classical covers of popular music from the front corner, the perfume from the floral arrangements hangs low in the air, and candlelight casts a soft glow throughout. And then, suddenly, my eyes find Nash standing up ahead, and I'm rendered breathless feeling something tighten in my chest, something I hadn't been prepared to feel.

He's dressed in a black tuxedo made to fit his body, and my eyes widen as I take him in from head to toe, and again my heart begins to stammer relentlessly in my chest. As if on cue, he turns his head, and our eyes meet, and a moment passes between us. His face is indifferent, impassive, and something flashes in his blue eyes. And in that split second, I'm not sure whether I've made the right decision in coming. Maybe he doesn't want me here. Maybe Anna was wrong. Maybe he really does hate me, and will hate me forever. Maybe I've lost him for good.

But, just as I begin to get carried away with my own thoughts of doubt, I spot the slightest hint of a smile sparkle in those blue eyes, and I release the breath I'd been holding as I watch him suddenly come to, snapping into gear before hurrying down the aisle toward me so fast he's almost running. He stops right in front of me, looking me up and down before studying my face, his eyes flitting between mine. "You came," he says through a trembling breath, as if he can't quite believe I'm standing right in front of him.

Tears prick my eyes, but I manage a smile, nodding.

"I'm *so* sorry," he whispers, shaking his head before moving in and wrapping his arms around me. And I'm fully aware as almost every person in the chapel turns their head in our direction, all eyes watching our exchange, but I lose myself within his embrace, burying my face into the crook of his neck and smiling through the tears threatening my composure.

"I *never* want to lose you, Murph," he says so softly, so gently, so tentatively.

I pull back just enough to look into his eyes, and I can see he's trying to contain his own emotion, tears catching the light as he sniffles quietly. I shake my head, offering him a knowing look before leaning in and whispering, "Forever and always."

Nash's shoulders seem to sag at my words and I know he's remembering the night we spent together when we were only 14 years old. Taking my hand in his, he leads me up the aisle, and I try my best to ignore the curious glances and the hushed whispers coming from the crowded rows on either side. I try to ignore the thoughts running through my head, that this could have been us. We could have been walking down this very aisle together as husband and wife. But none of those could've beens matter anymore because I know no matter what, Nash will always be a part of my life in one way or another. Stopping at the end of the aisle, Nash directs me to sit right beside his grandmother before hesitating momentarily, looking down at me with a look of apprehension in his eyes.

"Go!" I laugh quietly, giving him the encouragement he needs.

With a smile I haven't seen in a long time, one that takes me right back to the very first moment I met him when we were just 9 years old, Nash exhales a trembling breath, offering me one last knowing look before turning and hurrying back to his post at the top of the aisle, and I sit, fidgeting nervously as his grandmother whispers something to me about how beautiful I look, which is precisely the moment I suddenly notice Harley, finding him watching me from the small huddle of groomsmen standing right up there with Nash.

My heart stops. He looks better than I could have ever been prepared for. In fact, I can't even breathe right now as I stare at him completely unabashedly. His chestnut hair is swept back from his face, perfectly styled. The green in his eyes is illuminated, flickering shades of emerald and olive and flecks of gold with every lick of the candles scattered haphazardly around the altar. The stubble lining his jaw contradicts the perfectly tailored suit he's wearing, which fits his body like a glove. He's pure perfection.

Standing with his hands clasped behind his back, he leans in closer to Kevin, pretending to listen to whatever crude words are likely coming from his mouth, all the while watching me, his face a blank canvas despite the plethora of emotions flashing within his eyes. I try to offer him the smallest hint of a smile, but it's a sentiment he doesn't return, and that stings. Instead, he simply offers a curt nod before averting his eyes and turning to look toward the entrance as the telltale music begins to play throughout the space.

While everyone stands and turns to look toward the doors, I continue staring straight ahead as I make my way to my feet, wondering if that look was his way of telling me that it's over. We're done. Before we even had a real chance. And, at that sobering thought, my heart shatters, falling into a million jagged shards at the pit of my belly.

I swallow the pain and regret at the back of my throat, sniffling back the emotion as I watch Nash, witnessing that sudden look of adoration claim his face the moment he spots his bride at the end of the aisle. And it's a bittersweet moment. I used to imagine this day, the way he would look at me when he got that first glimpse of me in my wedding dress. And while he may not be looking at me, from the way his brow climbs slightly higher, to the way his blue eyes light up, glistening with unshed tears, to the way the corners of his lips curve upward just a touch, it's a beautiful sight. And I can't help but smile as I watch my best friend marry the love of his life.

As the congregation of wedding guests gathers out on the patio dusk settles over the pristine view of the manicured golf course. I stand alone with a flute of champagne in one hand and a canapé in the other, staring out as the sky turns a deep shade of magenta with sparkling gold undertones. Its beauty is captivating, and at that moment, feeling as empty and as hollow as I do on the inside, I envy the breathtaking sky.

"Hey ..." a familiar voice chimes from behind me, and I turn to see Emma looking at me with a tentative smile as she shifts from foot to foot, her eyes downcast, avoiding mine. She looks beautiful in a shimmering navy dress, her dark hair pulled up into a sleek bun, showing off her delicate neck and striking features.

"Hey." I smile, breathing a sigh of relief, thankful to know at least someone outside of the groomsmen. "I didn't know you were coming!" I wrap an arm around her, pulling her in for a brief hug.

"Yeah, I—um ... It was all real last minute."

My brows knit together in confusion at her words, and I watch as she obviously avoids my eyes. "What do you mean?" I laugh once under my breath before taking a sip of my champagne.

Finally, she lifts her head, her eyes finding mine, and she

releases a sigh so heavy, her shoulders sag as if she has the weight of the world resting upon them.

"Em?" I press. "Is everything okay?"

To be honest, she's starting to worry me. Emma has never been the kind of girl to take things too seriously. She looks like the whole world is against her, and my stomach is beginning to twist uncomfortably, because I just know something's wrong, and I have a sick feeling that that something might have to do with me. But, before she can speak and say whatever it is that's weighing heavily upon her, the throng of wedding guests is suddenly a flurry with excitement, and I glance over Emma's shoulder to see Anna's bridesmaids enter, accompanied by the groomsmen. And frustratingly, I can't help but smile when my gaze lands on Harley as he effortlessly commands the attention of the crowd with a dimpled smile and a wave of his beer bottle in the air.

My heart begins to race as he makes his way toward me, his eyes raking over me from my head to my toes, and I feel a swarm of butterflies flutter wildly in my belly. Maybe I was wrong before. Maybe it's not as good as done. But then, my heart sinks as those butterflies flutter off and abandon me the very minute he stops next to Emma and snakes his arm around her shoulders, leaning in to place a kiss against her cheek.

"Hi, babe." He looks down at her, a cocky smirk pulling at his lips. "You look sexy as hell in that dress."

Emma flashes me an uncertain glance, and I feel sick. Like I might actually vomit all over myself. The skin at the back of my neck prickles and itches, burns. My palms begin to sweat. And I just know tears are imminent. But I have no right to be upset. He's free to do whatever or, whomever, he chooses. I'm the one who screwed everything up.

Emma looks from Harley to me, and back again, nervously tracing the rim of her champagne flute with her fingertip, avoiding my eyes. "I'm so sorry, Murph, I swear I—" She shakes her head, stopping herself, staring down at her glass.

245

Harley balks, muttering something under his breath as he flashes me a look of pure disgust, a look that hurts like hell, before taking a big swig from his bottle of beer, and Emma flashes him a warning glare before finally looking at me. "Murph, I didn't— I mean, I know this is—"

"Em, it's *fine*." I force a smile onto my face, brushing off her inability to finish her sentences and her concern with a wave of my hand. But I don't dare look at Harley, because I know he'll see straight through me, so I ignore him as best as I can. Even Emma offers me a doubtful look, but I continue anyway, knowing she doesn't believe a single word coming out of my mouth. "He's single. He can do whatever he wants. And you two are good together, so ..." I try my best at a nonchalant shrug, even though I know I'm not fooling anyone. "Excuse me, I need to use the ladies' room."

"Murph, wait!" I hear Emma call after me, but I ignore her, pushing past Harley with a little more force than necessary.

I snake my way through the crowd, desperate for a reprieve from the shame and humiliation that is quickly overwhelming me. I feel hot tears hit my cheeks, and I duck my head, hurrying as fast as I can toward the nearest bathroom as if my life depends on it.

Chapter 33

I'm not sure if it's the champagne I've consumed on an otherwise empty stomach, or the beautiful song playing throughout the expanse of the ballroom, but the longer I sit all alone looking out over the dance floor full of happy couples swaying to the soft music, the more I begin to wonder what the hell I'm even still doing here.

I force myself to look away from Anna and Nash because I don't think I can bear to watch them share another meaningful kiss as they stare lovingly at one another and giggle softly between themselves. It's beautiful but sickening at the same time and, of course, I'm envious. Their happiness. That love. It's all I want. When my eyes find Harley dancing with Emma, his chin resting intimately on top of her head, it's like a knife straight to my heart. I close my eyes tight, feeling an overwhelming sense of regret settle low in my belly. Even Kevin is dancing with one of Anna's cousins from Long Island. She's almost as loud and obnoxious as he is but, to be honest, they're a perfect fit. I can't believe I'm actually jealous of Kevin.

With a trembling sigh, I stand and head toward the bar. I need something a little stronger than champagne if I'm going to make it through tonight.

"Hey, you."

I glance over my shoulder to see Nash smiling at me.

"Oh. Hey." I smile a real honest smile, turning to him. I take the opportunity to get another look at him. Because Nash in a tux is like a masterpiece in an art gallery—you just can't help but stare.

"Will you dance with me?"

My brows climb slightly higher as I look from him, to where I can see Anna at a table talking with an older couple seemingly unaware that her husband is asking the woman who tried to poison her with laxative cake to dance. I offer him an uncertain look. "A-are you *sure*?"

"Of course!" He laughs, taking hold of my hand. "I gotta dance with my best friend at my own damn wedding."

I manage a smile as he leads me to the dance floor, and I hold on to his shoulders while he holds on to my waist as we dance in time with the music, neither of us saying a word. I can feel his eyes on me the entire time, but I avoid his imploring gaze for as long as I can before it finally becomes too awkward and I know I have to look at him. When I do, I know exactly what he's thinking.

"You look *real* beautiful tonight, Murph."

I blush once again, ducking my head in an attempt at hiding my flaming cheeks.

"You do," he assures me with a nod. "But you're always beautiful. You just don't seem to realize it."

I press my lips together to stifle the awkward smile threatening me.

"I need to be honest with you," he begins, tentatively, and I meet his eyes, nodding as my smile falls at the sudden seriousness of his tone. "When you told me you and Harley were ... together," he says, his jaw slightly tense, "I was happy for you, but man, I was so fuckin' scared."

"Scared?" I ask, my brow furrowed in confusion at his unexpected admission.

"I was scared I was gonna lose you to him." He nods, pressing his lips together a moment. "I've always been terrified of losing you to Harley." I blink at him, sufficiently confused, but he just laughs at me. "He's been head over heels in love with you since we were kids." He chuckles. "It was only a matter of time before he stole you away from me, and I always knew that day would come."

My heart stops. And, for a moment, I'm not sure whether I heard him correctly. My brows pull together in confusion and doubt as I gape at him. "W-what are you even talking about?"

Nash laughs softly to himself, looking down a moment before meeting my eyes once again and nodding with a genuine smile. "It's true. He was so angry with me when I told him you and me kissed that very first time in your bedroom, remember?"

I nod slowly, still completely bewildered by what he's saying, but I do remember the two of them getting into a tussle while throwing the football around at our hideout, not long after that first kiss. At first, I thought they were just playing like they always did, but then it turned serious, and when I broke it up, Harley pushed Nash so hard he fell to his butt, and then he stormed off, flashing me a look I hadn't been expecting before disappearing off into the woods. I didn't think much of it at the time, but now ...

Nash laughs again, looking up in thought as a faraway smile remains on his lips. "He didn't speak to me for a whole week after that kiss."

"You're lying."

He shakes his head, offering an earnest smile.

"But Harley ... he—he *hated* me when we were kids. He said I stole you away from him. He was so mean." I think back to all the times Harley Shaw made my life a living hell. The teasing. The pranks. The constant practical jokes. He would go out of his way to do something mean and horrible to me at least once every day.

"No, he *never* hated you," Nash says with a defiant shake of his head. "He hated that you fell for *me*, and he hated me for stealing you away from *him*."

Suddenly I think back to all the times Harley has been there for me over the years. Moments I perhaps took for granted because I was too damn obsessed with Nash to realize. Graduation night when he took care of me because Nash disappeared. When he practically checked himself out of hospital after his football injury, just to come to home to help me because Nash couldn't leave New York. Hell, Harley was the one who saved me from Billy when we were 9 years old. It was never Nash.

As I allow Nash's words to sink in, I glance over his shoulder, and at that moment my eyes connect with an intense green gaze set steadily upon me from the bar, and my breath hitches in the back of my throat. I continue staring into Harley's eyes, and although we're so far apart, physically and emotionally, right at that moment, even with Nash's hands resting casually on my waist, it feels as if Harley and me are the only two people in the whole room.

"Don't let him get away, Murph." Nash's whispered voice pulls me back to the now, and I tear my focus from Harley to find a sincere, hopefulness in my friend's blue eyes as he implores me with an all-too-serious look that makes me realize just how right he is. "I meant it last night when I said the two of you are perfect for each other." He presses his lips together, taking a moment before managing a wry smile. "It hurts like hell to say that," he says with a soft laugh. "But it's the truth. Y'all have always been perfect for one another. I just stood in the way for far too long."

I seriously consider his words, but then I come to as the ache in my chest rears its ugly head. "But he's here with Emma." I shake my head, looking down momentarily only to hear Nash scoff. I lift my head to find a dubious smirk twisting his lips to the side.

"Oh, please. He called her an hour before the damn wedding

250

was supposed to start and *begged* her to come with him. He didn't even *have* a plus-one. The wait staff had to make an extra place setting at last notice." He chuckles, shaking his head.

"But … w-why would he do that knowing it would hurt me?"

Nash says nothing, and he doesn't have to. Instead he offers a knowing look, one of his brows quirked slightly higher. With a trembling breath, I glance back over toward the bar, but Harley's no longer there. I turn, searching the ballroom, scanning the tables, looking everywhere. But I can't find him. It's as if he's just vanished. Gone without a trace.

"You should go find him," Nash says, as if he can hear my thoughts.

I begin to shake my head, trying desperately to think of an excuse. But I don't have one. And when he lets go of my hand, gently shoving me away with a grin. I take an unsteady step backward, trying so hard to muster some courage, but it's pointless. I'm terrified.

"He's out on the patio."

I startle at the voice behind me. Turning so quickly I almost slip over on the shiny dance floor, my eyes going wide when I see Emma looking at me with a small smile, a knowing glint in her eye.

"B-but I—" I shake my head, looking her up and down. I'd have to be a fool to think I could ever compete with someone like her. "But what about *you*?"

Her head drops back and she laughs out loud, causing my brows to knit together in confusion at her reaction. "Oh, *please*, Murph!" she shrieks, her laughter fading to a soft giggle as she cocks her head to the side, reaching out and gently touching my arm. "Just go find him." She nods encouragingly. "He needs you, Murph. And, besides, Seth and I have been talking over the last few days … He's *really* sweet. He's driving down to visit me in Florida over the Memorial Day weekend!" She winks at me, and I gape at her as Nash laughs loudly.

I consider all of that for a moment, my heart racing in my chest to the point of pain. Swallowing hard, I take a deep breath, before turning on my heels and forcing my feet to move, despite my reservations. I have a choice to make; I either let him go and lose him forever, or I finally face the truth. This is it. It really is now or never.

Stepping out onto the patio, the silence and stillness of the night causes me to stop short, and I take the moment to look at Harley there by himself, appearing more alone than I've ever seen anyone look. Hunched over with his elbows resting on the railing, dressed in his shirtsleeves, the white cotton pulling tight across the obviously tense muscles in his broad back. He really does look as if he needs somebody. Whether that somebody is me, who knows. But here I am.

His head lifts from where it had been hanging low, and I can see through the dim light that his once perfectly styled hair is now sticking up all over the place as if he's been running his hands through it non-stop, and for some reason his melancholy makes my heart ache. Releasing the breath I've been holding since stepping outside, I smooth my hands down over my dress, hesitating momentarily before forcing myself to continue. But, of course, in true Murph-style, my heel catches between the flagstones, and I stumble sideways, knocking into one of the patio settings, causing an entire table to tumble, crashing to the ground in an almighty clatter.

Harley swings around, his face stark before his eyes narrow, finding me lurking in the shadows. Suddenly an angry-looking crease settles between his brows, and all I can do is stand there looking from him, to the table lying on its side before moving to pick it up.

"Don't!" he yells. "It's too heavy."

I pause halfway, watching as he makes his way over with a huff of a sigh, swooping in to effortlessly pick up the table and place it where it was before I'd clumsily crashed into it. He casts me a wry glance, brushing his hands against the seat of his pants.

"Thanks," I murmur, feeling my cheeks heat.

Harley says something unintelligible under his breath before turning and heading back to his spot by the railing. Reluctantly I follow, keeping my distance a few feet away as I look out at the view. The eighteenth hole looks almost magical tonight. The automatic sprinklers are on, the water a kaleidoscope of colors, illuminated by the flood lights in the ground that change from blue to pink, to green and purple and gold every minute or so. It's a beautiful backdrop, but I'm not here for the view.

Fidgeting nervously, I consider my words, but I'm far too conscious of my heart racing so hard and so fast, surely, he can hear it. I chance a sideways glance, but he remains impassive as he stares out over the night. The only thing giving away his emotion is that crease that seems permanently etched into his brow. I swallow hard, and I turn to face him, watching him intently as he does everything he can to pretend as if I don't exist.

"Why'd you bring Emma?"

He says nothing, ignoring me, but I can see his grip on the railing tighten, his jaw clenching.

"I know what you did," I continue, watching him, and I can see his eyes flit to the side, looking at me. "Did you do it just to hurt me?"

Harley scoffs, but says nothing more, shaking his head, and at least I know he's listening.

"Well, it worked ..." I say so quietly as I look down at my hands. "You successfully hurt me, Harley."

"Oh my fucking *God*!"

I startle from his booming voice and use of blasphemy, looking up to see him almost animatedly drop his head back and throw his fists in the air. "Every single thing you *do* hurts me!" he yells, and his proclamation is like a slap to the side of my face as it echoes throughout the night.

My jaw drops, and he turns to face me. I notice a look in his eyes I've never seen before, causing my brow to furrow as I study the confusing and contradicting expression on his face. I don't know whether he's angry, sad, worried or scared, but it only makes my heart race even faster.

"You wanna know why I brought Emma here?"

I nod, although now I'm not so sure.

He sighs heavily, scratching at the back of his neck the way he does whenever he's nervous or hesitating. Closing his eyes a moment, he bows his head before looking at me once again. "I brought her here tonight because I wanted you to fight for me the way you fought so hard for Nash."

Wait, what? I stare at him, my mouth opening and closing like a goddamn goldfish, but I'm at a loss for words. And thankfully, he breaks the awkward silence first. "But you *didn't* fight for me. Instead, you *walked away*. And that hurt like hell because I realized I'll *never* be the guy you fight for, Murph."

I stare at him, blinking once. Is he fucking serious right now? "Are you fuckin' serious right now?" Harley's eyes widen at my use of profanity, and I slap a hand over my mouth, ashamed of myself before I collect what composure I can. "I'm sorry. I didn't mean to say that out loud." I shake my head dismissively. "But *are* you serious?" He just stares at me, not even blinking, so I continue. "You were never *mine* to fight for, Harley!" I throw my hands in the air. "I told you I was in love with you last night, and it was *you* who walked away."

He scoffs once more, offering me an exasperated once-over.

"Why the hell would I fight for someone who never fought for me, even after all these years?" I add.

He's clearly taken aback by my words, and his brow furrows in confusion as his head cocks to the side, his eyes narrowing as he studies me. "W-what are you even talking about?"

"Nash told me the truth. *Everything*," is all I have to say, stubbornly folding my arms across my chest.

The revelation causes the hard look on his face to fall, and he glances down to the ground. I watch as he battles so obviously with his thoughts until finally he looks up at me with an expression of defeat, shrugging a shoulder. "You would've never chosen me over him. I saw it in your eyes that very first day, and then you walked off with him while I stayed behind ... fighting. For you."

My heart clenches at his hushed words so full of hurt and pain that I can feel through to my core.

"You were always so smart. You and Nash both were. Y'all were the two meant for each other." He shrugs again, sadness in his eyes. "I was just the dumb jock."

"Harley, you've *never* been the dumb jock."

He laughs once under his breath, looking down again and shaking his head as another heavy silence falls between us.

"Harley." I finally speak when I know he's not going to. He peers up at me through his lashes, a sheepish look in his eyes. "When I said I was in love with you last night, I meant it." I pause for a moment, before continuing, "I'm sorry for what I put you through this week. I'm sorry for *not* fighting for you. I'm sorry for *everything*. But mostly what I'm sorry for is not realizing sooner that you're ... you're the love of my life, because you have been for as long as I can remember."

His eyes widen at my confession, but nothing more is said. The silence is deafening, each second ticking away so slowly it's almost excruciating. I stare at him and he continues watching me, but no words are spoken until he finally exhales an almighty breath as a string of inaudible curse words fall from his lips. Placing his hands low on his hips, he bows his head and, most shockingly of all, his shoulders begin to tremble.

I look closer, narrowing my eyes. "A-are you ... are you crying?"

His head snaps up, and it's then that I notice the smile on his face.

"Oh Lord!" I throw my hands up in frustration. "Of course you're laughing. Everything is just a goddamn *joke* to you, isn't it, Harley Shaw."

His chuckle turns into a loud laugh before he's in full-on hysterics, and all I can do is roll my eyes while I wait for him to finish. "I'm sorry, Murph." He finally collects himself, clearing his throat and meeting my eyes. "I'm real sorry for laughing. But what the hell are we even doing?"

"Well, *you're* being a jerk, for starters ..." I mutter under my breath.

He flashes me a cocky smirk: his trademark. And damn him, I can't help but crack a smile of my own. I duck my head and bite down hard on the inside of my cheek to stop myself, but it's impossible.

"Come here."

Looking up, I'm not sure I heard him right. Maybe it was my mind playing tricks on me. But when I find him standing there with one arm outstretched, I offer him a dubious look.

"Murph— No, *Alice*," he corrects himself, and that cocky smirk morphs into a softer, genuine smile that hints at his dimples.

"What?" I stand my ground, looking him up and down.

"I'm sorry for being a jerk." He scratches at that same nonexistent itch at the back of his neck, giving away just how suddenly nervous he is. "And ... well ..."

I can tell the words are difficult for him to say, but I'm actually enjoying watching him suffer. "What?" I tap my foot on the ground, waiting, flashing him a warning glare, and quirking a brow.

He huffs a dramatic sigh, looking up toward the sky with his hands in the air, and I bite my lips together to stop my smile from showing through. "Fine!" he yells, his hands falling hard against his thighs as he glowers at me. "I ... *love* you." He says the words as if he's ripping off a Band-Aid, as if it hurts like hell but he's too damn stubborn to show too much emotion. But then

256

he softens, and his green eyes are suddenly full of sincerity. "I've loved you for a long time."

"Since we were 9 years old, to be precise," I correct him matter-of-factly, smiling like a smug jerk. "Nash told me *everything*."

"Na." He shakes his head, countering my smugness with a smart smile of his own. "When I was 9 I probably just wanted to touch your butt." I gape at him incredulously, as he continues. "I was *14* when I knew I was in love in with you." He flashes a smartass smile, his eyebrows waggling up and down, and I can't help but laugh. "Now, will you just come here so I can kiss you, goddammit?"

He opens his arms once again, taking a step forward, and of course, I don't hesitate in closing the distance between us, wrapping my arms around his neck. Our lips collide in a kiss that would otherwise bring me to my knees if he wasn't holding me so tight. His tongue glides against mine so soft yet so demanding, eliciting a soft moan from me, and when I rake my fingers through the lengths of his hair, pulling at the longer curls, he sighs heavily into our heated exchange, his hands moving down and gripping my hips through my dress.

"O-kay." I forcefully pull myself away, almost gasping for breath. "That's enough for now."

Harley stumbles forward, refusing to let me go, but I keep him at arm's length, flashing him a warning glance, which he answers with an eye-roll.

"So, what do we do now?" he asks, trying so hard to remain inconspicuous while adjusting himself in his pants, failing miserably.

I stifle my laughter, taking his hands in mine. "Now? We go back inside and we enjoy some of my delicious wedding cake, and then we—" I stop when I notice his face scrunch up.

"Ugh, no thanks. I'll pass."

I blink at him. "Ex-cuse me?"

"Are you forgetting something, Murph?" He shoots me a wry

glance. "Last time I ate your cake I literally shit my pants ... I had to leave my undies in the trash can in the men's room at Pane E Vino, and they had my name on them. I can *never* go back there!"

"You write your name on your undies?"

He deadpans and I can't help but burst into laughter.

"Oh, you think that's funny?" He launches at me again, grabbing at my sides where I'm most ticklish.

"Okay, okay!" I squeal, pushing him away. "Truce!" Holding his hands up in surrender, Harley laughs and my cheeks burn. "Can we please *never* speak of that night again?" I bury my face in my hands. "I still cannot believe I even did that!"

"Aww, c'mon now, Murph." Harley pulls my hands away from my face, kissing my flushed cheek before leading me back toward the party. "I'm never gonna stop with that story. It'll be brought up on holidays, birthdays. Family dinners. Our kids' graduations. On our—"

I stop dead in my tracks, looking up at him with wide eyes. "Kids, huh?"

He realizes what he's said and I spot a tinge of pink tinting his cheeks, his eyes widening before he quickly shakes his head with a dismissive scoff. "Murph, you're drunk! C'mon, baby. Let's get you some water before you say something else utterly ridiculous."

The way he calls me baby does unimaginable things to my insides, and I giggle as he ushers me in through the doors. And, once inside, I turn to Harley, wrapping my arms around his neck as we sway to the music playing throughout the party, but almost instinctively, my eyes find Nash over his shoulder standing across the way, watching us with the ghost of a smile playing on his lips.

"Thank you," I mouth, nodding at him.

In return he raises his glass in the air, offering me a wink before turning to his wife, and I smile as Harley rests his forehead

258

against mine, placing a soft kiss on the tip of my nose before whispering how happy he is, his lips brushing against my ear.

I close my eyes and smile to myself, because in this moment, despite the long and often painful road it took to finally find one another, right now, Harley and I are exactly where we belong.

Want more?

To be the first to hear about new releases, competitions, 99p eBooks and promotions, sign up to our monthly email newsletter.

Acknowledgments

Firstly, I'd like to thank Abi, my amazing editor, for taking a chance on an unknown author, and for being so patient when I've been clueless and stubborn and, quite frankly, impossible throughout most of this journey.

To my Twitter girls who have supported and encouraged me every step of the way—you know who you are—thank you so much, my loves.

Thank you to two incredibly talented authors—Zoe May and Belinda Missen—for helping me find my feet through this intimidating venture. A special shout out to Heather MacKinnon, a talented author and a wonderful friend who helped and encouraged me while writing this book.

Thank you to my family who have been my biggest advocates.

Finally, to my husband, Michael; thank you the most for allowing me to be selfish while I chase my dreams. Without your unwavering support, this would never have been possible. I don't say it nearly enough, but I love you more than life itself.

Dear Reader,

We hope you enjoyed reading this book. If you did, we'd be so appreciative if you left a review. It really helps us and the author to bring more books like this to you.

Here at HQ Digital we are dedicated to publishing fiction that will keep you turning the pages into the early hours. Don't want to miss a thing? To find out more about our books, promotions, discover exclusive content and enter competitions you can keep in touch in the following ways:

JOIN OUR COMMUNITY:

Sign up to our new email newsletter:
http://hyperurl.co/hqnewsletter

Read our new blog www.hqstories.co.uk

: https://twitter.com/HQDigitalUK

: www.facebook.com/HQStories

BUDDING WRITER?

We're also looking for authors to join the HQ Digital family!

Find out more here:
https://www.hqstories.co.uk/want-to-write-for-us/

Thanks for reading, from the HQ Digital team

If you enjoyed *Where We Belong*, then why not try another delightfully uplifting romance from HQ Digital?

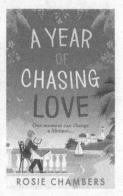

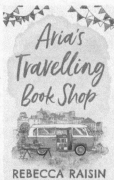